The Banquet of the
Lords of Night

Other books by Liz Williams include:

The Ghost Sister
Empire of Bones
The Poison Master
Nine Layers of Sky
Banner of Souls

The Banquet of the Lords of Night

and Other Stories by Liz Williams

Night Shade Books
San Francisco & Portland

First Edition

Night Shade Books
Please visit us on the web at
http://www.nightshadebooks.com

Contents

Adventures in the Ghost Trade

Detective Inspector Chen brushed aside the chaos on his desk and carefully lit a single stick of crimson incense. Smoke spiraled up into the air, contributing to the brown smear that marked the ceiling like a bloodstain immediately above Chen's desk. Chen bent his head in a brief prayer, then picked up the photograph and held it over the stream of smoke. The girl's face appeared by degrees, manifesting out of a dark background. She was standing in the doorway of a go-down, gazing fearfully over her shoulder. Her hair was still scraped back into its funeral braids, and her white face gleamed out of the shadows like the ghost she was. Studying the photo, and the expression on the girl's face, Chen was aware of the sudden hot glow of rage in his chest. How many more young women had gone the same way after their deaths, unnoticed and unmourned? But whoever was behind all this had made a mistake this time, choosing the daughter of Singapore Three's premier industrialist rather than some nameless prostitute. Chen held the photograph out to the woman sitting on the other side of the desk and said gently, "Do you think this might be your daughter?"

Mrs. Tang's grip tightened around the handle of her Miucci handbag as she studied the photograph. In a little whispery voice she said, "Yes. Yes, that's Pearl."

"Now, you say someone sent this to you?"

"Yesterday. I didn't go out of the apartment, and no one came in. But when I walked into the living room, the photo was sitting on the bureau. In a red envelope. I didn't know what it was at first. There was a note, telling me what to do." She gestured towards the spiraling incense. "You can see her face for a little while, but then it fades again."

"And did you notice anything—strange? Apart from the envelope?"

Mrs. Tang moistened dry lips. "There was some ash. I had to wipe it off the bureau before the maids or someone saw it."

"All right. Mrs. Tang, I know how hard this is for you, but at least we have a lead. You must try and be hopeful."

"You will find her, won't you?"

"Don't worry. We'll find your daughter, and we'll make absolutely sure that this time she completes her journey." Chen did his best to sound reassuring.

"Thank you," Mrs. Tang murmured. She pushed her expensive sunglasses to the top of her head and rubbed her eyes; they were rimmed with redness. "I'd better go. I told Hsuen I was going shopping."

Chen sighed. This was an added complication, but hardly an unfamiliar one. "Is there anything you can do to change your husband's mind?"

"I don't think so. I've tried talking to Hsuen, but he won't listen." Mrs. Tang gave a brittle, bitter smile. "He says it doesn't make any difference; Pearl's dead and that's that. You see, he and Pearl were never very close. He wanted a son, and after I had her, I couldn't have any more children. So he blamed her, you see. And she was always a—well, she was a lovely, lovely girl, but she could be a little bit difficult. Willful. She was fifteen, and I used to say to him 'What do you expect, these days?' They all go out with boys, and Pearl was very popular, he used to get so angry. . . . And I think the eating problem started about then. . . . "

Patiently, Chen listened as she talked on, building up a picture of the dead girl. At last Mrs. Tang said, uncertainly, "You've been very kind, Detective Inspector. I know you'll do your best in finding Pearl. I really should go now."

Chen saw her to the door of the precinct, then made his way slowly to the drinks machine. Sergeant Ma was bending over it, thumping the side.

"Damn machine's not working again. I—oh." He stood hastily back as he saw who it was.

"Take your time," Chen said, politely.

"No no no no no. It's quite all right. It's all yours," Ma said hastily, and made a rapid exit in the direction of the canteen. With a resigned sigh, Chen managed to extract a paper cup of green tea from the machine, and carried it back to his desk. As he turned the corner, he saw that Sergeant Ma had come back and was surreptitiously waving a blessing paper over the machine. Chen was used to this, but some days his colleagues' aversion to him got him down. He sipped his tasteless tea and contemplated the photograph for a few moments longer, then collected his jacket from the back of his chair and left the precinct.

It was only the beginning of summer, but already the heat had built to oppressive levels. Stepping out onto Jiang Mi Road was like diving into a warm bath. Chen glanced at the pollution meter on the wall of the precinct, but the results were too depressing to take seriously. He walked slowly down towards the harbor, lost in thought. By the time he reached the edge of the typhoon shelter, the weather had grown a little cooler. There was a storm building out over the South China Sea, and the air tasted of lightning and rain. Chen smiled, picturing Inari resting her elbows on the windowsill of the houseboat, avidly waiting for the thunder to break. His wife loved storms. They reminded her of home, she said. The ferry terminal lay a short distance along the quay, and Chen sat down on the bench to wait. Someone had left a newspaper, and he picked it up, beginning idly to read. Singapore was opening yet another franchise, this time along the Myanmar coast. Chen could remember a time when Singapore Three was the last in the franchise line; this new development would be the sixth city. Chen read on, learning that the city would be developed along the same lines as all the others, and he smiled, momentarily imagining another D. I. Chen sitting on an identical ferry terminal bench, several thousand miles to the south. A distant humming interrupted his thoughts and he looked up to see the wallowing shape of the ferry as it approached the terminal. Fifteen minutes later Chen stepped off at the opposite dock and into the labyrinth of streets that constituted Zhen Shu Island.

This was a rough area, and Chen walked warily, but no one bothered him. He supposed that he was anonymous enough; a middle aged man with an unremarkable face, wearing unfashionable indigo clothes. But occasionally he would see someone start and shy away, and realize that he, or at least his profession, had been recognized. No one liked policemen, and cops who were in league with Hell were doubly unwelcome. So Chen walked unmolested through the narrow streets of Zhen Shu until he found himself standing in front of Su Lo Ling's Funeral Parlor.

Unlike the neighboring shops, the funeral parlor was a magnificent building. The black, faux-marble facade boasted gilded columns on either side of the door, and red lanterns hung from the gable in a gaudy, tasteless display. This was not, Chen reflected, inappropriate, given the number of citizens who met their end in a similar manner. A narrow alleyway ran down one side, leading further into the labyrinth of Zhen Shu. The sign on the door proclaimed that the funeral parlor was shut. Undeterred, Chen kept his finger on the bell until blinds twitched from the shops on either side. Over the insistent jangling of the doorbell, he could hear footsteps hastening down the hall. The door was flung open to reveal a short, stout gentleman in a long red robe.

"What do you want? This is a place of rest, not some kind of—oh." His eyes widened. Chen never knew how people could tell; it must be something behind his eyes, some inner darkness that revealed his close association with the world beyond the world. When younger, though not usually vain, he had spent hours peering into the mirror, trying to detect what it was that made people so afraid.

"I'm sorry," the stout man said, in more conciliatory tones. "I didn't realize."

Chen displayed his badge. "Franchise police department. Precinct Thirteen. Detective Inspector Chen. Do you mind if I come in? I'd like to ask you a few questions."

With many protestations of the honor done to the establishment, the stout man ushered Chen inside. The interior of the funeral parlor was as ostentatious as the facade. Chen was shown into a long, mirrored room with a scarlet rug. Carp floated in a wall-length tank at the far end of the room, their reflections drifting to infinity in the multiple mirrors. The stout man clapped his hands, twice, thus summoning a small wan maid.

"Tea? Green or black?"

"Green. Thank you."

"Now, Detective Inspector." The stout man settled himself into a nearby armchair. "I am Su Lo Ling, the proprietor of this establishment. What can we do to help?"

"I understand you handled the funeral arrangements for a ceremony a week ago, for a girl named Pearl Tang. The daughter of someone who needs no introduction from me."

"Indeed, indeed. So very sad. Such a young woman. Anorexia is a most tragic condition. It just goes to show," and here Mr. Ling shook his head philosophically, "that not even the materially blessed among us may attain true happiness."

"How very wise. Forgive me for asking such a delicate question, but were there any—difficulties—with the funeral?"

"None whatsoever. You must understand, Detective Inspector, that we are a very old firm. The Lings have been in the funeral business since the seventeenth century, in Guangzhou before my father moved here. Our connections with the relevant authorities are ancient. There are never any irregularities with the paperwork." A small pause. "Might I ask why you pose such a question?"

"Your establishment does indeed possess a most honorable reputation," Chen said. "However, I fear that an irregularity—doubtless nothing to do with the manner in which the funeral was handled—has nonetheless occurred."

"Oh?" There was the faintest flicker of unease in Ling's face, which Chen noted.

"You see, it appears that the young lady in question did not in fact reach the Celestial Shores. A ghost-photograph of her has been taken, revealing her current whereabouts to be somewhere in the port area of Hell."

Ling's mouth sagged open in shock.

"In Hell? But the payments were made, the sacrifices impeccably ordered. . . . I don't understand."

"Neither does her mother."

"The poor woman must be distraught."

"She is naturally concerned that the spirit of her only child is not now reclining among the peach orchards of heaven, but currently appears to be wandering around a region best described as dubious."

"I'll show you the paperwork. I'll go and get it now."

Together, Ling and Chen pored over the documents. To Chen's experienced eyes, everything seemed to be in order: the immigration visa with the Celestial authorities, the docking fees of the ghost-boat, the license of passage across Night. He was intuitively convinced that the explanation for Pearl's manifestation in the infernal realms could be traced back to Ling, but the parlor owner's round face was a paradigm of bland concern.

"Well," Chen said at last. "This is indeed a tragedy, but I can see nothing here that is at all irregular. I realize that you operate a policy of strict confidentiality, but if you should happen to hear anything—"

"Your august ears will be the first to know," Ling assured him, and with innumerable expressions of mutual gratitude, Chen departed.

He was halfway down the street when the rain began, a torrent of water that hammered the dust of the pavements into mud and plastered Chen's hair flat against his head in the first minute of its descent. Hastily, he ducked into a doorway to wait out the storm, but he had no sooner taken refuge on the step of a go-down when the door was flung open. Chen turned. A long ebony spine whipped out and wrapped itself tightly around his ankle. Chen was thrown flat on his back and dragged through the doorway. Something tall and dark loomed over him; the hem of a stiff silk coat brushed his face like a gigantic moth. He groped frantically in his inner pocket for his rosary; finding it, he struck out with it like a flail. It connected with a bony carapace, producing a trail of sparks and the odor of scorched silk. There was a hissing curse and his ankle was abruptly released. Struggling to his feet, Chen began to tell the rosary; speaking the Fourteen Unnameable Pronouncements in a swift, urgent voice. His assailant sprang to the far end of the room, and Chen caught the glow of a string of hot coals as the demon produced a rosary of its own. Chen had a head start, but the demon spoke in several voices at once, Pronouncements clicking and snapping from its flexible throat. Chen speeded up and beat the demon by a single syllable. There was a blast of furnace light as a crack opened up and the demon was catapulted back to Hell, leaving a noxious wisp of smoke behind it. Wheezing, Chen stepped clear and the smoke crystallized into dust motes and fell to the floor, where it turned into a swarm of tiny red locusts that raced down the cracks in the floorboards. Chen leaned back against the wall. The rosary was red hot, but he didn't dare let go. Gritting his teeth against the pain, he limped back through the door of the go-down and out into the street, where the rosary hissed cold in the pelting rain. His ankle was swelling to alarming proportions. Cursing, Chen located his mobile and summoned transport back to the docks and the mainland.

Next morning, Chen's ankle had diminished to its normal state, although it still ached. It was lined with a ring of puncture marks; fortunately, his inoculations were up to date and minimized the effects of whatever diabolical poison the assassin had managed to inject. Despite the pain in his leg, Chen was conscious of a quiet elation. He was on the right track. Things were getting personal. He went to the precinct early and spent some time cross-checking the franchise death register. Eight young women had died in the last four months, all of them from anorexia, all from families in the city's industrial elite. Chen printed out the list and took it downstairs.

Jian was, as usual, hunched over the computer terminal with his eyes obscured by goggles. In the dim green light of the computer room, the technician looked rather like a large, misshapen carp. Chen tapped him on the shoulder.

"Hello, Chen," Jian said, without looking up. He was the most imperturbable individual that Chen had ever met; nothing seemed to faze him, not even Chen's infernal allegiances. They weren't exactly friends, but if it hadn't been for the technician, Chen would have been obliged to eat lunch on his own, every day.

"Have you got a moment? I need some help."

Jian turned. Behind the goggles, his eyes reflected strings of characters from the retinal display.

"Sure. I'm just running some stuff through the mainframe, nothing crucial. What did you want done?"

"Basically, I need to cross reference some names with the records of a funeral parlor. I need to find out how many match."

"Okay, that shouldn't be a problem," Jian said. What he was about to do was strictly illegal, but Chen knew that the technician wouldn't be inclined to ask any questions. He gave Jian the name and address of the establishment, and waited for a few minutes while Jian made his way around the Byzantine intricacies of the web.

"Got it. Surprisingly well protected, though. . . . Do you want these printed off?"

"Thanks."

Chen pored over the lists, and found an immediate match of some six names. Thanking Jian, and lost in thought, he made his way back to his desk.

It was never easy, placing calls beyond the living realms. Chen waited patiently as the line hissed and crackled, and he held the receiver a short distance from his ear to avoid occasional sparks. Finally the connection came through and a small, suspicious voice said, "Yes?"

"This is Li Chen. Am I speaking to the august personage of Number Seven Hundred and One, Ruin Street?"

"Forgive, forgive," the voice said, loudly. "You have the wrong number. Goodbye."

This told Chen that his contact had company. He waited patiently for a further five minutes, when the phone rang.

"You're still there?" the voice said. "Sorry I took so long."

"No, no, only a few moments." Sometimes the time differential between Earth and the infernal regions worked to one's advantage, Chen reflected. "Listen. I need some help. With a strayed spirit."

"Oh?" the distant voice was wary. "Who might that be?"

"Her name was Pearl Tang; she died about twelve days ago. She was supposed to enter Heaven, but she went missing on route and now there's a very strong possibility that she's in your neighborhood."

"Hell's a big place," the voice remarked.

"I think she's somewhere in the port area. I have a photograph." Chen turned it between his fingers as he spoke. "She's standing in a doorway of somewhere that looks like a go-down. There's a sign on a building nearby that reads 'Miu's.' I wondered if you recognized it."

"Miu's," the voice repeated. "Now let me see. No, it's not remotely familiar. Never heard of it."

"Ghon Shang, you are the worst liar I have ever met," Chen said, annoyed. The voice gave a hiss of pain.

"Don't use my name like that."

"Well, then, don't lie to me."

"Oh, very well. There is a place called Miu's in the port area. It's a demon lounge. It's well known among a certain clientele, but Madam Miu is apparently very discreet. I'm not surprised you've never heard of it; it only opened a year or so ago."

"A certain clientele. What does that mean?"

"People who want—specialized services."

"What sort of people? And what sort of services?"

"Your kind of people," Ghon Shang said, with a sniff. "The living. And demons too, sometimes. As for the services—well. Sexual ones, obviously."

"Are you referring to the ghost trade?" Chen said. A thin shiver of anticipatory distaste ran down his spine.

"What else?"

Chen thought fast. The pieces of this particular puzzle—the straying spirits of a number of well connected young women, the funeral parlor, the ghost-trade—were adding up to an unpleasantly obvious conclusion. He said, "If Miu's place specializes in the ghost-trade, then it must have a correlate here. Do you know of such a place? And what's the address of Miu's?"

"It's on Lo Tzu Street. As for its correlate in your city, I do not know. I have not walked in the living lands for a hundred years. And I have no plans to start now," Ghon Shang said, thinly.

"Try and find out," Chen said, and hung up. Then he took a fifty-dollar note of hell money from his wallet and scribbled Ghon Shang's address on it. Taking his cigarette lighter from his pocket, he set fire to the note, dropping it the ash tray when the sea green flame burned too close to his fingers. The ash drifted down in a fleeting spiral, winking out into nothingness as the note presumably remanifested into his informant's greedy claws. Chen took the map transparencies from the desk drawer, shoved aside the clutter of incense coils, papers and charms from the surface of the desk, and overlaid the two maps on top of one another. Hell changed its configurations rather more often than Earth did, but there were still close correlates between the two worlds: Singapore Three on Earth, and Rhu Zhi Shur in Hell. As he had suspected, the port area of Hell overlapped with the typhoon shelters and canals of northern Fu Lung, including Zhen Shu Island. When he matched the maps carefully together, the location of Miu's connected with the funeral parlor. Chen picked up the phone.

Finding volunteers for the stakeout was not easy. Law enforcement between the worlds was not a high priority; policy being that since the citizens involved were usually already dead, there was little reason to expend manpower. To Chen's secret amusement, the only officer available was Sergeant Ma. When informed of the superintendent's decision, Ma's round face became blank with dismay.

"Demons? The ghost-trade? No. I won't do it."

"Look," Chen said, trying to be sympathetic. "You won't be on your own. I'll be there."

"With respect, Detective Inspector," stammered Ma, "that's part of the problem."

Eventually, via the promise of massive overtime, Ma was induced to agree. Dressed in shabby clothes, he and Chen made their way to Zhen Shu Island. Obliged to sit next to Chen on the ferry, Ma was already pale when they arrived.

"I don't think anyone's going to show up," Ma said hopefully, three hours later. Chen gave a thin smile.

"It's early yet. Another hour till midnight."

They were sitting in a teahouse opposite the funeral parlor, nursing bowls of dragon oolong. The lanterns of the funeral parlor glowed through the dusk.

"Why would anyone want to come to a place like that?" Sergeant Ma wondered out loud.

"A funeral parlor?"

"No. You know. A demon lounge," Ma whispered.

"Don't ask me. Some people like breaking taboos."

"But such taboos. . . . "

"They say the clients of the ghost-trade are the connoisseurs," Chen murmured. "It's supposed to involve a rather subtle set of perversions."

Sergeant Ma blanched.

"Who'd want to sleep with a ghost? Or a demon, even worse."

"Not all demons want suffering and pain," Chen said, trying to keep his annoyance at Ma's prejudice out of his voice. "Some of them are almost human. They have the same needs and desires, the same capacity to love—" he broke off, abruptly. "Something's happening."

A car was pulling up outside the funeral parlor: a smart black Toyota with mirrored windows.

"Come on," Chen said.

Together, he and Ma stepped out of the teahouse. As they did so, Chen stumbled heavily, throwing an arm around Ma's shoulders, and leading him in a weaving line along the street. Beneath his arm, Ma's muscles were bunched into a tight knot of tension, but he went along with the drunken act nonetheless, and Chen's respect for him rose. Two men were helping a frail elderly gentleman out of the car. No one paid any attention to Ma and himself. Chen led the sergeant down an alleyway that ran along the side of the funeral parlor and stopped.

"What's going on?" hissed Ma.

"He's going in. Come on. We have to find a way in."

"What? Why would we want to do that?"

"Because I know who that old man is. Hsuen Tang. Pearl's father."

Hastily, he and Ma ran down the alleyway and found themselves at the back of the building. A high wall, topped with razorwire, separated the alley from what was apparently a courtyard. At their feet, lay the cover of a drain. Chen looked at Ma.

"Give me a hand."

Ten distasteful minutes later, they were standing in the courtyard at the back of the building. The rear end of the funeral parlor was considerably less imposing than its facade. A narrow window faced the courtyard. Chen held up his palm.

"It's guarded. Never mind—" Gritting his teeth, he took a sheathed scalpel from his pocket. Before Sergeant Ma's horrified gaze, he slashed a character across his palm, then held his bleeding hand up towards the window. The guarding spell hissed into dark steam and nothingness. Sergeant Ma's eyes were as round as teabowls. Hoisting himself through the window, Chen landed in a narrow hallway. Checking to see that Ma was still behind him, he slipped down the corridor until they reached the door of a room which Chen estimated to be the main parlor. Muffled voices came from within.

"Wait here," Chen said. He went swiftly up the stairs and found himself before a row of doors. Each of them flickered with a quiet light and Chen felt the rosary begin to grow hot in his pocket. His skin flushed cold. Each of those doorways was an entrance into Hell. Taking the photograph of Pearl Tang from his pocket, Chen blew on it, then glazed it with a thin smear of his own blood. Balancing the photo on the palm of his hand, he placed a feng shui compass on top of it. The needle swung wildly for a moment, before settling in the direction of one of the doors. Pearl's spirit was here.

Cautiously, Chen held out his palm to display the still-bleeding wound and released his second spell of the night. Soundlessly, the door swung open. With the rosary wrapped tightly around his knuckles, Chen stepped forward. Even with the protection afforded by the rosary, his skin began to prickle and burn: a sure sign that the room was no longer entirely in the realm of the living. Across the room, a girl lay upon a divan. Her eyes were closed, and she was curled around herself like a cat. Her skin was as white as ash.

"Pearl?" Chen whispered.

She did not stir. As Chen reached the divan, a demon leaped through the door. It was one of the more humanoid of its kind: a pale mantis face and slick black hair, wearing a long silk coat. The coat was marred with an ugly burn, Chen noticed. They had met before. The demon's taloned fingers grasped a bloody katana. It came forward in a sudden rush; the sword raised above its head. Chen spun down, hitting the floor beneath the arc of the katana and sweeping the demon's feet from under it. He whipped the rosary across the demon's wrist, making it howl. Its curiously jointed fingers flew open, releasing the katana. Seizing the sword, Chen drew back for the final blow. But as he did so, a shadow fell across his shoulder.

"Look out!" Ma's panicky voice came from the doorway. Chen turned in time to see the ghost of Pearl Tang, a skinning knife in her hand, crouched to spring. Her pale gaze was locked on his own throat. He brought the demon's katana down upon her, splitting the spirit from head to crotch and spilling her essence out across the floor in flakes of fragrant ash. And then he turned in the direction of the demon. The being was sitting on the floor, nursing its wounded wrist, but as Chen stepped in for the kill it hastily snatched something from an inner pocket of its silk coat. A black badge. The demon said mildly, "Seneschal Zhu Irzh. Vice Division, Fourth District, Hell. Can I have my sword back? When you're ready, of course."

"Cigarette?" asked the demon, languidly.

"No, thank you. I don't smoke." Chen was methodically winding a bandage around his injured hand. The azure lights of the police car outside spun in endless refraction from the mirrored parlor. Inside the car, Ma was still questioning Su Lo Ling.

"Too bad. Helps you relax, you know. How about you?" Courteously, the demon offered the packet of thin black cigarettes to Hsuen Tang, who still sat, head bowed in shame. "No? I'm assuming you don't smoke, either," he said to the prisoner, who favored him with a furious glare from an eye somewhere around the level of her waist. Zhu Irzh lit the cigarette with a touch of his taloned thumb.

"She was Su Lo Ling's accomplice," the demon said, nodding in the direction of the prisoner. "In fact, Ling claims that the pimping was her idea. She used her access to her father's pharmaceutical products to dispatch her friends, knowing that most of them would be brought here for burial—it is the most respected establishment of its kind, after all. Then Su Lo falsified the visa documents so that virtuous girls bound for the Celestial Shores would end up—elsewhere. Working as ghosts in Miu's brothel, of which the parlor is a counterpart. Human customers would come here to visit the ghost girls under the guise of enquiring at the funeral parlor; people from Hell would come directly. But her dad found out, and poisoned Pearl to protect the family honor. Except that she must have found business to be twice as lucrative from the other side." He glanced across to where the prisoner was sulkily weaving herself back together again.

"So who sent the ghost photograph to her mother?"

"Some rival operative, maybe. Hell's a jealous place." The demon yawned, displaying sharp gilded teeth. "Sorry about assaulting you, by the way. I mistook you for one of Ling's clients; I was hoping for information. My department's billing yours for the damage to my coat."

"So what's your interest in this?" Chen asked. "Surely not the quest for law and order?"

The demon stubbed the cigarette carefully into the palm of its hand.

"Imperial Majesty, no. I'm sure you know that the Seneschal forces of Hell don't work in quite the same way as the police force in your world. No, our only concern was that Pearl Tang was operating without a license, so she wasn't paying any tax. And taxes," said the demon, with a beguiling smile, "are the only certainty in this life or out of it. Since not even death's reliable any more."

Outremer

It was a night in the embers of winter and the fog was pouring up from the river, lying pale over the water and a dull orange above the dockyard gaslights. My brother was out looking for me and even my name on his tongue was too much to bear. I drew back against the grain canisters when I heard the echo of his footsteps out of the cold air, but the beating of my heart seemed to fill the world. I waited until his voice faded away and ran down to the wharf. I thought of the ship, of the message I had sent on the day of my father's death. In seven months' time, the captain had said. When we come back from the Indies, I'll take you with me. In seven months, when the moon is new. But then, a wind rose from the treacherous sea and veered upriver, driving the mist before it, and as the sky cleared I saw that there was no ship waiting by the wharf. He had not come, after all. I would have to go back.

Leaving the darkness of the shipyards, I hastened back to the place that was no longer a home. Each guilty step I took rang like a bell in the empty streets; I thought of my brother, following me with smiling, greedy patience. When I reached the end of the row, I ducked into the mews and ran along the cobbles until I got to the back wall of the house I'd hoped never to see again. Hitching up my long skirts, I dropped over the wall, but I slipped on the wet earth and fell heavily, biting my lip. I lay there for a moment, breathless. The blood was bitter in my mouth, as sour as failure. Forcing myself to get up and go inside, I found that the kitchen door was still on the latch. I pushed it open and as I did so, the gas lamp hissed into light. My brother Jonathan was standing in the doorway. He said nothing. I licked the blood from my lip; instinct always saves. I knew how it would affect him. He said, gently enough, "Where have you been? I couldn't find you in the house."

"There was a fox," I said, lying. "In the hens, again. I thought, if I went out without the lamp—"

"Yes, yes," Jonathan said, impatiently. Of course he knew where I'd been. He had followed me down to the wharf. I hoped he couldn't guess the reason why I'd gone, but how could he? It was the one secret I'd managed to keep from him.

He said now, "You've hurt yourself. . . . "

I forced myself to keep my voice light.

"I walked into the door," I said.

Coming over to me, he brushed the cut with the tip of one finger to leave a thin scarlet smear. Then he said, "You'd best go to your room. Make certain that you say your prayers."

It was always like that: kind words, and the cruel current running beneath like the tides of the estuary. I nodded, as submissively as I could, and ducked past him to run up the stairs. Once I reached my room, I shoved my muddy shoes under the bed, pulled on my nightgown and pulled the counterpane up to my chin. I left the door open. I had locked it once. Now, a month later, I still remembered the bruises. It was easier to leave the door open, and endure, and wait. As I heard my brother's footstep on the stairs I kept the thought in my head: tomorrow. The ship is late, nothing more. Tomorrow it will come, and I will be saved and safe.

After he had left me I lay as still as I could and waited for the Sabbath dawn. When at last the sun rose up over the sill it was as pale as a shadow. It drew the cloud up with it and soon it was gone into the winter day. I went downstairs and cleaned the ashes from the grate. Soon, the mouse of a maid came from the lower town where she lived and set about preparing the breakfast.

As usual, I accompanied my brother to church. Sitting at the back of the congregation it seemed to me, as it always did, that everyone could see, that everyone knew, but perhaps this was only my own shame making me lie to myself. My brother was a good citizen; a good man, they said in the town, like his father the minister had been. The men approved of Jonathan's florid respectability; the women liked his soft voice and plump hands. Jonathan might have inherited the house and the wealth, I told myself, but never our father's Christian charity. I had loved my father, now resting in the green churchyard beyond these uncaring walls, but at that moment I could not help hating him for dying, for leaving me, for not taking me with him.

The service ground to its interminable close and the congregation filed out into the cold. Meek as the lamb they say we should become, I followed my brother home. That afternoon, I sat in the parlor and pretended to read my Bible. The words swam across the page as though the room was filled with water. They didn't mean anything to me any more; my faith in the Book had died with my father. I could think only of the ship, the rigger, sailing out on a dark wind when the moon is new. I thought of the prayer I had whispered down into the grave. If you want something badly enough, my father used to say, then it will come, but you must be careful of the form it takes. You must mind what you wish for, he said, but I no longer cared.

The evening wore on. I sat in the parlor with the unread Bible on my lap. I could feel my brother's eyes on me. Murmuring something, I put the book aside and rose.

"Where do you think you're going?" he asked. His voice was light and kind.

"Just to the—outside for a moment," I said. I lowered my eyes, hoping that he would think I was ashamed, or afraid.

"Make sure you take your shawl," he said. "It's a cold night."

Outside, I banged the door of the outhouse as if I had gone in there, and crept back into the darkness of the kitchen. Jonathan stepped past me, unseeing. He called through the back door, "Cecily? Sis? Are you there?"

He crossed the yard and as he stood peering uncertainly into the dark I ran swiftly through the kitchen and out through the front door, closing it softly behind me. My slippers skidded on the icy road but I did not look back. It did not take long for me to hear the beat of his running feet behind me, but his soft life had slowed him down. I ran as fast as I could, and when I reached the wharf I was gasping. The pain ran up my side like lightening. It seemed far away, a separate part of me. I could hear my brother's steps along the wharf. I prayed that the ship would come, drawn by the beating drum of my heart through the fog which once more rose from the river. I reached the grain bins and had to pause to catch my breath.

Out above the river the gulls wheeled and cried in the darkness. In the town, they christen them 'Davy Jones' Chickens,' but my father, a fisherman as well as a minister, called them the daughters of God and said that they were the souls of fallen women consigned to the forgiving waves and free forever. I could hear my brother's voice as I stood on the wharf, shouting for me once more, and it seemed to me that I had been listening to that voice all my life.

Before the fog had fallen to suffocate the estuary, the storms had battered the coast for a day and a half. I was afraid then that the ship had foundered out on the North Sea, missing the safe channels, torn apart by the currents. My eyes strained to see the mast-lights through the mist that rode on the night like a banner, but I could see no further than the harbor wall. I thought I could hear something; the soft lapping of water against the wharf, as though a craft was stealing upriver. I was so desperate to see that I was out on the edge of the wharf before I knew it, and there my brother found me. He grasped me by the arm and dragged me from the water's edge. I stood and faced him, and he slapped my cheek, knocking me to the ground.

"Whore!" he shouted. "My sister a whore and out waiting for a sailor, you dockyard slut. I'll drown you like a kitten!" He hit me again as I tried to rise, bruising my knees on the cobbles, and railed at me for a portside harlot, a disgrace in the eyes of the Lord.

"If I am a whore," I cried "then it's you who made me one!"

He hit me in the mouth and I fell across the wet stones, rolling to the edge of the wharf. Jonathan stepped forward to strike me, but a sight that I had not yet seen stopped his hand and he stood appalled on the dockside, a small and wicked man. The ship that is the bride of the sea rode above us on the river. She was a wreck in the night; her sails hung in tattered rags and pennants on the skeletal rigging, her hull was staved in, and her boards were the color of bones in the darkness. Her figurehead remained, the figure of the whore, ivory faced and bloody-lipped, though her colors were faded. I looked for the gilded name of the ship, but I could no longer read what it might be. It didn't matter what it was called. She belongs to us all who are fallen. I could see the faces of the women as they clustered along her rotting sides and they reached out their hands to me through the mist, crying out in sympathy.

I scrambled painfully to my feet. My brother was backing away to turn and run, but before he could bolt, I threw my arms around him. I do not know where I found the strength, nor do I remember falling locked in his arms from the wharf, or the crushing weight as the hull of the wreck drove us down into the cold and the darkness.

The bride of the sea is an old boat, and she rides the tides forever. We are sailing north now for the winter; beyond the sea, to the place called Outremer, but there are many ports of call along the way, many graveside promises to honor. It is work to which I feel fitted. I even have my own cabin, and the captain, a Dutchman, is patient and forgiving, like my father. The daughters of God, the gull and the albatross, sail with us in the empty seas. I sit on the prow and watch the mist stream by in these northern waters, and if anyone should ask where I have gone, why, you must tell them I have run away to sea.

Skindancing

Anyone can make a monster these days, Ivan Vorlund knows, but it takes more than science to breathe life into the waiting flesh. It takes the alchemical processes of power and desire; the conjuring of a soul out of bone and blood. He looks down at the body of the girl, neatly placed upon the veined marble slab, and reflects that it does not matter how the thing is done. Perhaps he and Siri are in a laboratory, somewhere in the outskirts of Tokyo or Novy Rus, and he has watched the sheaths and filaments of skin unravel slowly from the weaving spider of artificial DNA. Or perhaps Siri is the legacy of an ancient transformatory skill: carried from drowned lands to the Middle Kingdom, cradled across the centuries until it reaches its apotheosis in the basement of some old house in the Jewish quarter of Prague. It does not matter how Siri has been made, Vorlund reflects, as he leans down to whisper in her ear the secrets of her soul, and she opens blue and empty eyes.

Later, when she is able to stand, Vorlund takes her home; traveling through the night to Berlin and the house in Kreuzberg, where she is to be trained before entering society. Here, he carefully prepares Siri for her work in the torture gardens of the newly reunited city. She's a quick learner, it seems. Soon, she's ready to entertain clients—well, they're more friends, really, because Vorlund is not in this for the money. He is already a wealthy man; one who has the resources to indulge himself in the darkest of the arts of pleasure. He teaches Siri all the subtleties of masochism: how to submit, how to express torment in the most elegant way, the way that will give the greatest delight to the dominant. The processes which created her ensure that the amount of pain she experiences can be controlled: fine-tuned to the dominant's desires. At the end of her training, Siri will do whatever is required of her, and the existence of her soul makes Vorlund's triumph the more complete. For without a soul, after all, how can someone truly suffer?

Siri does not show the same aptitude for everything. At first, it seems that language is beyond her, but Vorlund gradually teaches her a simple form of Sign. At length, she can manage basic conversations, speaking with her hands, and she seems to understand what he says. Initially, Siri also demonstrates some slight indication of independent thought, which pleases Vorlund. Unless the submissive is to some extent an individual, the dominant cannot experience true power. All the same, it's a delicate balance, and has to be encouraged in an appropriate way. Vorlund decides to direct any latent enthusiasms that Siri might possess towards the arts. He takes her to the Opera, and to the galleries which are proliferating throughout Berlin. She clings to his arm and smiles, and her fragile beauty wins admirers wherever they go. Vorlund introduces her to other arts; hiring dance teachers to train her in the suitably brittle forms of ballet.

Soon it is evident that Siri loves to dance, and this intrigues Vorlund. She spends hours at the bar, moving just within the betraying edge of human capability. When she dances, dressed in black leotards above which her face is as pale and grave as the ghost of a child, her hands tell Vorlund that she is utterly his creature. And yet, and yet. . . . There have been incidents; cracks in the perfect veneer. The time, for example, when Vorlund enters the bedroom to find her hunched in the chair, bent over her arm, doing something.

"Siri?" and looking up she smiles, hiding the thin thread of blood beneath her sleeve and putting the manicure scissors back on the table. "What are you doing?"—but she only holds out her flawless, innocent hands.

"Siri, come downstairs, please. They're waiting for you," and she nods vaguely, but not before he has seen something whisk furtively away behind her eyes. The thought occurs to Vorlund that his galatea might be all the better for a little diversion, and so he takes her dancing, to the Engine Room in Kreuzberg.

After a turn around the floor, they watch the show in silence. It's an avant garde performance, which even in liberal Kreuzberg manages to raise a few eyebrows. Vorlund is interested in Siri's reaction; he steals a glance at her as the dancers on the stage put each other through elegant and unnatural rigors. He cannot help hoping that it might give Siri ideas;

for although he has trained her well, there's always room for something new. Siri's face betrays no expression whatsoever, but at the end of the performance she rises and walks over to the stage before Vorlund can stop her.

Her eyes are blank, as though someone has switched off the life inside her, but she is smiling. The crowd gives a collective sigh as she steps onto the stage, and sits back to watch. Siri is perfect: a porcelain doll with hair the color of old blood. Vorlund shifts uncomfortably in his seat.

Siri holds out her hands to the crowd, inviting adulation, then begins to dance in a sequence of fluid arabesques. She keeps the performance within limits, but there's something not quite right about the way she moves: she's too flexible, somehow, too sinuous. Reaching down, she picks up her evening bag and takes something from it. Vorlund can't see what it is, but it glitters as it catches the light, and then Siri raises her hand.

Resting on her palm is a pearl handled scalpel, which Siri wields with all the obscene precision of a robot arm. There's something reassuring about this clinical evocation of the operating theatre, as though things are under control. And sure enough, the first cut is tiny, no more than a nick in the flesh, as if to prove that nothing vulgar's going to happen; that Siri won't start slashing at herself like some deranged mutilatory doll. Vorlund sips his blended Ukrainian scotch and watches numbly as Siri makes a sequence of intricately delicate incisions across her forearm. There isn't a great deal of blood; only a smear of pale scarlet beneath the spotlight. Siri ambidextrously turns her attention to the other arm. She undulates coyly across the stage, in a parody of coquettish seduction. Soon she is banded and dappled with blood: protective coloration, Vorlund thinks, then wonders where the thought has come from. The drops scatter around her bare feet like the petals of a flower.

Some of the crowd, Vorlund notices, are holding little bowls made from a pale, frosted porcelain, the color of the dancer's own skin. Puzzled, he soon realizes that these are the ashtrays belonging to the Engine Room. Siri sighs a little and drifts down to the floor, plucking at her arm. Her skin tears from her fingers in a series of fragile strands, and as she progresses down her arm it begins to peel away in a single stripe, like a tight glove. Her face betrays nothing, least of all pain. Yet it seems to Vorlund that he can feel what she can not, as though it is he who is up there on the stage, easing his flesh away. He doesn't feel the pain in skin or bone or blood; it lies deeper than that, beyond the body. It's not supposed to be this way, he thinks through the haze of suffering. It should be the other way around. The faces of the crowd are tense, approaching a genteel satiation. Now that the muscles of Siri's arm have been laid bare, she tugs the scalpel across her wrist. Vorlund's teeth clench in involuntary anticipation, but there is no sudden gush of blood: only a few slow drops. The audience press forward and collect it in their little bowls, then discreetly withdraw, leaving Siri to sag bleeding to the floor.

The manager of the Engine Room offers medical assistance, but Siri waves it away. They place her on the couch, where she lies in almost regal state, her raw arm covered by a blanket. Gently, Vorlund lifts it aside and sees that the new dermis is already regenerating itself, filming the revealed muscles in satin translucence.

"She'll be all right," Vorlund tells the manager, possessively. "You can go now." When the man has gone, he looks at Siri. He can think of nothing to say. His creation stares back at him, equally mute, then she gives Vorlund a look which bears the faintest trace of disdain and turns her head. Vorlund is unexpectedly pierced to the heart.

"Siri, Siri," he manages to say. "Why are you doing this?" and then he adds, though he does not know why, "I'm sorry."

After the first performance, the question of why Siri should do such a thing takes immediate possession of Vorlund. He asks her over and over again, in all the languages he knows, but he must be asking the wrong questions, for Siri only sits, and smiles, and heals, and says nothing. Eventually Vorlund gives up and stares at her in unhappy bewilderment, but Siri is already asleep.

Vorlund tries to keep Siri confined to the house, but she eludes him with frightening ease. At last he takes to attending her performances, and each one makes him more depressed. It isn't so much the bloody content of her art, but the fact that he is so pointedly excluded from it. He's no different from the rest of her audience, he tells himself, but whereas Siri enjoys a smiling and secret complicity with the other watchers, she ignores Vorlund. Her gaze meets theirs, but shuts him out. He longs to know what they see behind her eyes. His own pain does not diminish with each performance, but retreats further within, traveling further and further with every drop of blood she sheds.

Eventually Vorlund's determination breaks and he goes out to buy a bowl. He sits in supplication with the others, and when it comes to the climax of the show, he shuts his eyes. He reminds himself, disgusted, of a child waiting for a present, but his feigned innocence doesn't do him any good, for when he looks down into the bowl it is as white and clean as the polished arch of a skull.

Frustrated, Vorlund starts hanging around the dressing room door. Siri won't let him in any more, and she never comes home. He sends associates to bring her back, but somehow they always fail. Vorlund is not alone in his longing, either, for the crowds have begun to swell as some tacit, half-understood message passes through the city. It costs the equivalent of $200 to get into the Engine Room, and most people can't afford it, but there are still tides and eddies of worshippers waiting patiently outside the dressing room as Siri rests within. It seemed that it doesn't take much, after all, to turn the Mozart-loving, mink-furred sophisticates of old Berlin into medieval supplicants. Suddenly, bankers and diplomats are claiming wide-eyed that the latest cabaret star can raise the dead and heal the sick, turn the sun on its head and stars in their paths. Some word of the needs of ordinary people must have reached her, for soon Siri starts doing free shows.

Vorlund discovers this by accident. He sees her from the limousine, one wan afternoon, as he is coming back from the Siemens plant. She is standing on a patch of wasteland, where the old Wall used to be. The Wall has been gone for a while now, but some memory of limitation or boundary must remain, for this is where Siri has chosen to perform. Vorlund only catches a glimpse of her, but it is enough. He orders his driver to stop, and runs back. He's too late. By the time he reaches the wasteground, the crowd is already trailing away, carrying the bowls and their precious contents in gloved fingers, and Siri is crumpled across the broken earth. It's November now, and the frost still lingers in the dark places beside the fractured concrete. Vorlund kneels by Siri's side and touches her face. She is colder than the day. Blood seeps from her in a widening pool; her pulse is silent. Vorlund feels breathlessly cheated; after all his devoted care, she's still managed to give him the slip. He stares blindly around the wasteland. Apparently it is one of the city farms encouraged in Kreuzberg. The earth along the fences is combed into neat strips, and the last atrophied heads of sunflowers are averted from the sky. Vorlund turns and finds Siri sitting up and watching him. She has a faint, smug smile like a cat's, as though she's done something unforgivably clever. Vorlund is so relieved that he hugs her; she stays stiffly in his arms for a moment, then pulls away. He could almost have borne it if she had been angry with him, but there is nothing in her face. Rising, she walks away, her hand to her throat as it seals.

Vorlund has no idea how she does it. He does not understand her evolved ability to treat death as a door. He performs a number of tests, rushing her lifeless form into hospital at the end of her latest stage performance, and there's no doubt about it: she's gone. There isn't even a trace of brainstem function; none of the ambiguities of coma. This time, she seems to be irreversibly dead; she won't come back in answer to his whispered, urgent pleas, but he still feels that she can hear him. He's convinced that she is sulking, somewhere in the long wastelands beyond the flesh, and sure enough, once her lifeless body is taken from the hospital and returned home, she comes neatly back to life again, rising from the bed and stalking into the bathroom without a backward glance at her miserable creator. Vorlund wonders whether any god could feel as hollow as he does now.

After this, Siri vanishes for long stretches of time. Vorlund follows her, and tries to have her followed, but she eludes him every time even though he knows roughly where she goes: a different location each day, to the old places where the Wall used to stand, where barriers and boundaries have fallen. One day he finds her, more by luck than accident, in the woods around Wannsee, with a crowd gathered before her. The trees are bare now, and there's a wind blowing out of the east from the river. The faces of the audience are white with cold, but Siri has pared herself down to a lattice of bone and when she turns Vorlund can see the intricate scaffold of ribcage and spine. He glances away, only for a moment, but when he looks back the crowd have gone and Siri is lying whitely among the dead leaves. He cannot understand how there can be so little left. She might be mimicking the lost dead of the last war; it might not even be Siri at all.

With revolted fascination he watches her rebuild herself, cell by glistening cell. No one should have to see so much, he thinks. No one should penetrate so far into the mystery of the body, and fail so completely to understand. At least her audience has the decency to leave her alone after the show, but Vorlund isn't satisfied, he thinks with bitter self reproach; he has to see more. Siri blinks eyes that are as blue as the winter sky and walks down towards the river.

In an attempt to forget for a little while, Vorlund invites one of the floorshow girls from the Engine Room to come home with him. Somewhere in the night he wakes and finds her pressed against his side; her skin is hot and damp and human. Vorlund looks down at her shadowy shape and thinks how much better she would look without all that weight of flesh. He begins idly to plan, still half asleep, dreaming a butcher's dreams. A sound in the street brings him to his senses; he steals from the bed, retrieves his clothes and walks uncertainly out into the morning city. His hands are shaking; he wonders whether this loss of control is going to happen again, or often. Unfamiliar thoughts pass through his mind. Women, he believes, are conditioned to submit, men to transgress. Yet Siri, who is neither artificial nor natural, strides boundaries with ease, even the ultimate violation of the divide between life and death. What she does, after all, is no more than anything men have done to women since history began, sending them down into torment. It is what Siri was created for: why then should it be so intolerable when she savages herself, terrorizing her own secret flesh? But even as Vorlund asks himself these questions, he knows the answer: it is because Siri has taken control. He has assumed that she is damaging herself as some form of protest; he realizes that he is wrong. Siri's reactions lie beyond his comprehension. He remembers how he felt at her unnatural birth; how he would train her for the dynamics of objectification, yet teach her how to be human. He has given her a soul, after all; neural dreams distilled from images and experiences. The earth under the pines, wet with rain; the taste of snow at dawn in the mountains above Yerevan; the red wood of Nakano temple on the lamplight. He remembers concertos and arias, mathematics and spells, the understanding of power and pain. He has infused her with all that a soul should be, and even at the time he wondered whether it was enough. But isn't that what they all want, in books and films and animé? Robot/cyborg/alien/other, all with the simple tremulous desire for a human self beneath their monstrous carapaces? But Siri, it seems, has other plans; desires so remote and unfathomable that Vorlund might as well have tried to teach a stone or a star.

Vorlund has started smoking again; it seems to anchor him as he stands at the back of the crowd, watching as Siri spins her enchanted dance. His vision blurs through the smoke. There are two dancers tonight; a girl has joined Siri on stage. She twists and turns in mimicry of

Siri's impossible fluidity, but when they both crumple to the floor, only Siri rises. The crowd sighs with release. Vorlund can't watch any more; it seems he's losing his taste for forbidden pain. He leaves the Engine Room without speaking to anyone, and spends the day by the river. When twilight begins to fall, he heads for the wasteland, drawn by a magnet which he does not comprehend. At the city farm, there is the glow of a fire. Vorlund pushes aside the dead sunflowers and there is Siri, standing on a concrete block, quite still. One by one, her audience is stepping onto the makeshift stage. Vorlund cannot see what happens then; they seem to pass and fade into the darkness behind her. Forcing his way through the crowd, he stands at the foot of the block and looks up. As usual, Siri ignores him. What is she? Vorlund wonders, yet again. Avatar, demon, goddess? Anyone can make a monster, these days, but Siri is something else: something that makes a mockery of the categories of the world, who has twisted its ontology to her own impenetrable ends.

At last, the crowd has gone, and Siri and Vorlund are alone. After what seems like a very long time, she bends her head and looks at him. Her eyes are golden in the light of the flames, but behind them he can see the void: the heart of chaos from which all violation comes. It is not Siri's soul, Vorlund realizes, that has been at issue, but his own. Siri reaches out and takes his hand. As he looks down at their interlaced fingers he can see that his own flesh, too, is starting to burn away, and the world is bright as fire as his redeemer smiles.

A Child of the Dead

One

I've walked down Jiangsu Road almost every day of my life, ever since I was a little girl. Going to school with my brother Tso, my grandmother would hold our hands and together we'd look in the restaurant windows at the steamed buns and the egg rolls, at the flat stretched chickens which Mr. Hsiun told me were wind-dried. I work in that restaurant now, and I know how the food's prepared, but I used to imagine all these poor hens blown about in a roaring gale until all their feathers had gone and they were stiff and thin. It's funny the ideas you get when you're a kid. Grandma knew everyone then, and they'd come out of the doorways to talk to her. Sometimes we'd go round to see people and I'd sit with a Coke while Grandma fixed something or other: she was always good with machines. Now, no one talks to anyone, and my grandmother stays at home. It seems to me that many things have begun to change, down Jiangsu Road. The sunlight doesn't seem to reach it any more, and last night when I came home from the restaurant, I looked up and saw the stars. I've never noticed them before above the city, because of the lights, but one night at my great aunt's house out in the country Grandma sat on the porch with me and pointed out all the constellations: the shepherd boy, the maiden, all of them. When we went home to Shanghai I got a book and learned them off by heart. But these stars that blaze above me now are different and I don't recognize a single one.

Sometimes the people change, too. I walked down Jiangsu Road yesterday on my way to work, as usual. There wasn't a soul in sight, but just opposite the entrance to the market I turned round and saw that all the doors of the shops were open and everyone was watching me. At first I didn't recognize anyone, but then, to my relief, I realized who they were. They were the dead. I could see old Mr. Hsiun, who'd told me about the chickens, and who died about four years ago when we had that cholera outbreak. He was smiling and nodding at me, so I waved. Some of my relatives were there, too: I saw my great uncle Leo. I went over to have a word.

"So you're still living here?" I said.

"Yes, yes, we're still here; we haven't moved," Leo said. "We heard your prayers. Thanks." He smiled at me, but there was nothing behind his eyes. He looked as two-dimensional as a paper doll, and then the wind shredded him into tatters, so I walked away. The restaurant was still in its usual place, but the chickens that were hung up in the windows had gone and in their place were things that looked like ribcages; human ones, I suppose, but I'm not really sure. Anyway, after that it all melted away and I was back in the normal world and late for work. I'm trying to ignore these odd episodes; there are too many other things to worry about at the moment. I'm working double shifts at the restaurant now, because we spoke to the doctors yesterday and they said that we're behind with the payments for Tso's treatment. We can't very well abandon the treatment halfway through, so it's a question of either taking out a loan, which I don't want to do, or trying to catch up. I suppose we'll just have to manage. At least if one of us can get proper treatment, it makes things seem a little better, and it has to be Tso, because he's a boy.

Two

My grandmother, as she sits in front of the flat eye of the old computer screen, tells me that I should put my faith in machines rather than the chancy flesh. Perhaps she's right; I don't know any more. I'm just going from day to day at the moment: working at the restaurant, cleaning the flat, taking Tso to the hospital once a week. I took him up there this morning. They had him in the viral unit for almost two hours, while I waited outside. I tried to get tea out of the machine with a plastic chip they give you at the take away, but it broke off and stuck in the slot so I had to sit there, guilty and thirsty, while everyone gave me dirty looks. Then when Tso came out we had to spend ten dollars on a taxi because he was still a bit groggy. After that I went to the restaurant and started my waitressing shift, but I was late again and they docked my wages. It's not been a very good day, today.

Three

When I got back last night, Grandma was still up, sitting with her ear to the lifeless terminal.

"You know what?" she said. "Sometimes, if I listen hard enough, I think I can still hear them."

"Who?" I asked.

"All those voices. In the old days, you could log on, you could talk to people. Thousands of voices. . . out there, everywhere." She gave the terminal a little shake, as if it needed only a little encouragement to get it going again.

"Yeah, you said." Grandma used to tell me stories about the e-net, but it didn't sound much to me. All you could hear was a lot of people and static on the other end of the line, crackling and bouncing off a strand satellite. She never had a very good machine: only the little home-made portable. Well, those days were long gone and there was the future to think about now. I drew a deep breath.

"Grandma? Listen, a couple of days ago I stopped off at the market and spoke to Tony Tang. I don't know how you're going to feel about this, but he thinks he might be able to get me a cheap deal."

I muttered the words, but I got her full attention. She gave me a beady look.

"What sort of cheap deal?"

"Well, you know. . . . He thinks he could get me some equipment. Just some basic stuff. . . . "

"And how do you propose to pay for it?"

I wished I'd never started the conversation. I should have just got on with it and said nothing, but I couldn't tell her now that I'd already done a deal with Tony. A fait accompli, I think they call it. Reluctantly, I said, "The thing is, I'm thirteen now. So I don't really want to wait much longer, because, I guess, it won't be long before I'm too old. To learn how to use the new technology. You know?"

She was quiet for a while, and then she said, "Li Hua. . . we were talking about the old days just now. I can't help feeling that things were better then. Maybe I just don't understand this new technology of yours. I trained with machines, you see? Chips and neural nets and A-life, but things moved on so quickly. Two years after I graduated, Genreng Pharmaceuticals started to develop neuroviral interfacing—the bioweb, the Hsingtao, whatever they call it these days—and I found out I was obsolete. I was too old to be put through the new program. Past it, you see. I was nineteen. And in the old days, at least you had the hope of another job when your technician career was over. I don't like this modern technology, Li Hua. I don't trust it, and I don't want you hanging round Tony Tang and his cut price under-the-counter deals."

I said, "Okay. Look, I'm going to bed. I'll see you in the morning,"—and I left her staring at the blankness of the screen. I hate arguing with Grandma. It always makes me feel guilty, because I know she paid a lot of money for Tso and me. She wanted a child so badly, but she couldn't even have that. There was something wrong with her ova, some genetic thing, and they had to terminate her pregnancy. But fortunately, when they checked the fetus, they found its ova were fine, so they just fertilized two of them and transplanted them into a breeder and Grandma got Tso and me. That's all my poor mother was, a scrap of meat in a jar, and my father maybe less than that. I sometimes wonder if that's why I seem to be seeing ghosts all the time, being a child of the dead; but I know that isn't the real reason.

Four

I went to see Tang again this afternoon in his shop at the back of the herbalist's. He was bent over the desk, doing something with a culture dish. He had one of those dried snakes that they make pills out of sitting on the desk and when he saw me he rattled it at me, hissing.

"Cute," I said. I pulled up a stool and watched him as he worked. I drew a finger down the snake's skeletal spine: it felt as light and dry as air.

"So, did you speak to your grandma?" Tony asked.

"Yeah. Well, I tried. She wasn't very keen, to be honest. She's old fashioned, Tony, you know?"

"Sure. She's an old lady. When she was your age, they just didn't do this kind of thing. Times change. Your grandma knows that." He paused, concentrating on the contents of the dish beneath the microscope.

"Do you still want to go ahead with our deal?" he asked.

I said, "If I decided to back out now, could I? I mean, is it too late?"

"No. No, it's not too late." He looked up, and his round face was earnest. "And you should know something, Li Hua, I wouldn't charge you for the equipment you've already used. I mean, I wouldn't do that."

"I know," I said. "It's okay; don't be silly. I want to carry on with it. Can I have a look at this?" I squinted down the scope while he held the microdermic. I could see the little blob, and the tip of the dermic penetrating it.

"That's all it is." Tony said.

"So how long will it take?"

"Ten minutes."

"Oh, okay, not so long, then. So I could go in on my way to work?"

"Whenever. I've made an appointment for you at the doctor's on Xiang Road. She's a woman; I thought you might prefer that."

That's one of the things I like about Tony Tang; he's thoughtful.

"Thanks," I said. "What about tomorrow?"

"If you like. Stop in here on your way back, let me know how it went. You'll need more of the equipment then, anyway."

"Okay, see you then." I said, picking up my bag. I didn't want to tell him about the hallucinations; I was scared that he might think it was a bad omen and get cold feet. I left without saying anything.

"Keep the snake," he said, on my way out the door.

Five

The session at the doctor's wasn't as bad as I'd thought. The doctor was really nice, and afterwards she gave me a can of paracola, which she needn't have done.

"Do I have to do anything else?" I asked her.

"No, that's it. You shouldn't have any complications, but if you do, you come right back and let me know. You said your periods haven't started yet?"

"No, that's right." I said.

"Okay. It might have a slight effect, but there shouldn't be any problems." She helped me down from the couch. "There you are. You're all done."

Six

I guess Tony might have felt a little sorry for me, because as well as the equipment he gave me twenty dollars. Then at the weekend, it was New Year's and I made nearly three hundred in tips. It was more money than I'd ever seen before. Grandma and I counted it up today, before we stashed it under the bed, and Tso watched us from the bunk bed, smiling. I'm so relieved. Now we can pay off the hospital fees and in a month or so Tso can start work. I suppose I'm sorry, in a way, because we won't see much of him once he's got a job. Tso's doctor has been helpful; he says that he might be able to get Tso a place at an institute in Harbin. It's a long way away, but it's worth it.

I took my grandmother out this evening. Mrs. Eng came in to look after Tso, and Grandma and I went out to dinner. I told her to order anything she liked, no matter how much it cost.

"You're a good girl, Li Hua," she said.

"Isn't it great? Tso's treatment, I mean." I couldn't stop talking about it.

"Yes," she said, but she still looked sad. I reached across the table and squeezed her hand.

"Don't worry," I told her.

"Oh, I suppose I'm pleased for Tso, if that's what he wants, but it just seems—I'm sorry, Li. I know I'm old fashioned, but things were just different in the past, you see." Suddenly, I could see, she was angry. I knew that she wasn't mad at me, but I kept quiet, anyway. It was as though she was talking to herself. "All those machines, Li Hua, all those wonderful machines. Then Genreng invent the bioweb, and computers aren't any use any more. Machine obsolescence. Suddenly there's the bioweb, and how do you access it? You've got to be part of it, your whole body, through a neuroviral interface. And you can't do that unless you get dosed up with one of their synthetic viruses, and you've got to be young." She snorted. "You can't tell me that there's nothing wrong with that: making yourself ill so that you can be part of the global communications network."

She fell silent and I stared at the table. I couldn't quite see what the problem was. I thought of Tso, in a month's time; lying in a cot in Harbin, sailing the viral pathways, able to reach out to everyone else who was infected. A disease is a system, I understood, and I thought it was a great mark of progress: that we no longer needed to invent machines, computers, for the resources had been with us all along. Tso would be another link in the great chain of the neuroviral web, and it in turn would convey all the information he needed: the world as one great mind, unified.

"And then what happens?" my grandmother murmured. "He'll work for a few years, and then what? How do we know he's even got a future after that?"

"It's not like that, Grandma! The doctors told me. They just give you a cure, it's all perfectly straightforward."

"Maybe." She did not sound very sure. She reached out and patted my hand. "At least you'll still be here, Li Hua."

I didn't want to tell her, then, that she was wrong. Even with the low grade viral equipment that Tang's given me in exchange for the ova, I should be able to get a job in some webshop somewhere, and then I'll be able to reach out across the thousand miles to Harbin, and beyond, and my brother will be there. Grandma doesn't understand, you see, that you have to accommodate yourself to life, to Tao. It's like water, you have to go wherever it takes you, and you can't stop it for long. She always wanted to leave the body behind, soar out into the electronic sunlight, but you can't do that. You have to go the other way, into darkness, into the body itself. But I didn't want to argue with her, and this was something we could talk about later. I reached out and poured more tea into her cup. I smiled at my grandmother and I could tell from the side effects that Tang's virus was working, for outside the window the faces of the dead clustered in the shadows, beneath the unknown stars.

The Sea of Time and Space

I have seen stars that have the redness of an eye, formed from the great and glittering dark. I have seen the suns that shine at midnight, and the hand of God reach down to touch the hand of man. I have seen a great many things in the sea of time and space, but I have seen nothing like the visitor who came to me, one winter day. On several occasions, I have had to account for the painting that illustrates that visitor, yet this is the first time that I have brought myself to tell the true story.

I had gone to see a customer that afternoon, to fetch a manuscript to proofread. I hoped to begin setting it in my little print shop on the following morning, and I was glad to be coming home. I intended that evening to work on certain pictures, granted to me through my visions, and I was anxious to continue this work: for to me, this was the reason and purpose of my life and not the mundane print tasks that I was compelled to undertake in order to support my own needs and those of my wife. Though the thought of the work was warming, I shivered as I crossed the river. It was a cold evening, with frost ringing hard beneath the horses' hooves on the earth of the London streets. My breath streamed white in the air, and as I entered the house I heard the bells of St Luke's ring out the hour and realized that I was late for supper. I could hear my wife's irritated footsteps clattering to and fro across the wooden kitchen floor as I hastened up the stairs to change my outdoor coat.

Just before the landing, however, I chanced to glance down and saw that an eye was watching me through a crack in the skirting. The eye was the size of a small apple; a dark, burnished crimson like a coal in the ashes. It looked like the eye of the Devil himself. Stepping hastily back, I tripped on the stair and dropped the manuscript. The eye winked, once, and retreated into the blackness beyond the wall.

"William!" called my wife's voice from the bottom of the stairs. "Whatever are you doing?"

I looked back towards the crack. There was nothing there. I said, "Catherine? I think there is something in the wall."

She snorted. "Of course there is. Rats, Mr. Blake." My wife only called me that if truly annoyed, which was rare. She went on, "The house is alive with them, as anyone could see who doesn't live entirely in his own head. If I've told you once, I've told you a thousand times—we really must get a cat. I suppose you weren't listening, as usual. I shall go to Mrs. Smallwell's and purchase one tomorrow. And your supper's getting cold."

Slowly, I gathered up the pages of the manuscript and descended the stairs. I did not know to what manner of being the eye might belong, nor was I eager to find out. I wondered whether it had been a manifestation of the visions which so frequently veil my waking sight, like the spirits of dreams, or simply the low, late sun glinting through a window-pane and catching some fragment embedded in the wall. There are times when I find reality and illusion hard to differentiate and indeed, I maintain that there is little difference between them; that what to the run of mankind is held to be a fancy, is itself the truth.

As the days went by, I became increasingly preoccupied with the great work on which I had so recently embarked. I sought nothing less than the depiction of the human soul itself, but though I could see this so clearly in my vision—a brilliant petaled growth like the lotus of the East—I somehow could not quite grasp it through the medium of paint. I became immersed in my work, only coming out for meals and sleep, and then reluctantly. Catherine, who was as a rule the most patient of women, declared herself tired of my absent rejoinders, often delivered many minutes after her original question had been asked, or not at all. She would, she informed me, be removing herself to her mother's for the next few days, leaving me to steep in the juices of my own imagination. I confess that I greeted this pronouncement with some relief. When this curious state that is such a mixture of blessing and affliction comes upon me, I am best left to myself.

Catherine went, therefore, and I was alone. I fear that I hardly noticed. Ignoring the manuscript that I had promised to typeset, I worked all that day in a fever, painting furiously as the vision possessed me. And yet I could not capture with mere daubs the form that I perceived so clearly, nor describe the phosphorescent transformations of the light through which it moved. Perhaps words might more readily ensnare them. . . and with that thought, I threw down the brush and sought the sanctuary of sleep.

It was already late into the night and the arms of Morpheus eluded me. I tossed for a while, then sank into an uneasy doze. When I next awoke, I was no longer alone. Something was crouching by the side of the bed. I lay still for a moment, still hazed by sleep. My left hand was enclosed in a hot dry clasp, but I could feel the rasp of something like a dog's tongue across my inner wrist and then a sharp sting of pain as the thing began to sip my blood. Gripped with sudden, belated horror, I tore my hand away and struggled upright. My assailant rustled back into the shadows, but I could still see the scaled arch of its brow, the curve of its massive shoulders and the pursed mouth, so akin to those soft anemones found in the rock pools along the south coast. It was taller than a man. Its eyes sparked coal-hot in the firelight. I could not utter a single word.

The creature dropped its great head for a moment, like a dog chastised by its master, then it rose to its feet and padded softly from the room. It is hardly startling that I slept poorly, if at all, for the remainder of the night. I lay in a kind of trance, clutching my wrist, and my head filled with a dull ache. Towards dawn, when the first thin winter light fell across the floor, I arose and went numbly down the stairs.

The visions that had so besieged me over the course of the previous day were now wholly absent, and I felt as heavy as the clay of the London street beyond. The only emotion which I could muster as worthy of the name was an increasing sense of dread as the December evening grew on. I was, indeed, most reluctant to go to bed at all, and at length resolved to remain sitting in my armchair before the fire, with the lamp and the firelight to comfort me. Congratulating myself on my wakeful vigilance, I promptly fell asleep.

Yet once again, I awoke to the stealthy touch of an unhuman hand upon mine, and opened my eyes to meet its crimson gaze. The creature and I stared at one another for a few moments. Its thick hide was the color of old blood, and its eyes were filled with sorrow, and something more. As I sat motionless before it, its tongue flickered out in a convulsive, greedy movement, and then it looked away.

"What are you?" I asked hoarsely, finding my voice at last. "What is it that you want?"

"Blood," it said. Its own voice sounded rusty, as though rarely used.

"Are you some demon, then, sent to persecute me from the heart of the Pit?"

It shook its armored head from side to side.

"I am nothing," it whispered. "Nothing at all. I want only blood." Its harsh voice rose to a roar and I shrank back into the armchair. "Blood!" it cried, and was abruptly gone. I sat, shaking, until the dawn. That morning, I resolved that if it were to come again, I would be ready for it.

The sleepless nights, and the stress and terror of the creature's visit, were taking their toll upon me. Normally a man in the most excellent of health, I felt weak and ill, and my very bones seemed to grind in their fragile casing of flesh. I could not afford a further depletion of my exhausted resources. If my nocturnal visitor wanted blood, I decided grimly, then blood it should have.

I dragged myself into the street and summoned one of the urchins who haunt the print shop in the hope of earning a few pennies by running errands. A boy came eagerly forward, for I was known to be generous with money—hoping thereby to ensure that my commissions would arrive safely at their destination and not be permitted to fall into the gutter during the pursuit of some more distracting game.

"Mr. Blake," the boy called as he approached. "You've work for me, then?"

"Yes, indeed," I told him. "Though I am afraid it is of a rather different order to your usual errands. I want you to go down to Smithfield for me, and procure—" I broke off, aware of how it sounded.

"What?" the boy asked, puzzled.

"I want you to bring me a large bowl of blood."

The boy looked nonplussed, as well he might. "Blood, Mr. Blake? What sort of blood?"

"Pig, cow, sheep—it doesn't matter. You see," I improvised hastily, "You know that I do paintings and drawings, things of that sort, don't you? Well, I am experimenting with a new type of pigment, and it has come to my mind that with a proper fixative, blood might provide me with the color I'm looking for."

It sounded like a lunatic explanation to me, but the boy's puzzled gaze seemed to clear. It seemed that my reputation for artistic eccentricity was standing me in good stead.

"Very good, sir. I'll go now, shall I?"

"That would be most helpful," I told him, thrusting a few pennies into his small pale hand. "Here's some wages in advance, and the rest when you return."

The boy ran off, and I went slowly back inside the house.

An hour later, there was a knock at the door. I confess that it startled me considerably; I had fallen into a doze at the fireside and when the sound came I leaped like a scalded cat and looked wildly around me. Then I recalled the boy's errand, and went hastily to the door. He was standing in the darkening street, holding the bowl before him. There was a smell of snow in the air but the blood steamed with the odor of hot iron.

"It's fresh," the boy assured me. "Pig."

"Excellent," I said. I took the bowl from him and placed it carefully on the step while I paid him the rest of his commission. Then I carried the bowl indoors and took it upstairs. I glanced in upon it several times over the course of that uneasy evening, but the blood remained undisturbed and undiminished, merely congealing in the chilly air. It was growing colder, and the fire seemed to make little difference to the temperature of the room. Shivering, I took myself to my bed fully clothed and sat there, sleepless.

I did not see him come. One minute, there was only myself amid the firelit shadows, the next moment, the creature was there, bending over the bowl of blood like a hound at the end of the chase. I saw the long serrated tongue flicker out once, scattering drops of pig's blood across the whiteness of the wall, and then the creature turned to me.

"It will not do, you see," he said, sadly.

"You said you wanted blood," I whispered. He padded across the room and crouched by the side of the bed. His head was level with my own, yet he seemed different, somehow: more skeletal, his skin dulled brown like rust or a scab. He said, "Thank you, for what you have tried to do for me. But it will not do. The blood must be that of a man."

"Tell me," I said. "Why should that be so? I see in your eyes that you do not wish to harm me—" and as I spoke, I knew it to be true. The creature sighed.

"It is part of my punishment, to sip the blood of men, even though I have come to hate such a craving."

"I asked you once before," I said. "What are you? What manner of thing?"

"I told you once before," he said. "I am nothing. I am the smallest of all small things that are. I am the ghost of a flea."

I gazed at the huge, bowed head and the hunched muscles of the shoulders and back.

"Small," I said, "Is not the word that comes most immediately to mind."

"Nevertheless," the creature replied. "That is what I am. Yet I was born a man, long ago, in a hot and ancient city. I lived my life in the service of one whose name is known to you in the holiest of books, a king. They knew me as the one behind his throne; my power was limitless, and I did not scruple to abuse it." He paused and something old and dead flickered behind his eyes.

"To abuse it?" I asked. "How?"

"I craved the blood of others since I was little more than a child. I would seek it out, in the public executions, and in more. . . private. . . amusements, such as a child may make unobserved. When I grew to the stature of a man, and earned my place in the city, I would have those who had taken my fancy brought to me, and entertain them far from the eyes of others."

I swallowed. I said, "Entertain them? Do you mean you tortured them?"

"I told you," the creature said. "I craved blood." Our eyes met. He went on "And then there came a time when I was witness to more blood than lay within the depths of that yearning. The city fell, to an army from the south. The king fell beneath enemy swords; the halls of the palace ran red. I tried to flee, but I was not long in following my master. They cut me down as I ran. I choked on my own blood and I thought it was the end, but the faith in which I had never believed proved truth after all."

"You do not mean the Christian faith," I stated.

"I do not. I felt my soul split into three and whirl out across the desert sands like shadows, and the last little core of that soul was brought before those who judge." The creature frowned. "Even now, I remember only darkly. Great presences, in a greater hall, and my soul plunging down against the balance of a golden feather. . . . But they sentenced me to life, not death, and granted me my greatest wish. They told me that since it was the blood of others that I had yearned for and sought, my yearning would be fulfilled. They cast my soul into the spirit of a flea, to sip the blood of men and learn to hate it." The creature grimaced. "And so I was dead, and free to go, and I walked on my silent ghostly feet from the halls of the dead and out into the worlds that lie beyond. I wandered through the vastnesses of the universe, but somewhere, out in the wastes that lie between the stars, I lost what little soul I still possessed. It slipped away from me, and I was nothing more than a ghost at last, a shadow that could speak and move and touch, but had no place." The ghost paused. Its crimson eyes grew quiet, like a coal that falls through the grate to die in the ashes. "My first and only love drew me back to the world. I scented human blood, running red from war and murder, and I came at last to the lands of the living. I wandered in the city for a time, stealing blood where I could find it, and then one day I met someone. He was not a human. I do not know what he was; he was bending over a dying woman in the streets of Tyburn and his face was filled with light. I caught him by the corner of his robe and pleaded for his help. He stared at me for a long time when he saw me, and then he smiled.

" 'If you can find a man,' he said, 'Who can help you find the soul you have lost, then he will put you on the road to Heaven.'

" 'Who?' I asked. 'Who amongst the living can even see me, save as an incubus in the night?'

" 'There is such a man,' he said, 'A visionary, one who walks between the worlds. His name is William Blake. And temptation will be placed in your way: to steal his blood—and more. If you take his blood, then you will steal his soul also, at the moment of his death.'

" 'That is not what I want to do, ' I protested.

" 'Then let us see if you can indeed resist it,' he said, already fading into air, and soon he was gone. Dejected, I made my way back out into the city, and several nights after that, I heard a man speak the name of William Blake: a madman, a mystic, he said, who experienced visions, and lived in the city. Thus I sought you out." The ghost fell silent.

"And you want me to help you?" I asked. "Help you to find your soul?"

The ghost nodded. "They say that you among all men may see where others cannot. All the way to God, so they say. But I can no longer contain my need for the blood that has drawn me back to the world, and holds me yet. I have sought you out and sipped your blood; I could not resist it, it has been too long. I am tied to you now. And if I steal your blood at the moment of your death, then your own soul will be mine." His eyes shot sparks in the darkness, and I was even more afraid.

"Listen to me," I said. "It is true that I have talents that few others seem to possess, although it is also true that these are granted to me by God's grace alone and no innate quality of mine. I will try and help you. I will travel to the world beyond, and see if the Lord in his infinite wisdom may grant me an answer. But there is one thing that you must understand. If I am to place myself into this state of trance, I must not be physically weak. I will not have you fastening on me like a leech. I want your word—not the word of the flea, nor of the man you used to be, but your own promise, as you are here and now."

After a long moment, the ghost bowed his head. "You have that promise. I will not take the smallest drop of your blood. Not now. But if you should fail. . . . "

"Very well, then," I said. "And now you must go."

When it had gone, my head felt clearer than it had for some time. I rose from the bed and went to kneel by the window, there to pray for guidance. And somewhere around dawn, when the light was touching the eastern sky with the color of resurrection, that guidance came.

The everyday world around me seemed to grow suddenly thin, as though it were nothing more than a membrane separating myself from the true reality. With infinite slowness, it began to peel away, layer by layer, until the very fabric of the universe was revealed. I was kneeling in the sea of time and space. Before me lay a wasteland of stars: suns boiling into being and shedding their light within the space of a few seconds, and the flickers of life around them nothing more than sparks that were soon gone. I looked into the whirling spiral void of the universe and knew that I was seeing things as a God might see them, each millennium nothing more than the blink of an eye. How, I thought despairingly, in the midst of that vast expanse where the greatest sun was nothing more than a pinprick flicker of light, how was I to find something as infinitesimally minute as the soul of a flea?

But moments, or millennia, passed and gradually I became aware that I was not alone in this cauldron of creation. Immense presences passed by, striding from one sun to another in a single step. They had been there all along, but they were almost too vast for me to see. I looked down, though the term had little relevance, and saw that what I had mistaken for the corona of a galaxy was the trailing hair of a Presence. Angel or demon, it filled me with awe and I paused for a moment, before setting thought firmly aside and letting myself plummet into the void. An instant later, and I was among the coils of hair, like a flea in the mane of a horse. Struggling upwards, at last I glimpsed the curve of a cheek and a vast and glittering eye. A spark of acknowledgment entered it, and Someone paused. A voice that filled the vaults of the universe itself said, "What do you want?"

I would have thought my own voice would be too small to be heard, but it seemed to ring out nonetheless. "I seek the soul of a flea."

"The soul of a flea?" the Voice repeated. "However do you hope to find so tiny a thing?"

"I do not know," I said. "I only know that it is this that I must find, to set free someone who has been punished for so long that they cannot help themselves." And to save my own soul, I thought, but did not say.

"Look at what you see," the Voice said, in merriment. "Here among infinity, where a sun is nothing more than a speck of dust, you seek a soul? Are you a god, to know where such a thing may be found?"

"I am nothing more than a man."

"Then I suggest you look in the nearest place where a soul might be found," the Voice said. And with that Someone twitched in the manner of an impatient steed, and flung me free. I fell through worlds, drawn by the pull of my own frail flesh, but just before the vision left me I saw the figure turn and stride away; its crimson wings outstretched among the stars and suns sent spinning with a flick of its tail. Then I was back in the housing of my own body, and falling to the floor.

I regained consciousness towards evening. Hauling myself stiffly to the bed, I lay down, to ponder on what my interlocutor had told me. After a time, I thought I had an answer, though it was not one that filled me with joy. Yet were my dreams and visions not sent to help my fellow man, whatever form they might take, or whatever meanness they might embody? Blessed is he, who gives up his life for a friend—yet what would this mean to me, who so regularly passed between the portals of life and death? No, the sacrifice that was asked of me was greater than my life, because of the gift that I possessed, but perhaps it was also less dreadful than I feared. For it came to me then that in the old desert religion to which the ghost had once belonged, they spoke of the soul as being in three parts, not one. . . . I lay lost in thought, and as twilight fell the ghost congealed out of the shadows.

"Well," he said, sadly. "You have failed, then." His hot-coal eyes were haunted.

"No," I said, smiling at him. "I have not failed. I have found you a soul. Or at least, enough of one to give you your freedom."

"My soul? Then where is it?"

"I did not say that I had found your soul." Look in the nearest place where a soul might be found, the Presence had said. I held out my hand. Wonderingly, the ghost placed its own within it and I felt something leave me like a breath, so that I was suddenly as hollow and empty as a stripped reed. The ghost seemed to waver, as though heat had passed between us, and the eyes that looked into mine were no longer red as fire, but dark and human, like the eyes of the man he should have been had evil not reached out and touched him with its tongue. His skin flushed golden-green; he became as a lizard in the sunlight. The ghost smiled, and was abruptly gone. And I was more alone than I had ever been before.

I have not explained the nature of my illness to my wife, telling her only that I may have caught a chill in the absence of her devoted care. I have closed the print-shop for the time being, and spend my time wrapped in a blanket and staring into the fire. I was not, I think, mistaken about the nature of my sacrifice. God has taught us that it is necessary to give in order to receive, and it seems to me that now spring is almost here, I can detect the presence of new growth within the fractured parts of my soul, like a seed from a scattered flower. I think of it growing into that many-petaled lotus which I used to see so clearly, but only now truly understand. The visions are absent, for now, but I have no doubt that they will return, when I, and my new-grown soul, are ready for them.

The Daykeeper

One

At the river's edge, the ice was no more than a layer of cold skin across the shallow water, fracturing as the woman stepped forward. The mist closed behind her; if Ainé had looked back, she would have seen nothing. The oak grove, bare now and laced with snow, the long white reach of the meadow and even the dun itself, silent beneath the frozen earth; all had gone into the mist from the river. The woman walked on, breaking the ice with each step, and in her arms the child cried once, a single sharp note like a gull, before falling quiet.

Ainé walked on, and now the mist was beginning to clear. She could see the gleam of sunlight, and the high stone towers of Otherness, and her steps quickened.

"Not long now. . . . " she whispered to the infant girl in her arms. She hoisted the child more securely against her shoulder. The child smelled familiar, a pervading odor of dead leaves and bonfires, and for a moment Ainé faltered, but the exchange had to be made. She gazed up at the great stone tower for a moment, then slipped inside. The baby whimpered all the way up the stairs, until Ainé found the place she was looking for. Another child was crying within, and Ainé smiled. She could smell him, now: not the decayed scent of her own infant, but healthy human flesh, and blood as hot as summer sunlight. The door opened easily, and Ainé stepped inside.

Later, her own child left behind in the cradle and the human boy in her arms, Ainé made her way down to the mound of muddy grass that approximated to the dun in her own world. She bent to lay her hand flat on the barren earth, and waited for the shift. Beneath Ainé's fingers the mound felt suddenly as warm as skin; a flexible membrane that stirred beneath her touch. She drew her hand back through the ghost of grass and earth, adjusting the baby in the crook of her arm. He whimpered as she moved him, so she bit her thumb, then slipped it between his lips. The child fell silent. Smiling, Ainé gazed up at the faint shadows of the towers as they rose around her. At their height, their windows caught the last of the sun and as Ainé watched, they flared as the light was gone. She could taste the summer twilight like a mist in her mouth. Silently, the baby tugged on her bloodied thumb. She paused a moment longer as the world around her faded, then stepped through. The skin of the mound parted and the child gasped at the different air.

Ainé looked about her. Below, the river meandered along the edge of the water meadows, quiet beneath the green haze of willows, and in the grove the oaks had already begun to send out their spring shoots. Ainé, standing on the slope of the dun, watched with satisfaction as the year grew on.

Two

"What's that?" Callum asked, staring into the pool.

"Ah, nothing. . . . " Ainé trailed her long fingers beneath the water, watching as the shadowy fish streamed through them and were gone.

"Look," the boy said, losing interest in the fish. A cluster of hazel nuts drooped into the water. "Can I have them?"

"You'll have to get them yourself," Ainé told him and so Call waded across and broke away the thin bough, ignoring the few drops of blood that span down into the pool.

"Careful, Call. . . . Don't hurt it, now." She glanced up into the fading brightness of the Summer Land's sunless day. "And be quick. . . . "

"Here you are," the child said, He handed her the bough and she stood, switching it impatiently through the long grass.

"Time to go," Ainé answered, uneasily. She took the boy's hand and together they walked up through the meadow towards the dun.

"Ainé? Tell me the story?"

She gave him a sidelong smile.

"Which story would that be, then?"

"You know. . . . "

"Well, now." The golden grass brushed her shins as they walked, releasing pollen into the evening air. "You want to hear about how I went to the stone city, and how I found you in a high tower—a palace, Call, with walls to last a thousand years and metal doors, like iron. And your name-mother had left you crying, so I carried you away. . . . "

"And then?"

"And then we came here, back to the Summer Land."

"Can I go back? One day? It isn't far, is it?" the child persisted. He could not read the thoughts behind Ainé's slanted look. "You said it was just over the river. . . . "

But she did not answer his question, saying instead, "Hurry now. . . . " She glanced over her shoulder at the shadows gathering along the valley. "It's almost twilight. Remember what I told you."

Call followed her gaze. "Are those hounds, down there?" He thought he could almost see a white body, slipping between the shadows, but he could not be sure.

"Perhaps the Hunter will come," he said, half fearful, half in hope.

"Hush," Ainé said sharply.

"But I've never seen him. . . . "

"And if you ever should, you must run. And if he should ever catch you, you must give him what he wants."

"What does he want?" Call asked, curious, and his mother replied in a sharp whisper, "Blood."

She meant to frighten him but he dragged at her hand, lingering back with excitement, until they were at the dun. Ainé held the protesting child tightly, murmuring necessary words, and the skin of the dun peeled away to envelop them in the world's flesh, while in the valley below the shadows gathered and grew.

Three

"A nice enough child, I suppose," Sister Olivia said doubtfully, to the social worker. "But not academic, if you see what I mean. . . . "—for Bronagh McCluskey did as little as possible in class, though her pale eyes remained fixed on her teacher in unnerving, unblinking concentration, except when the weather changed and her gaze drifted out through the window to watch the rain or sudden sunlight. "And—I know this is a terrible thing to say when the poor child's no more than thirteen, and didn't get off to the best of starts—found in another child's cradle, of all things, and then fostered—but you can always tell, you see. About the ones who'll be—well, who are likely to be a problem."

Yet Bronagh did not see herself as a problem; knowing only that this was not her own place, not home at all, but simply somewhere to bide her time. She avoided the other children, preferring her own company or that of the older girls, the ones who were always in trouble, as though drawn to the magnet of difference. But she spent most of her free time down by the canal, where the hawthorn grew white as frost at the end of the spring and the water was constantly changing under the altering sky. The canal was neither one thing nor another, not a river, but a place with its own moods and transformations, especially at dusk. Bron was not supposed to go there. The nuns talked about Men, capitalized so that they seemed as huge as God, and Eleanor, her case worker, was constantly telling Bron that if anyone, anyone at all, tried to make her do anything that she did not want to do, then she was to tell Eleanor at once. Bron's conscience, that the nuns had so assiduously and unsuccessfully tried to instill, was therefore clear, for she was quite happy to do anything. It did not matter; why should it, for it was only the flesh, after all, and she knew how to make that disappear into shadows and air, changing with the day. So she continued to walk by the canal, watching as the slow seasons turned and the grass grew long and died again, and she knew deep within her bones that if she waited for long enough, someone would come for her, across the water, and take her home.

Four

Now that he was older, Call spent less time with Ainé. There were no other children, only Niamh's small, pinched child, which whimpered its unhappiness all through the day and only fell silent when the dun closed over it, filling its mouth with the earth's flesh. There were plans for the child, Call knew. Now, he listened to the women talking as they sat with their spinning in the shade of the oaks. Ainé was winding a golden thread around the spindle; her sisters, Niamh and Macha, were busy with their own work. Down in the valley, the cattle drowsed in the summer heat, untroubled by flies. Niamh's child had been fractious all day, whining like a hound at the fireside, and Ainé's mouth grew tighter and tighter as the day span on.

"You'll have to do something about it," she snapped at last. The golden thread in her hands sang tight and broke against her fingers.

Niamh's eyes filled with sudden tears and she bent her head. Call watched, silent and sympathetic, but he did not say anything. His mother's moods were swift to change these days, and not for the better. Niamh whispered, "I can't. . . she's so young. And there's the veil—it's like being burned. It frightens me."

Aíné pulled the thread taut, tugging angrily at the edges of the material. "You can't keep her. She won't live. Do you want that, Niamh? To wake one morning and find her withered and shriveled beside you, like a leaf in the soil? Or do you want another child, a strong child, who'll grow and flourish and the world with it?"

She gave Call a fierce, proud look and he glanced away in embarrassment. Macha bowed her head closer to her sewing, and Niamh said nothing. Aíné continued, "Take her to Otherness and leave her there. She'll die in good care; they look after their young these days. And you can get another one. It's for the best, Niamh." She looked up to where the oak leaves were already growing brassy with the onset of autumn. "Look. Summer's almost gone; even Call can't make it stay. We need another life. . . . "

She passed an ungentle hand over the baby's head and it fell suddenly silent, staring at her. "Get rid of it, Niamh. Soon."

Call had heard enough. He sprang up and ran through the leaves in the direction of the valley. Behind him, his mother's laughter echoed unkindly until he reached the river meadow and it became lost in the humming of the bees among the briars.

Five

The young man's hands were very gentle. He said

"There, you see? It's easy. . . . " and he was right. It was the easiest thing in the world, now that he had shown her what to do and all that remained was for her to lie there and let the clear rush of the drug run all the way to her heart, watching as a cloud passed in front of the sun. Idly, Bron sent it away, causing the sunlight to deepen to a darker gold. Motes of dust, trapped in the rising draft from the window, span in the changing glow and Bron, enchanted with the effect, made the air darker yet until the bedroom was bathed in a light that fell as slow as honey through the air. But not enough, she thought through the haze, it was not enough. She could only play with shadows; she understood, without knowing why, that it should be possible to do more. Longing burned inside her, for a place and a power she had always known should be hers by right.

"You see?" the young man murmured, smiling at his latest convert. "It really changes things. It really does. . . . " Bron smiled back at him, catching his thought that the sudden ebb and slowness of the light was only an effect of the heroin, and knowing that he was wrong.

Six

Call walked with Niamh to the edge of the meadow. Looking back up the slope, he saw Ainé crouched at the top of the dun. The banner of his mother's head, once as red as a fox's coat, was now no more than a rope of gray wool and Ainé's eyes had faded to the color of a chilly sky.

"She's growing old," Niamh whispered, fearful. "All of a sudden. . . it happens like that."

"What then?" Call asked. He had never seen anything die before, and the thought of losing his mother was unimaginable.

"One day she'll just—go. Become a shrieking voice in the wind, nothing more." Niamh's blue gaze met Call's. "We're growing fewer and fewer, Call. When I was young, a girl, summer lasted for a hundred years and winter was no more than a shadow over the sun, but now winter's coming back. Ainé is dying; Macha is old. I'm growing old, too, and so are you. . . . We're taking the summer with us."

She had never said so much before. Call stared at her, numbly.

"Ainé said I'd stay here forever."

Niamh laughed and there was no humor in it.

"Ainé lied. She wanted a last child to lighten her last years, bring the summer back for a while. She thinks to do the same for me; she still pretends, you see, that everything will be all right."

"A last child," the boy repeated. He looked back towards the dun, where Ainé still crouched like a crow at the top of the mound. "There were other children, then? Before me?"

Niamh's eyes were pale with spite.

"Oh, yes. Every time the Hunter gave her a child, she'd exchange it. Do you know what happened to those children, Call? From your birthworld? The Summer Land always takes, never gives. Death in exchange for life. . . . Do you understand?"

"No," Call whispered. For a moment it seemed that he could smell blood on the wind. He opened his mouth to ask Niamh what she meant but before he could speak she said with sudden determination, "I'm not coming back, Call. Once I'm through the veil, I'm staying, whatever happens to me and the baby." Turning, she seized his arm and her grip was hard as iron. "Come with me."

Call thought of the story that Ainé had told him, of the great stone city, and the wonder of it pulled at him. He did not like to think of Niamh wandering lost in that strange other place, but then he thought of his mother, old and alone.

"I don't know," he said, doubtfully.

A mist was rising from the river, as though the water breathed, and the air was growing colder. Niamh climbed down the bank, the baby in her arms. She stepped forward, the water eddying about her ankles. Call felt the mist rise about him, choking him, and he turned and ran, fleeing back into the drawing twilight.

Seven

Bronagh waited until Sister Theresa had turned the corner, then ran out through the gate and down the road to the underpass. Behind the school stretched the estates, going on for miles into the wasteland around the city. Bron liked the estates: a desolation of concrete that made no demands on her, perfect for the play of light and shadow against the pale walls, but this evening she was heading once more for the canal. She clutched the precious twist of foil tightly inside her pocket. A group of youths stared at her as she ran past, calling something, but Bronagh neither heard nor cared. They seemed hardly real; shells of speaking flesh, and she left them behind, running on towards the water.

Eight

Call stumbled through the mist, out onto the side of the dun. He seemed to have been walking for hours, moving in circles through the thickening air, until he finally reached known territory. There behind him were grove and meadow and river, but the dun was as closed as a grave and dappled with frost. Ainé and Macha were nowhere to be seen. Mist congealed among the stripped branches of the oaks and the trees themselves seemed smaller and twisted.

"Ainé?" Call whispered, ice in his heart. "Mother?" and he clawed at the side of the dun until his fingertips bled. He could hear his own heart beating. The world was very still and very cold. The mist was fading, now, retreating back into the trees. Winter rising, he thought. He remembered, uneasily, what Ainé had told him about the Hunter.

Down in the valley, patches of darkness were rising from the grass. Here, on the higher ground, the light was still opalescent but soon it would be too late. He would be snared in nightfall. He glanced down to the uneven mass of darkness filling the valley floor. He could not be sure whether he glimpsed the white body of a hound, or only a trick of the unstable light, but he did not wait to find out. He scrambled to his feet, running back towards the river, with the branches whipping at his face and the dun, silent once more beneath the frost, falling behind him.

Nine

Along the tow path the hawthorn smelt sweet and decayed. That afternoon it had rained and the air still bore the metallic scent of water. Bronagh crouched beneath the damp may blossom, waiting. The man had paused, uncertain, at the point where the steps led up to the road. Minutes earlier, she had passed him on the towpath, feeling his eyes on her back as she walked away, so she conjured a second form out of rain and the darkening air, and the musty sweetness of the hawthorn. It drifted along the path and up the steps, distorted a little by the watery pull of the canal, but it was enough to trick him. Alone again, Bronagh fumbled in her pocket for the strip of foil. Her hands shook; she had to concentrate so as not to spill the powder out onto the wet ground. Then, a few minutes later, the enchanted needle like a bee sting in a pinch of flesh and she could sleep, she thought, for at least a hundred years, sleeping while the slow water ran beside her and the world peeled away.

Ten

Ainé had been right. It was a wonderful place, this world from which he had been stolen. He had stumbled out beside a narrow river, the mirror of the one behind the veil, except that its waters were channeled between high stone banks, green with weed. Call ran up the steps and across a wide stone path, and when at last he stopped he found himself in a wide courtyard, surrounded by towers, and it was just as his mother had said. Call gazed around him, amazed. It was a marvelous place, but when he stooped to put his hand on the stone ground, he found that it was quite hollow. There was no warmth, it did not breathe; it was dead and old. Thoughtfully, Call stood and began to walk towards the towers.

Eleven

Bronagh sank into the shadows beneath the hawthorn and listened as the drug sang inside her blood. She did not want the night to grow around her and so she held it back, calling the day in, but something was wrong. She could not hold the day; it was running from her, falling down towards night with unnatural speed. The drug was giving her power, stripping away the conscious mind, but she could not control it. Beyond the canal was the glitter of frost. Father, Bron thought, without knowing how she knew. And my mother is dead. She seemed to have been waiting for this for a very long time. Across the water, the Hunter raised his head. She could see the gleam of antlered bone in the shadows as he quested to and fro. The white hounds milled at his feet; the white mare pawed the ground, impatiently. Slowly, ice began to film the waters of the canal until it lay glassy in the darkness and the Hunter's mare stepped forward.

Twelve

It was evening before Call found his aunt. Niamh was lying in a drift of blown leaves and dirty newspaper against the tower wall, the child still clasped tightly in her arms. Her hair, like her sister's, had become the color of smoke. Call crouched by her side, unbelieving. Ainé had come to this world, and returned again, and remained young for years, but then Ainé had never stayed for very long. Call found it difficult to judge time in this new place, but surely they had been here for almost a day. He was roused from his reverie by a touch at his shoulder. He turned to look into wary blue eyes.

"She dead?" the young man said, uncertainly.

Call nodded. He brushed his hand across Niamh's cheek and it crumbled into ash, leaving the leaf tracery of bone beneath.

"Jesus. . . ." the young man said, backing away. Call listened sadly until the running footsteps faded and then he walked slowly back between the towers. He could sense his winter-locked home running beneath and beside: that mound, covered in scanty grass except where the soil had worn through, was the dun. Uneasily, he wondered again about the relationship between the two worlds. Aine's land seemed to draw its strength from Otherness; was it leaching this world of life, or was the link between them a subtler one, less one-sided? He thought uneasily of those other stolen children, his changeling kin. There were none in the Summer Land, so surely they must have gone back into this world, unless they were dead. His mother had never really told him anything, he realized now. Feeling hollow and bitter, he climbed the shallow slope of the mound and waited, but nothing happened, only the day turning down towards night and the place around him still solidly, horribly real. He could smell winter on the air, and then, towards the river, his mother's voice raised in fear. Without thinking, he ran towards it.

Thirteen

The drug within her, coupled with her own latent power, was making the world change, drawing together fallen rain and the cold starlit air, binding it with her own fear. The glamour shadow fled down the towpath, veering like a bird in flight, but the Hunter only laughed soundlessly, throwing back his head. Stumbling to her feet, Bronagh turned to run, but the drug slowed her and she fell down among the thorns. The blossom was falling, too, all around her, filling the place between the worlds; hiding the black branches and the pale heads of the hounds. Her hands grazed the earth, but it felt like cold skin, the bones lumpy and twisted beneath. Then someone was crying out and the pack turned to flow past her and away.

Fourteen

They were following him. Call swerved between the high towers, mapping the unfamiliar landscape. He stole a glance over his shoulder. The pack ran as though they moved through water, slowed by the different air. In their midst was the nightmare image of the Hunter, his wolf skin cloak flowing out across the pale flank of his horse. Call had been running for hours, it seemed, but time still stretched and held, the dusk still spreading all around him. He ran through both worlds at the same time: ghosts overlaid upon each other and none of them real. He stumbled out onto the wide stone road, and realized that he had come almost full circle. He could see the glint of ice through the trees and as he ran towards it he could see his own country, sharp and clear beyond the river. Far away, the hills shone at the edge of the world. Call ran on, staggering through the snow towards the river.

Fifteen

Midwinter cold: earth as hard as iron, water like a stone. The wind blew drifts and eddies of snow across the estates and through the city as the tide of the year unnaturally turned. The canals stretched in a network of frozen arteries; the streets were glazed with ice. The Hunter was summoning the wolf wind, Call knew: the dark wind from the beginning of the world. The thorn brake lay ahead and there, a little to the left, his mother lay. He stumbled. The muzzle of a hound grazed his leg and when he glanced down he saw that he was bleeding. Call felt nothing. He threw himself to his knees, between the hounds and the body of his mother, and the world opened.

He was kneeling on the riverbank. A white hound, red eared, lay dead at his feet and across the stone circle lay his mother, very still, but young again. Then her eyes flickered open and he saw with sudden uncomprehending dismay that she was not Ainé at all. Her gaze was as green as the spring, and focused on something behind him. He turned, and the Hunter was there.

"And if you should ever meet him, you must run. And if he should ever catch you, you must give him what he wants. . . . The Summer Land always takes, never gives." The women's voices echoed in his ears and at last Call understood. With a last glance at the girl, he knelt, and bared his throat.

Sixteen

Underneath his hands the earth felt soft as flesh in the sun, but perhaps it was only his own blood that warmed them. He blinked. It was high summer, now, with the honey sweet scent of heather all around, but snow still lay in his shadow. Macha and the girl were kneeling by his side.

"Who are you?" he asked the girl, but his voice was an empty thread on the air. He was, he realized, already dead, but she heard him anyway.

"Bronagh. Ainé's child."—and Macha added, "You see, to keep the seasons in balance, you don't just need life, but death. You're the sacrificial son, Call. Ainé would never agree, she thought she could break the rules. You need the blood of a willing victim to restore the land: life and summer here, death in Otherness. . . . Didn't you feel it, when you were there? Didn't you feel it was winterhearted?"

He wanted to say: but what gives you the right to bleed that other world—my world—of its vitality, while you live on in the sun? He looked up into their faces and their eyes were bright and cold.

"It's the Summer Land that matters, Call." Macha said. Bending down to the fast melt of the snow, the girl took a handful of ice crystal and blood and cast it up. It was no longer snow, then, but the falling blossom of the may and he watched with the last of his sight as she stood beneath it, changing the day, turning the year around as her mother had done, when she and the world were young.

Dieudamour

They say I have done things that are beyond the ability of humanity to forgive: acts that betray what it means to be human. Yet through all the dark years, I believed that I could be redeemed. Isn't that what they say about God's love, that it can save even the greatest sinner? I now know that this is the last lie of all.

My superiors had at last admitted that the war was over, but I knew that for me this was not and would never be true. I took pains to erase as much of my old identity as I could, but I needed to find somewhere to lick my wounds for a while, somewhere unexpected, and so one October morning I took ship from Piraeus and came to the coast of Cyprus and the monastery of Bellapaix. That name, the combination of beauty and peace, drew me to visit it: an irony, now that peace has been stripped from me forever.

There were very few monks left when I arrived. Most of the young men had deserted, abandoning their life of contemplation to defend their homes, and now only the old men and a few boys remained. The current Abbot, Father Michaelis, greeted me absently and ignored me from then on, but I was not the only guest at the monastery. My fellow visitor was an Englishman, named Nicholas Giddings; a silent man with a round, unhappy face. We fell into the uneasy complicit truce of men who both have a past that they would rather remained concealed.

For the most part, I spent my time reading. The late autumn days lay cool and gray upon the coast, suiting my mood, and I sat for hours in the courtyard beneath the dying vines with a copy of Pliny or Virgil from the monastery's meager library. The past has always been my escape, ironically enough; a time more distant than my own sorry sum of years. Usually, I was left in the peace for which I craved, but one day the

Abbot made it clear to me, in his unfailingly polite way, that guests were expected to attend at least one of the services. So on the following morning, for the good of what had once been my soul, I joined the congregation. The practices of the Orthodox church come from an earlier and richer age than the cold faith beneath which I had been raised. The solemn lines of old men and boys filing into the church were reminiscent of some medieval allegory; the ochre sunlight blurring the shadows and softening the sight. I tried to lose myself in the drifting incense and the lament of the liturgy, but it was no use. Whatever might be present here now was no longer open to me, if indeed it had ever been. I have only ever truly believed in one thing—I suppose you might call it a faith—and not for very long.

The service could not hold me, and my gaze began to wander idly over the assembled worshippers. At the very end of the furthest line, one of the boys raised his head. The angle of the window cast his face into shadow, but his eyes seemed to burn into mine. I felt as though I had been doused with cold water; it seemed to last only a moment, but now the service was over and they were all filing out again. Dazed, I rose and strolled back into the sunlit courtyard to resume my reading, but my thoughts returned to the boy again and again across the course of the day, without understanding why.

I still recall his first visit as though it were yesterday: the memory of that night returning to me faithfully, now that I am old and have no other love. I have no recollection of him entering the room, but woke from an uneasy dream to find him sitting quietly on the edge of the bed. I can remember almost everything: the darkness of his eyes, more akin to the animal than the human, the slowness of his smile, the gentleness of his hands, but try as I might, I cannot conjure up his face. The lamp cast uncertain bronze shadows across his face, so that his features were blurred. He said nothing. Raising myself on one elbow, I reached out my hand, took his chin between my fingers and turned his face towards the light.

"Let me see you properly," I said. To my own disgust, my voice was hoarse with sudden desire. He ducked from my imprisoning grasp; I thought I saw him smile.

"What's the matter?" I asked.

"Nothing," he replied shyly, in Greek. He brushed my cheek tentatively with the palm of his hand: it felt as light and soft as feathers against my skin and without knowing what I did, I pulled him down. Then, the sharpness of the memory fades. All that is left to me, and perhaps it is more than enough, is the remembrance of swan's-down skin, the honey sweetness of release and the golden lamplight spreading and rushing over me in a great wave, like fire.

When I awoke, the sun was breaking around the edge of the shutters and he was gone, presumably to his duties in the monastery. For the first time since the beginning of the war, I felt empty of both contrition and pain. I walked barefoot to the window and threw the shutters open. It was a borrowed day: warmth and gentle air at the edge of winter. The straits were calm beneath the sun and the mainland lay beyond, the mountains striped in ochre and mauve. I remember thinking that perhaps it might be possible, after all, to begin again.

Downstairs, the monks were going about their affairs. I searched for my visitor in every face that I passed, but he was nowhere to be seen. Perhaps he was not an acolyte after all, but a boy from the village. That afternoon, for the first time since my arrival, I left the monastery and walked down into the little nest of streets surrounding the monastery. It was very quiet, peaceful in the sun, as though the tide of the war had simply rushed around it and then ebbed. Hearing a distant hum, reminiscent of a large wasp, I looked up and saw the tiny cross of a plane moving towards the mainland; it seemed utterly wrong, displaced by centuries. The afternoon air was scented with the incense of laurel and cypress, the resinous corollary of death, enticed out of the wood by the warmth. Here, in the sunlight and the heavy silence, I no longer possessed a past.

This sudden sensation of freedom was a little constrained when, hearing voices, I turned the corner and found myself in the middle of a raging argument. It seemed to have blown up out of nowhere, in the manner of a summer storm. The Englishman Giddings stood in the middle of a crowd of villagers, remonstrating. His face was lobster pink: he had unwisely come out without a hat. In unison, like a swarm of bees, the villagers turned to me and murmured 'Kopriaste,' in the mechanical Greek welcome to the stranger, before returning their attention to the pleading Giddings. For a moment, I thought that his crime must surely be in direct proportion to the amount of ire it had raised: the rape of a villager's daughter, perhaps, but from the snatches of conversation I realized that his only sin was to have underpaid a taxi driver by a couple of drachmas. It was also at this point that I realized the limits of Giddings' Greek. I could hardly leave him there, stuttering his innocence to the incipient lynch mob around him, and so I sought out the self-proclaimed victim, thrust a generous amount of money into his palm, and announced to the crowd that he ought to be ashamed of himself, begrudging such a miserly sum to a man who had almost lost his life defending Greek honor and Greek lives. For all I knew, Giddings had never been further east than Belgium, but there was a brief and impressed moment of silence and then everyone turned on the cab driver and began to berate him instead. I took the bemused Englishman by the arm and marched him around the corner to the nearest cafe.

"What did you say to them?" Giddings asked, apprehensively.

"Nothing of note. But if anyone mentions your war record and offers to buy you a drink, I suggest you go along with it."

"My—? Well, anyway, thanks," he said, with some embarrassment. I ordered a bottle of retsina and a couple of glasses, and we sat in companionable silence until the wine arrived. As I have said, ordinarily I would have kept myself to myself, but the curiously redemptive visit of the young man last night had inclined me towards being well disposed, a sensation which I had taken care to stifle over the last few years. I poured the retsina and touched my glass with his. Giddings said, with a slightly nervous laugh, "I thought they were going to tear me limb from limb."

"No, no. It's all a good excuse for a drama, breaks the monotony of the afternoon."

"I didn't mean to shortchange him. I thought I'd got enough money. But I had to give the porter something to go into the castle; I suppose it was more than I bargained for."

"You've been down to Kyrenia?" I asked. One could see the castle from the monastery; a scrap of shadow against the great, rolling land.

"I wanted to see it again. I've always been something of an amateur historian and this island is so rich in the past, in legends. So old. . . . " He stared out across the sunlit square. "I always promised myself that when the war was over, I'd come back here. I spent a summer in Cyprus in the mid-Thirties and I've never forgotten it." He turned to me and said in the rush that sometimes force a person across the gap of loneliness and inhibition, "And you, Mr. Ravn? What makes you stay?"

I shrugged. "Just a wish for peace and quiet, like yourself."

Giddings said, still a little diffidently, "I've wondered where you're from, actually. I thought, from your accent and your name, you might be—mid European?"

The unspoken word rang between us like a bell. He did not want to ask if I might be German. I said, "I'm Danish, as a matter of fact. From Frisia." Wryly, I watched him relax.

"Oh, I see. There was a bloke in my regiment from your neck of the woods. Svensson. A decent sort; I liked him."

There was a brief silence.

"So," I said. "Tell me about Cyprus. You see, I don't know the island very well, although I've spent time on the Greek mainland."

I've always been interested in other people's passions. I suppose that's why I'm a good listener. Certainly, people tend to confide in me. Well, the history of this part of the Levant was Giddings' passion and as he talked, letting his retsina sit untasted beside him, I learned that Cyprus was to the Greeks the most beautiful and blessed of islands; that it was from her cerulean waters that foam-born Aphrodite had stepped, the seawater turning to pearls as she came ashore to the adoring arms of the Horae. She was worshipped here for centuries, before a more modest goddess replaced the queen of pleasure and the suffering figure of the cross assumed the throne of her son Eros, the lord of desire.

Embarrassed by his own eloquence, Giddings broke off abruptly and took a sip of wine. It was growing late. The sun had already slipped down behind the mountains and the long shadows of the cypress pointed into evening. Giddings and I returned to the monastery and our beds. I had lost track of the retsina I had imbibed, and although I was not yet drunk, I could feel the golden weight of the wine within me, its warmth making me languid. All I could think of was whether the boy would come to me that night. I was so far away, lost in desire, that I did not even hear the door open, nor feel the slight shift as he sat beside me on the bed. I could not seem to open my eyes, even when he kissed me, and the darkness seemed full of soft shadows and the breath of wings against my face.

The following days passed almost in a kind of trance. It was as though he did not leave before morning, but stood just behind my shoulder as I walked in the courtyard, or walked in the somber, fragrant air of the cypress groves. Once, I remember that I turned my head and for a moment a face looked into mine. It was familiar, but old and drawn with pain, almost skeletal. Startled, I stepped back and it was abruptly gone. I suppose I had earned the right to be haunted, but it made me uneasy, even so.

I knew nothing about him. Although, naturally, I asked his name, and told him mine, he always evaded my questions. During the restless hours of daylight, I could not even recall his face, though I could conjure up with ease the curve of his shoulder, and the line of his throat, and the pale skin within wrist and elbow. Knowledge sets limits; without it, the imagination is released, and I had already infused him with everything I'd ever wanted. He was utterly responsive to my mood; sometimes seeming older than I, in comfort and reassurance, and sometimes it seemed that it was not a youth that I held, but a girl. Well, I suppose that I need not tell you what I felt: I was in love.

I took to sleeping for much of the day, to dream and wait for night, and now that winter was moving across the Mediterranean there was little reason to stir beyond the walls of Bellapaix. Giddings remained in the monastery, following his own pursuits, which consisted principally of research into the locality. He was writing a short paper on the fortifications at Kyrenia; and I remember proofreading it for him before he sent it away to London.

"It's very old, the castle," he told me one evening over dinner. "The Crusaders called it "Dieudamour", after Aphrodite, because a temple to her and to her son is supposed to lie somewhere around here. The porter said it might have been Bellapaix, but there's no evidence for that. He also said—" here Giddings lowered his voice, in case he shocked monastic sensibilities, "that the worship of Aphrodite accounts for the large number of hermaphrodites on the island. They bred them, apparently."

"I hadn't noticed," I said.

He grinned. "Well, you wouldn't, would you? I would think it calls for a rather more intimate acquaintance with the local youth."

Well, I certainly had that, and the very young men of the Mediterranean often have slightly feminine characteristics, but I could hardly say so in front of Giddings. Although they do call it the English disease, I suppose. I turned the conversation towards less contentious matters, and we lingered for a while over the monastery's resinous wine before retreating to bed.

At first, as I have told you, my ignorance of my lover only enhanced my own contentment, but as love settles into place, it leaves room for other sensations: unease, and then jealousy, and finally fear. I lay on my bed during the long afternoons, watching the steely light die behind the window and thought of what I must say to him when he next came. For several nights, however, I was too afraid to voice my apprehension. He sensed this, I knew; stealing the questions from my mouth, but even he could not hold the inevitable at bay for long.

During the day, the first storm of winter had swept up the straits, blocking out Kyrenia and the little square of the castle in a haze of rain. I lay and listened to the wind rattling the shutters. At last one of them broke free and banged open, letting in a cold breath of air. The smell of salt and rain washed away the drowsy warmth in which I lay and abruptly I was awake and clear headed. The boy lay beside me, still as the dead. Gently, so as not to wake him, I reached for the lamp and touched a match to the wick. Holding the lamp between us, I turned his face towards me.

In the old story of Psyche and Eros, they say that the girl feared what she might see when at last she looked into her lover's face. He had visited her night after night, until her sisters in envious suspicion urged her to hold a lamp above his sleeping face so that she might see what manner of demon had been courting her so assiduously. She saw no demon, only a person more beautiful than any she had ever imagined.

I wish I could say the same, but for me, it was the other way round. I looked for beauty and saw instead the monstrous. The lamplight fled over his face, driving the shadows before it, and his features rested for a moment in sharp perfection before they changed. The faces came and went in a seemingly endless procession; I knew every one. I saw every prisoner who had passed through the interrogation chamber: Jewish citizens, members of the French resistance, all of them known to me. For many of them, I was the last thing they ever saw, yet there was no reproach in their eyes and they were silent. The dead are blind, and have no voice; it is the living who must supply the lack, through guilt and regret. At the end, the face beneath me underwent its final transformation and became my own, looking back at me, as the dead had seen it. I saw what poor, blameless Psyche had feared to see: a monster, myself. Then the familiar, unseen visage of my lover replaced itself, smiled once and then was gone into the darkness and the winter rain. Someone was hammering at the door.

Matters resolved themselves swiftly after that. The Allies had not taken so very long to find me, and I accompanied them without surprise or complaint. That night, down in the long, empty hall of the monastery, I made a full confession to one Colonel Connolly and in the morning I returned with him to Berlin, to stand trial and begin my sentence.

I never saw Bellapaix again. Following my release, I found a changed world, and one that I had little to offer. I live now in Damascus, where I write articles for the local press under an assumed name. The only pleasure I have is in memory, and as I sit in the cafe and watch the other old men play backgammon in the dusty evening, I consider the choices I have made. When I joined the Gestapo, I convinced myself that there was no longer such a thing as love, that duty and the state were all that mattered, and even common human compassion could be put safely aside. The young man at Bellapaix, whatever he was, convinced me otherwise, but on that last night my capacity to love went with him forever.

Sharecropper

One

Jirhan slept in the rocks above what had once been the city of Semi-Palatinsk, with the gun tucked hard beneath his hip and his grandfather's Koran clasped to his heart, and there he dreamed of wheat. In his dream, he stood at the very edge of the field and gazed out, marveling that where there had once been nothing more than dust and scrub, there was now only grain. The fields rolled before him, the wheat as golden-pale as a snow leopard's coat, all the way to the horizon. And in his dream, the perimeter fences and the guards and their guns were gone, blown away on the gentle wind. Then he saw that a man was walking lightly through the wheat, and it did not bend at his passage. As he drew closer, Jirhan recognized him and his heart leaped, for the man was Jirhan's great-grandfather. Jirhan, dreaming, did not stop to think how he knew this, for he had never seen his great-grandfather in life, and the family photographs had been burned years before, when the law against images had been enforced. The old man carried the book that had made him famous. Jirhan could see his name on the black cover, Bakhtizhan Nazaraev, and the title of the book: *Traditional Agriculture in Uzbekistan: 1850–2010*. Both name and title were written in Russian, a language with which Jirhan's people were no longer so familiar, but the book itself had rested beneath the Koran ever since he could remember; the one work that the family had managed to salvage from the raids thirty years before, when all literature had been banned.

His great-grandfather smiled when he saw the young man, and pointed into the distance beyond Jirhan's shoulder. Jirhan turned, and the sea of wheat swung like a tide before his eyes, catching him up and carrying him back to waking.

❧   ❧   ❧

The desert air was cold on his face and the stars lay above his head like a bright harvest. It was not yet dawn. Glancing through the rocks, he could see the fences and the guard posts, the turret emblazoned with the NRG logo, and then the grain, just as it had been in his dream. But now he turned away from the endless wheat, and shouldering the gun, he began walking north through the desert, towards the place where the laboratory was said to lie.

Two

Jirhan had now been gone for fifty days, swallowed by the forbidden, endless lands to the north of Tashkent. On the evening of the fifty-first day, Armin Nazaraev stood high on the minaret, watching for his son. From the pinnacle of the minaret, he could see for miles across the haze of the city; as far as the road that led towards Samarkand, shimmering with dust cast up by the wheels of the NRG tankers and the military traffic. Later, when the sun was nearly gone, the snowlit peaks to the north would turn the color of rose sherbet and tremble in the distance. These were times when, to Nazaraev, the whole planet seemed to turn on the pivot of the minaret like a wheel around a spoke, and he had to grip the railing tightly to prevent himself from spinning over and falling into the well of the world.

At such times, too, Nazaraev always thought that he could see his son in the streets below. The mirage invariably appeared at the in-between times: the cool dawn or the depths of sunset. Sometimes the figure rode a horse or a camel, sometimes it fled on foot, and once he saw it standing at the wheel of an ancient ATV. Nazaraev knew that it was never real. It always faded just outside the wall of the mosque, like a ghost.

The evening wore on and the curfew fell across Tashkent's old quarter, but Nazaraev still waited on the minaret, listening to the cracked voice of the imam as the old man recited the litany of the muezzin. Allah, the compassionate and the merciful. . . . Prayers, it sometimes seemed to Nazaraev, were all they had left. Amplified by the speakers, the words sank like stones into the still evening air and Nazaraev bowed his head, pleading silently with God to bring Jirhan home. If he brings nothing, if he has failed, if his hands are empty. . . . It no longer matters to me. Only let him be alive. . . . The muezzin drifted away. The imam came to stand by Nazaraev, and placed a gentle hand on his sleeve.

"It's nearly dark," the imam said.

"If he does not come tonight—" Nazaraev said, and heard his words trail away. If he does not come tonight, then I think he will never come. He is already a week late. He could not bring himself to say the words, but Nazaraev and the imam, Serzhan Beyildi, understood one another's silences.

"Armin, don't worry. The boy can look after himself. You did well with him."

Nazaraev gave a small, bitter smile.

"So did you. You were the one who taught him to read. If it hadn't been for your madrasa, he'd never have found the passage in my grandfather's book."

The imam sighed. "We all do what we can, Armin. We'll need people like your boy. This regime can't last forever, this unholy alliance between our government and the Western biocompanies." He looked towards the road, where the grain trucks still rumbled. "I was born under this regime, and so were you, so how can it seem so unfamiliar, so wrong? How did we come to this pass? A rapacious, starving West and yet another government of peasant boys who make a mockery of Islam. Who ban books and twist the holiest book of all to their own ends, yet sell drugs to black marketeers and everything else around us to foreign multinationals. . . . Hypocrites and fools. I haven't been outside this town for twenty years, and I'm fifty-six now, an old man. I doubt I'll ever see the mountains again. I envy your son, in a way." He touched Nazaraev's sleeve. "Don't worry about Jirhan. He's KGS trained, he knows a lot of tricks."

"But that's what worries me, don't you see? If he's been captured and they find out he was with the Specials..."

"They won't. And anyway, even if he is taken, why should they make the connection? We set him up with a new identity, didn't we? We were as thorough as thieves. As far as the KGS knows, Jirhan Nazaraev is dead."

Beyildi's grip tightened on Nazaraev's arm, then the imam turned and made his way slowly down the stairs of the minaret. Nazaraev followed, moving carefully, with an old man's slowness. And then, as the filigreed door closed behind them, he heard a shout from the northern gate of the mosque. Hope hammered at Nazaraev's heart. He turned, and began to stumble towards the gate through the half-dozen students hurrying out of the mosque's madrasa. A name was spreading like wildfire: Jirhan.

Nazaraev's first thought, however, was that it was not Jirhan at all, but a stranger. The man at the gate of the mosque was surely old, crouched gasping on the steps, but then he glanced up to meet his father's eyes, and Nazaraev recognized him. He stepped forward and took his son's hands. The crowd clustered around them, clamoring.

"Jirhan? Did you find the place? Did you bring anything back? What happened, Jirhan?"

Jirhan Nazaraev opened his mouth to answer, but the old imam raised his hand.

"Enough, enough! Do you want to attract the KGS with your racket? Let the boy see his father and get a decent meal inside him. There'll be time enough for your questions later."

Murmuring, the crowd drew aside and Jirhan followed his father through the evening streets, keeping to the shadows. As they hurried, a helicopter whirred overhead, searchlights panning across the old town. Jirhan stood blinking upwards like a rabbit, and his father drew him swiftly back into a doorway.

"Jirhan?" Nazaraev could not quite keep the sharpness from his voice.

"Sorry," the young man muttered. He shook his head, as if trying to clear it, and Nazaraev noted with a sinking heart the bewilderment in the boy's eyes. The helicopter passed over again; illuminating the minaret.

"It's just the curfew sweep, it's nothing to worry about. You used to do it yourself, remember?" Nazaraev murmured, trying not to sound as uneasy as he felt. "Come on. Let's get you inside."

As they approached the house, Nazaraev's wife hastened into the courtyard, the youngest girl limping at her skirts. Her mouth opened in a soundless zero as she saw her son. Gaping like a fish, she embraced him, while the child looked on wide-eyed.

"Inside," Gulzhan Nazaraeva commanded, wiping her eyes with her apron. Jirhan stepped into the courtyard and his brothers rushed out of the house. The young men stood grinning foolishly and slapping Jirhan on the back.

"The bread!" Gulzhan said, and ran for the kitchen. Nazaraev knew that these first few moments of hospitality were sacred under the will of Allah, but he couldn't keep the question from his eyes. Jirhan saw what was in his father's face, and seemed to straighten. The bemused look left him and he gave a slight, grim nod. Nazaraev felt the breath rush out of him. Until now, he realized, he had not truly believed that Jirhan stood a chance of success.

Gulzhan returned, bearing the traditional lepeschka loaf that she had bought on the day of Jirhan's departure, weeks before. She thrust the round loaf, stamped with the hallmark of NRG-Grain, towards her son, and Jirhan took a piece. It was as fresh and easily broken as though it had been baked only an hour before. Nazaraev remembered his grandfather years before, mumbling at the soft bread and telling the children how the loaves baked in his day had been as hard as iron the next morning. And he remembered his grandfather throwing the soft patented bread to the kites which clustered along the courtyard wall, calling it a sin in the face of Allah. Sudden tears welled in Nazaraev's eyes; his grandfather would have been proud of Jirhan, if he'd lived to see the boy. But he had died in his fifties of a tumor, like most folk then, and now. The young men tore the bread between them and Jirhan handed a piece to his father. Nazaraev let the fragment rest on his tongue for a moment; it tasted of nothing, of air.

In the moment before they went through into the main room, Jirhan turned and placed something in his father's hands: a heavy rectangle, wrapped in thick cloth.

"Here."

"Where's the best place for it?" Nazaraev whispered.

"Somewhere neither hot nor cold. Somewhere dry."

Nazaraev took the container into the workshop that adjoined the courtyard and placed it on a shelf. But before he left, he unwrapped the cloth and stood staring down at the container. It was made of some kind of metal, with a smooth, gray surface, and a transparent panel at one end. A faint iridescence showed where it caught the light. It was of a different order of technology to the machine parts that lay around the floor of the workshop and which were mere scraps welded together in the approximation of a whole. The container was flawless; a gift from another world. Nazaraev bent forward and peered through the panel. A cluster of something pale lay within, nested in a honeycomb of cells. Nazaraev sighed, and it was only when the panel misted over that he realized he had been holding his breath. Wrapping the container in the cloth once more, he returned to his family and celebration.

Nazaraev had decided not to press the boy for immediate answers, but the younger lads had no such inhibitions. They leaned across the table to touch Jirhan's hands, as if checking that he was real, and they clamored questions.

"So how was it? Did you really find the laboratory? Are the stories real?"

"What are the people like? Are they like us? Have they changed, as the southerners say? Are they really taller than trees and stronger than lions?"

For the first time, Jirhan laughed, but it sounded raw.

"Yes, I really went to the laboratory; it really does exist. It's somewhere in the wasteland to the north of Semi-Palatinsk, where they say that air still sparkles and burns. It isn't true. The climate is soft and mild, and I saw a wheatfield five hundred kilometers long, drifting into the distance like a Russian girl's golden hair."

Jirhan's brothers' eyes grew round, and Nazaraev suppressed a smile. His eldest son had always known how to spin a good tale.

"Five hundred kilometers? Of wheat?"

"Of growing grain, yes." He leaned across the table and tapped what remained of the lepeschka loaf. "Where bread like this comes from."

"I know that," the smallest boy said with scorn. "Everyone knows that. It's why you went, isn't it?"

And Jirhan nodded. "Yes. It's why I went."

After the meal, Nazaraev followed Jirhan out to the workshop and took the container from its hiding place. Father and son stood looking down at it as it lay in Nazaraev's hands.

"Such a small thing," Nazaraev said, half to himself. Jirhan nodded.

"It doesn't look like much, does it? It nearly cost me my life." His mouth tightened, as if in memory. Nazaraev said nothing, and after a moment the young man went on, "You've no idea, the kind of security they've got up there. On the fields, I mean. And it goes on forever: there's a watchtower every half kilometer or so, with heat sensors and monitors and guards with guns. Father, when I first joined the special forces, I thought I knew it all. But I've never seen anything like the security they've got on the NRG fields." Jirhan ran a careful finger along the surface of the box. "We'll have to take good care of this. Separate some, and hide the rest."

"So what about the laboratory?"

"It's there. Just as the old stories said. There wasn't anyone there; it was deserted. I found this," He weighed the box in his hand. "In an empty room filled with dust."

"Forgotten," Nazarbaev whispered. The pride came back into Jirhan's eyes.

"Not by my grandfather. He remembered. . . . I've said a prayer for his soul every night of my life. It was as though he was with me on my journey."

"He was," Nazarbaev said softly. "Now. I need to speak to Imam Beyildi; he's seeing the others tonight."

Jirhan smiled. "It's the spring equinox tomorrow. Navrus. Not such bad timing, then."

"It's a good time," his father said. "Time for the planting; time for a summer harvest." Their eyes met.

"A good time," Jirhan echoed, but suddenly he did not sound so sure.

Three

That night, home in his own bed, Jirhan once more dreamed of wheat. He stood again at the edge of the field, gazing out across the grain. A locust whirred across his vision, towards the wheat, but as soon as its ungainly flying form touched the air above the grain, it buzzed and fell. Jirhan stepped forwards to look, but the locust was already decaying, killed by whatever genes had been implanted in the crop. And suddenly he saw that the magnificent field was crawling with life: scorpions clustered upon every stem like spiny fruit, and he could see inside the stalks, too, where the black specks of artificial diseases crawled like lice. Jirhan turned in disgust from the field and looked down at his hand, to where a single golden seed rested in his palm. Stooping, he tucked it into the soil and watched it as it grew. It was a pale, pallid shoot, but it belonged to no-one, contained nothing except its own frail strands of DNA. He looked up to see his great-grandfather staring at the shoot, but the old man's face was somber, and the cancer that had killed him was clearly visible, hanging from his throat like a scorpion on the grain.

Jirhan woke up with a gasp. The muezzin rang out across the silent town, and he rolled automatically out of bed to pay his devotions. It was still and cold and dark. As he crawled gratefully back under the covers he realized that it was Navrus, the equinox, and a moment later, his father was knocking softly on the door.

"Jirhan? We should go."

Following his father through the door, Jirhan stepped into the court-yard to see a figure in the shadows. It was the imam. Jirhan clasped his hand, but the imam did not speak. He was looking at the box, which Nazaraev was carrying carefully from its hiding place.

"You're both going?" the imam whispered.

"No," Jirhan said quickly, before his father could speak. "I'll go alone. It's too risky, otherwise."

"Yes," Nazaraev said, as though Jirhan had said nothing. "We're both going."

Jirhan started to argue but the imam took his arm in a surprisingly firm grip.

"Don't argue. If your father wants to go, then neither you or I will be able to stop him. It's your legacy, after all—both of you. Your great-grandfather would have wanted this. And anyway," he added, "Your father knows the old fields, and you don't. They're hard to find—do you think you can just walk up to them, up the mountain? If you could have done that, then you could have gone there straightaway and not risked coming back into Tashkent. We talked about all this before you left, Jirhan."

Jirhan fell silent, knowing that the imam was right, and besides, in an hour it would be dawn. They could not afford the time to argue.

"You've arranged a vehicle?" he asked.

"Yes. You'll find it at the end of Abai Street, past the roadblock behind the market. You'll have to get past the guards, though—you should get there in time for the changeover. But you won't have long."

Tashkent was quiet, still under the predawn curfew. They saw only one man, a cleric, and not one of the imam's people, going into the mosque on Ferghana Road. Jirhan and Nazaraev crouched beneath a wall. Jirhan could not help feeling that the box was emitting its own faint, betraying light.

"Pity we can't do this within the city walls," his father murmured.

"There's nowhere big enough to grow a crop, and how would we hide it?"

Nazaraev did not reply. They'd already had this discussion a hundred times. They slunk around past the rows of whitewashed houses. Starlings began to shriek in the trees with the coming dawn, and Jirhan wondered what this neighborhood must have sounded like in his great-grandfather's youth: clucking hens, ducks, goats. Each house with its own small garden: its own cherries and apples, carrots and cabbages. And now they were forced to buy everything in the sanctioned market-place; the vegetables and fruit bursting with obscene health, the meat glistening with by-products. A century ago, Jirhan's countrymen were smuggling gold and drugs and guns, and now their ambitions had contracted down to black-market carrots.

They had reached the guardpost. Jirhan could see the guards, huddled in the chilly light. One of them lit a cigarette and Jirhan grimaced: that came from the West, too. The old local tobaccos had been made illegal years ago. The guards were walking towards a truck; their backs were turned. Jirhan and Nazaraev slid painfully under the razorwire and rolled down into the muddy ditch.

"What now?" Nazaraev whispered.

Jirhan motioned to the left. "Along the ditch." Halfway between one outpost and the next, a gully led down to the narrow river. The imam's vehicle would be waiting on the other side, out of sight in the bushes, but Jirhan was nervous. Things rarely went to plan. They scrambled along the ditch, and just before they reached the halfway point Jirhan heard the siren signaling the end of curfew. The sun was just touching the edge of the distant mountains, spilling light over the world. They raced down the gully, and threw themselves into the muddy waters of the Chirchik. It was neither deep nor wide; in minutes they were across and into the trees. The vehicle, an old army jeep, was waiting. The man inside wore the uniform of the Uzbekistan Defense Corps and Jirhan's heart skipped a beat, but then the man turned and he recognized his old schoolfriend from the madrasa.

"Shoqan!"

Shoqan smiled, then gestured. "Get in the back under the seat. There's a false base, in case anyone looks. I've got papers as far as Yangiabad; we'll take a side road off before we reach the village. After that, you'll have to walk."

"We'll follow the river," Nazaraev said. "It takes us up into the Chatkal."

The journey fell into a pattern: start, stop, start, stop. Jirhan counted twenty roadblocks between Tashkent and Angren. It was close to noon when the road beneath them, always bad, began to worsen. Jirhan was able to peer through the gaps in the vehicle's floor, to where the dusty, pot-holed track span away. The air, filtered in through the vehicle's sides, became thick and stifling with coal dust from the local mines. Finally, they slowed and stopped. The seat was hauled up, releasing them into the clear coldness of the mountains.

"Go," Shoqan said. "And keep as close to shelter as you can." Without waiting for Jirhan's thanks, he jumped back in the vehicle and spun the wheel. Jirhan and his father trudged stiffly across the stony plateau, to where the Angren river tumbled between steep banks. They began to follow it up into the heights, and gradually the air became colder and the trees more thickly scattered.

"Are you sure this is a good place?" Jirhan asked. "Won't it be too cold?"

His father shook his head. "Too cold here, but the path drops down into the pastures, the old zhelau. They're sheltered. Good growing land, and—" the sound reverberated from the rocks, sending a flock of birds whirling into the sky.

"Down!" Jirhan pushed his father to the ground, as the helicopter roared overhead, its dragonfly shadow racing over the riverbank. They were in full view, and in the next moment, Jirhan knew that they had been seen. The helicopter turned. Nazaraev scrambled to his feet. They splashed across the river and up the other bank, running across the open land towards the trees.

"You are trespassing on government property! The penalty for violation is death!" Distorted by the loud hailer, the voice echoed from the mountain walls. Gunfire spat a line across the earth, and Nazaraev stumbled. Filled with a sick dismay, Jirhan turned, but his father was already clambering up. Blood stained his side. Jirhan slid an arm around him and dragged him into the trees. The helicopter spun overhead. Bullets splintered the pines, sending a resinous waft through the air. Jirhan and Nazaraev reached the end of the trees, wavered on the edge of a steep, fronded gully, then plunged downwards. They plummeted through tall bracken and stunted trees, into a thin line of cold water. Panting, bleeding, their clothes torn, they looked up. The helicopter was nowhere to be seen.

"Given up?" Nazaraev asked, hoarsely and hopefully.

"Maybe. Perhaps they took us for poachers. You're hurt."

Nazaraev grimaced. "My ribs. It swiped me. It didn't go in. We've got to go on."

"Dad—"

"Didn't the imam tell you not to argue?" Nazaraev's face was as tight as a fist. Jirhan opened his mouth to speak, but his father was already up and heading through the gully, brushing low through the bracken. Jirhan, still clutching the box, followed.

Towards the early part of the afternoon, they reached the high pasture. There had been no further sign of the helicopter, but Jirhan and Nazaraev kept as far out of sight as they could. If it had not been for the constant threat, Jirhan would have enjoyed the walk: the silver birches marching down the slopes, the grass filled with flowers. He wondered how long it had been since anyone had come up here. The government had said this land was poisoned, but there was no sign of it here. The sloping aprons of the zhelau, the old pasture, slid gently down the lower slopes. Once, Jirhan knew, this grazing land would have been filled with cattle or horses, but now all the herds were strangely bred, and under UDC control. At last they reached a long slope, sheltered by a ridge of high ground. Nazaraev pointed.

"Here."

"Are you sure?"

His father nodded. Together they scraped back the earth to form a long oblong and then, carefully, Jirhan opened the box. The grain rested inside, looking as though it had just been scattered from a stem of wheat.

"It's an experimental strain in itself, of course," Nazaraev said. "Engineered for strength, according to grandfather's notes."

"But not patented. It's strong, it will grow, and it won't last for just a single generation, either. It can be harvested, planted on. This is just to get it started." They stared at the grain, marveling, and then they put two handfuls in the ground and covered it over. Then repeated it, further down the slope, until ten oblongs marked the ground, hidden by the long grass. They stood, and looked at one another.

"I'll go with you to the rendezvous," Jirhan said. "Just in case. Come and see me in the summer."

"You're sure you'll be all right up here?" Nazaraev said.

"I'll be all right. It's unlikely anyone will trek up here, and I'll avoid the helicopter sweeps, stay out of sight. But someone needs to stay and tend the grain. And in August, we'll harvest it, and so will all the others. And then we'll try and find a field."

They returned to the rendezvous place, where Shoqan was impatiently waiting. Jirhan embraced his father, feeling the blood stiff on Nazaraev's shirt. Nazaraev's scarf was still bound around the graze, and when Jirhan pulled away, he saw for the first time that there was a swelling on the side of his father's neck. Nazaraev saw him looking, but neither of them said anything. When they had gone, it was already twilight. Jirhan made his way back through the trees, now humming with early cicadas, to where the bare earth waited, like a grave.

Nightside

"Illness is the night-side of life…"
— *Susan Sontag*

Deep in illusion's halls, Serena dreams of Cassini: imagining him hastening through the city, not risking the underground, heading east towards the Docklands. Serena shivers then, thinking of night and the cold, and the dream is abruptly banished. Rising from the couch, she walks to the window and stares out across London. The triple glazing reflects the lights of the city in a series of trinities: endless refraction, eternally fractured. Beyond the curve of the Thames she can see snow clouds massing, their summits lit by the moon. Below, London sleeps, and to Serena's artificially stimulated imagination the whole city is visible: the fortresses of the Docklands, and beyond them the protective wall which rings the city as far as Dartford. And after that lies the unimaginable wasteland of flood and fen and ruin, which Serena has never seen and hopes she never will. The city is frightening enough. Serena knows, deep in her heart, that the European Empire is entering its last days, sealed off by the constant encroach of winter, and she knows, too, that the masques and balls and parties of which her peers are so enamored are no more than the last flickers of the sun, before summer goes out like a candle. She hides such knowledge away in the secret places of the head, drowning it in dreams.

Crossing her fingers in the folds of her pashmina robe, Serena prays to the Virgin that Cassini will come back safely. As she prays, she holds her breath, and the effort makes her cough, racking her lungs with fire until a single drop of blood stains the soft folds of her robe. Stigmata, she thinks, for luck, and turns back to the winter city, waiting for the masque and Cassini's midnight gift.

She has felt a little better today, only occasionally tasting the flat salt blood of hemorrhage in her mouth, but she has nearly finished this month's supply of the preparation. Opening the padded box, she gazes down at the last little phial. It's almost three-quarters full; Serena has been saving it for the masque tonight. She'll be appearing in front of London's highest society, so it's vital that she looks her best. Besides, it's Christmas Day tomorrow and Cassini, moved by an uncharacteristic whim, has promised to supply her with more of the preparation as a kind of Christmas present. Serena will still be paying for it, and it isn't cheap, but she supposes that it's a kind thought.

She has spent the past few days thinking about Cassini, and of the dangers that he undergoes for her. Serena has only a hazy idea of what these dangers might be: she knows nothing of the world outside London's pampered inner courts, and has no wish to know. The origins of her precious preparation, the franchised city of Singapore Three, seems as distant as the moon. Serena's world lies in the heart of London, wrapped like a pearl in its layers of fortifications against the broken lands beyond. This morning, however, she has been a little adventurous.

The Thames has been frozen for over a month now, and today Serena's friends took her skating. She remembers watching them as they swooped over the marbled ice like summer swallows, then flocked to the v-booths that lined the shore in search of more vicarious entertainments. Serena herself, too frail for such energetic pursuits, stayed in the coffee house on the Embankment, where she sipped hot chocolate laced with morphiates, and watched the skaters pass by.

The river is untroubled by commerce. This far into the winter, the icebreakers are running down-river only as far as India wharf; merchanters trailing obediently in their broken wake. The contact from Singapore Three is arriving on one of these ships. Cassini has told Serena that he has arranged to meet the man in a warehouse off Peking Street—a go-down, Cassini calls it. Serena's friends have told her that this is a term used frequently in the Far East. This adds to Cassini's glamour, and makes Serena just a little more afraid of him: a sensation that she enjoys, as long as it doesn't become too threatening. She's ill, after all, and she tires easily. But whenever she gets bored, which is often, Serena tries to find out more about Cassini: obsessively tapping into the veins of the Web and running down the traces of his systems. Cassini, however, has been careful; she finds nothing. She wonders, fretting, whether he has reached the go-down yet, or whether he is still out in the London night. She wonders, too, whether he is thinking of her, and at that thought, she smiles.

'Serena?' a voice says. Serena looks up and sees her mother standing in the doorway. Against the darkness of the hall, her mother seems almost young; her blonde hair coiled precariously about her head and her slight figure wrapped in a silk robe. But when she steps forward into the light, Serena can see the lines that a lifetime of getting her own way has etched onto her mother's face, and the determined set of her jaw. I could look like her, one day, Serena thinks, and her own mouth tightens at the thought.

"Aren't you dressed yet?" her mother says, fussing. "Honestly, if I didn't know better, I'd think you didn't want to go. Has Premya put out your dress?"

"I don't know."

"Well, go and look," her mother says, and rings the bell for the maid. "You know Jamie Buchanan's going to be there tonight, don't you?"

Serena nods, and although she tries to hold it back, she starts to cough. Her mother's lips compress into a thin line, but as usual she avoids any mention of Serena's condition.

"He'll hardly want to see you—less than your best," is all that her mother says, under her breath.

"He won't," Serena says, with icy precision.

"Very well, then."

The masque is to be held somewhere behind the secret walls of Highgate: a fortress within a fortress. The theme of the masque is summer. Serena wears lace as golden as fire, velvet as soft as flesh in the sun. Just before she leaves, she takes the last precious drops of the preparation, and not a moment too soon. Already, the silk of her handkerchief is mottled with hemorrhage as she steps through the door of her father's house to the hired car. The limousine is too hot; stifling with the smell of leather, but outside the temperature is dropping further beyond zero. When they arrive Serena, wrapped in furs, hastens to the mansion, but a chill still snatches her breath from her throat. Then she's through the door and enveloped by warmth.

The room in which the masque is held is suffused with the perfume of roses. The blooms have the excessive quality that is characteristic of gen-enhanced organisms: the roses are too crimson, too sweet. Serena's sensitive faculties detect the faint undernote of opiated pheromones. She sighs, but the sudden taste of blood in her mouth bisects the pleasure. Delicately, she touches her handkerchief to her lips. Heads turn, then turn away. Serena moves slowly among the crowd, pretending not to notice their covert glances. They are staring at her because of her illness: the sickness which presents with such discreet elegance in a few drops of blood and the translucence of her skin.

She strolls to the window, where she finds herself standing next to Juliet Arden. Juliet's family are wealthier than Serena's own. They have a place in the Shires, tucked away in a Cotswold fold behind gun turrets and shark-hounds. Juliet's people have their own transport, too; a rarity these days. Serena has always considered Juliet to be a little vulgar: old money, yet rather flashy with her robust good health, but as she looks at Juliet now she sees with a jolt of shock that Juliet, too, is betraying the signs of illness. There is a heightened glow to her skin, a sheen of sweat that has nothing to do with the hot-house warmth of the room.

"Juliet?" Serena says, and the girl replies, with a small smile

"It's nothing."

The message passes between them, unspoken. They share a secret, and Serena wonders how many people, here in this luxurious place, are hiding similar sicknesses. All sorts of things are rife in London these days: new manifestations of fevers and syndromes. Myalgic-encephalitis and the other pollution-borne viruses of the last century; older accompaniments like tuberculosis. At the thought, Serena coughs delicately, just once. In response to Juliet's concerned glance, she manages a smile and turns back to the panorama of the city. For a moment she almost envies Cassini. What must it be like, to be able to move freely about the world, unconstrained by illness?

Pleading fatigue, she goes to sit on a nearby divan, where she can watch the crowd and count the signs: secret traces on the landscapes of the flesh. Her reverie is interrupted by the arrival of another friend—well, perhaps not precisely a friend, but certainly an acquaintance. Serena has not seen this woman, Nola Elgin, for over a year. She never quite knows what to think of Nola, who is the only member of Serena's immediate social circle who travels: to Paris, Prague, and to places whose names are only vaguely familiar to Serena. No-one travels much these days, and certainly not for pleasure. Nola, however, even has a job: working for an aid agency which hosts charity events to generate relief for the stricken southern hemisphere. Serena sometimes goes to these events, but not often. They upset her too much and besides, she is ill and cannot be expected to worry about the suffering of others. But she is a little nervous of Nola, who now sits down heavily beside her on the divan and gives her an unreadable smile.

"Well, hello," Nola says, wryly. "How are you? No, don't tell me—as well as can be expected, I suppose."

The last words are laced with sarcasm and Serena does not know quite what to say. She feels as though the rules of the game have been changed, somehow, and no one has told her. She gives a little nod.

"I'm fine," she says, trying to sound brave. Nola says nothing, but stares down into the pale depths of her champagne with something that could almost be distaste. Serena notices that Nola's pale forehead is shiny with perspiration beneath the lacquered arch of her hair and the hand that holds her glass is shaking a little, almost imperceptibly, but Serena has sharp eyes and has learned to recognize the signs.

"Nola? Are you all right?" Serena asks, still playing the game of illusion, expecting the customary evasions, but Nola says bluntly, "No. No, I'm not all right. I've got Sumari fever."

Serena blinks, appalled. Sumari is one of the new diseases; rare, but almost invariably fatal unless it's contracted in a particular configuration. She's read about it, of course, but never thought that she might meet someone who actually had it. Bitterness wells up within Serena and she stumbles over the words, "How–I mean, if you don't mind me asking—how did you get it?"

Nola gives her a long level look and Serena's gaze drops away with unexpected embarrassment. At last Nola says, "It's not what you think, Serena."

Now, it's Serena's turn to stare. She thinks for a moment that some-one must have opened the window, then realizes that it's only her own face growing cold. Nola continues, "I caught it in Paris, from a Somalian refugee. There are so many new viruses these days—once one gets out of London, that is. Don't worry, Serena," and there's more than a touch of mockery in Nola's voice, "It's not contagious."

Serena says, desperate for conviction, "But there must be something they can do about it, isn't there? I mean—surely there's a cure?"

Nola says simply, "No. No, there's no cure."

She gazes around the room with an oddly complacent satisfaction, her gaze sliding from face to fevered face.

"But there must be," Serena says, desperately seeking reassurance, denying the truth all over again.

Then Nola's angry eyes meet her own and Nola says, very low, "You've no idea, have you, what illness really means? How lucky you are. . . . " Nola's voice sharpens. "I promised myself I wasn't going to lecture anyone tonight. I wasn't even going to tell anyone what's wrong with me, and then I overhead you speaking to Juliet Arden. You're a wonderful pair, both of you. A brace of languishing consumptives, preoccupied with your own little world of cybershopping and gossip and parties that might just as well be virtual, for all the life than anyone ever shows. And the pretence, Serena, the pretence—all the careful discretion of your artificial, manufactured illnesses, each one of you feigning to be worse than the rest, all an excuse, so you can be so delicately glamorous, cared for and cherished, never needing to take any real decisions. . . . Symptoms without cause and no damage except a little nervous adrenaline and a little harmless blood loss. Well, I must be the height of fashion, mustn't I? Because I'm really sick. And I'm really going to die."

The room has fallen silent now, and everyone is staring in Nola's direction.

"Go on, then," Nola says venomously to the room. "Go ahead and stare. I'll give you something to stare at," and she wrenches open a sleeve to display her ulcerated arm, lesions clustering across the ruined skin. "How chic does that make me, then?"

She reaches out and presses a hot, moist hand against Serena's appalled face.

"Merry Christmas, my dear. I doubt I'll be wishing you another one."

And then she rises and leaves. The crowd parts before her as she stalks through them like the leper she's become. Serena's chest hurts in earnest now; she realizes she's been holding her breath. Behind her, Juliet Arden's loud, over-bred voice says, "Well, really!" and the chatter of conversation gradually starts up again as the guests, with consummate skill, pretend that nothing has happened, and the party goes on. But Serena walks like an automaton to the window and throws it open to let a cold rush of air into the stuffy room, and leans out into the night so that she can breathe again. Then she turns away from the window, ignoring the stares, and slips out of the room to where the car is waiting. Outside, she lingers for a moment, standing in the snow until it soaks through her expensive slippers, staring up at the distant stars.

When she gets back to the house, she finds that a package is waiting for her: Cassini's Christmas present, a parcel of artificial sickness. Carefully, Serena opens it and stares numbly at the row of little phials. In each resides a dose of fashionable symptoms, a barrier against the pain of living. Serena sits with the box on her knees, and then, one by one, she takes each phial and throws it into the fire.

Dog Years

All down the long days of summer's end, I listened to the dead. They began to speak to me one night, when the warm wind tasted of salt and gasoline fumes from the refineries along the Clyde estuary. It was the hottest August I had ever known, or perhaps it was just the fever. My mother said I was sick, and stroked my long hair back from my face and called me her Sylvie, her little girl, but I don't remember the illness so much as the voices which whispered from the dark. They grew loudest towards dawn when, perhaps, the light of the sun reminded them of what they had lost, and with its rising they grew silent. That day seemed to pass with anguished slowness: the heavy sunlight dragging itself over the sill and each drop of sweat as hot as blood. In the night, the voices returned. I don't know if they realized I was listening. I was only a child then, and I did not understand the languages of the world beyond the world. I did not realize that a soul does not speak with a single voice but with many, at the same time. It is as though they carry their voices with them from life to life, so that when they speak it is like listening to the static of a radio badly tuned, to a station that is no longer there. Maybe the dead grow tired of hearing themselves, and become lost in static and sound. But gradually, as the year grew on and grew colder, and still I did not get well, I found that by degrees I could understand what the dead were saying.

used to take the apples down to the press and he'd catch a rat and drop it in the barrel like seasoning

followed her down the road from the kirk, but she never once turned her head and I

hated him even as he lay dying and he never knew

The voices scratched away at the air and the shadows; memories caught in time like flies in amber as the dead sipped away at the edges of life. I struggled up in bed and lay against the pillows, listening avidly as they spoke. I don't know why I wasn't more afraid; it must have been the illness. I remember thinking that it would be a wonderful thing to be able to speak to the dead, and have them listen to me in turn. My mother had four more children to care for, and though she used to sit with me, she still had a hurried air, as though she was just pausing between tasks. Farm life is hard: quotas to be met and subsidy forms to fill in, as well as the work in the field. My brothers and sisters were at school during the day. And when it became clear that I might in fact die, they did not visit me quite so often. It was as though they were practicing for the day when I would no longer be there, or as though they feared a reminder of what might happen to them. Sickness may be avoided, but death is catching, or so it seemed to me. So I did not fear the dead, and to my young mind it seemed a good idea to make friends with them when I was still alive, so that they would be familiar to me when I died. It was at this point that I began to talk back to the dead.

I conversed in whispers, as they did. My mother used to put a night-light by my bed, and my words seemed to link with the shadows that danced over the white walls of the room. I replied to the words that the dead spoke, the fragments and snatches of phrases, telling them that I remembered these things too, or that I'd had similar thoughts. And after a while, the dead started to listen to me, instead.

Gradually, I realized that they were beginning to cluster around me, hanging avid on my every word. Sometimes I felt a brush of air against my mouth and my lips would become cold, as though the dead were sipping the warmth from my words. I liked that, in the hot heart of the fever, and I began to tell stories to the dead, murmuring to them, describing everything I saw and remembered. I should have known that it would be too much for them to resist.

One evening, shortly after the blue dusk filled the land, someone came to me. My mother had left the window open and I could see a square of twilight sky over the ridge of the hills. As I lay there and watched it, and whispered, a figure began to etch itself onto the hazy air. I fell silent and waited. The figure was slight, not much taller than myself, and the air within its outline seemed to move, distorted by the evening breeze. Gradually, it solidified, and turned to face me. It was a girl, of more or less my own age, with long pale hair. Slowly, she smiled.

I've been listening to you, she murmured. My skin prickled like static.

"Are you a ghost?" I asked her.

Yes, she said, after a pause, and tilted her head to one side. *Yes, that's what I am.* Her smile grew sweeter. She stepped forwards. Wondering, I could see the shadows of flowers in the places where she stepped. She added, *We like to listen to you, you know. You tell marvelous stories.*

"It's just what I see. And I don't see much. I've been in bed for so long. . . ."

My voice had a quiver in it; it is one thing to hear voices from the other side of life, another to look their owners in the face. I told my fevered mind that it was nothing more than a dream, and that made it easier. The girl frowned.

Are you ill, then?

I was surprised that she did not know this; I thought it was obvious. "Yes," I said. "They don't know what's the matter with me."

Coming across to the bed, my visitor sat down and rested her hand on my forehead. Coolness drifted across my skin in waves, alternating with the heat of the fever.

So you are, she said, still smiling. *What a pity.*

"I think," I said, and swallowed hard, for the thought was suddenly a frightening one, "I think I might die."

Oh, my visitor replied. *That would be a shame. . . . You'd be one of us, then, and I don't suppose we'd find you at all interesting.* She leaned closer, but I could feel no breath against my face, only a pervasive sweetness underlain with decay, like the scent of hawthorn. *Wouldn't you rather live?*

I looked into her eyes. They were very pale, and the light flickered in their depths as if within a distant mirror. I said, "Yes. Yes, I'd rather live."

She took my hand, as if in sympathy, and again I felt nothing except a faint coolness.

We could help you, the girl said, softly. *Take the fever away, so that you can run out into the sunlight again, play in the rain. Would you like that?*

Her hand on mine was growing colder. Once, when I was very young, I'd touched a line of barbed wire in the middle of winter and my skin had stuck fast, only to tear and bleed when I pulled free.

But if we help you, she added into my ear *You must do something for us, in return.*

There's always a bargain to be made, so I have learned; it only depends on the price. But suddenly life seemed the most important thing of all, in comparison with this chilly, faded halfglow.

"What do you want?" I whispered. I'd read enough fairy stories by then to think I understood. "My soul?"

The girl's head tilted back and her mouth opened in a burst of slow, soundless laughter. A draft which I could not feel lifted her hair and it floated around her face like water. *Your soul? We'll have that soon enough, why should we want such a thing? No. We'd just like to borrow your body for a little while, look through your eyes. To see what you see.*

"Borrow my body? Like possession?"

It's not true that spirits can possess. We can't animate you. We can't move your flesh. It would be more than I could do to keep your heart beating and your lungs pumping in and out. But in this world, in this form, I am almost blind. And in the country of the dead, nothing is more than a gleam. You can't know how tired one becomes of a world of shadows and smoke. . . . Lend us your eyes for a little time each month, when you're closest to living and death. Lend us your eyes when you bleed. And we'll let you live.

I could not think what to say. She rose from the bed and drifted back towards the window.

"Wait, wait," I said, in a panic in case she should be gone. "All right. I agree."

She smiled at me, came close again. Without saying a word, she bent and kissed my brow and in the instant when she drew away she no longer looked like a girl, for a flickering instant, but something else. Something else, with an animal's eyes. I gasped, and then she was no longer there. I don't remember falling asleep, but the voices were silent and I do not think I dreamed.

Next day, I awoke and everything had changed. I felt hollow inside, like a reed with the pith sucked out, but the fever had gone and so had the pain in my limbs. I made my halting way to the door and called for my mother. After the first few days, my recovery was swift. The ghost had kept her word, and so did I.

I was sent back to school, but a month after that my periods started. On the day that they began, I went down to the stream in the evening, and crouched by its banks to watch the water run clear and cold over the speckled rocks towards the weir. It was November now, and growing dark early. I waited in the half light, and there was a sudden tension in the back of my mind, as though someone had pulled a wire taut, matching the cramp in my stomach. I blinked, and found that the stream had widened. The opposite shore was now more than three strides away, yet somehow closer. It was like looking at two scenes at once, superimposed upon one another. I reached down and trailed my hand through the water. It was icy: snowmelt running fast from the hills. The water was tinged with red in the last of the light. I looked across at the far shore and saw a woman crouching on the gravel with a linen band in her hands. She could have been my own reflection, but as I gazed she glanced up. Her face was covered by a mask, which had the smooth pallor of bone, and beneath it her eyes gleamed black as oil. I felt a chill run from the crown of my head to my feet, as if I had held up my hand and pulled back lightening.

"Who are you?" I said, but I spoke without a sound. And then there was only the little stream, running swift through the dark valley, and a crowd behind my eyes, avidly drinking in every aspect of the scene. I don't know how long I sat on the banks of the water, but when the dead retreated, sated at last, I saw that the moon was rising.

I went home to fury. What was I thinking of, my mother cried, to spend more than three hours out alone on a freezing winter night? Did I want to get ill again? And after a pause, because for the first time I had caught a glimpse of what my unnatural bargain might mean, I answered No.

After that, it happened again and again, usually three or four times during the course of each period. I became used to slowing and stopping, nodding off to a glimpse of elsewhere, while the spirits of the dead clustered behind my eyes like flies on carrion, watching. I saw the school counselor, but what could I tell her? She would think I'd gone mad. And then we began to notice something. My sisters and brothers were growing up, voices deepening, faces changing, but I seemed to have stopped at the age of thirteen. My parents took me along a gauntlet of doctors, who did CAT scans and neurological tests. Tentatively, they suggested narcolepsy, epilepsy, ADD, but none of them seemed to have any real answers. At last we settled on arrested development with episodes of catatonia; it seemed to cover a multitude of sins. It didn't appear to effect my intelligence, or even my ability to function. I won a place at university in Glasgow, to study English Lit. And it was around this time that the dead began to grow greedy.

Until my move from home, the shadows who borrowed my body

had seemed content with what I offered them. They would cluster and gaze, staring out across the drowsing cornfield, or the corner of a room, or the television: anything seemed to satisfy them, as long as it was in the world of the living. But when I moved to the city, the dead seemed to wake and take an interest. The spirit had told me that they could not possess a living soul, and I do not think that she lied, but they could influence. They steered me like a ship, gently nudging me in the direction of danger or horror or pain. Like scavengers, they seemed able to sense blood, and their assumption of my reluctant flesh was no longer confined to the peak of my menstrual cycle. I'd find myself standing in front of a road accident, gazing like a ghoul, or wandering down the corridors of the hospital until someone would ask me sharply where I thought I was going, and break the spell. Maybe the dead could see something that I could not: the moment when the breath leaves the body, the parameters of pain. I glimpsed myself sometimes, reflected in shop windows: a small, pale figure, hollow-eyed, flitting through the rain. But all I really wanted to do was to look at the sunlight, summer fields, blue sea and pleasant things, and if I became resentful enough the dead would relent, and leave me in peace for a few ordinary, welcome days.

Strangely, this obsession which was not my own gave me a career rather than hindering it. When I left university, I got a job at the local paper, making my way up through the journalistic ranks until I got my first posting as a war correspondent, in Lebanon. I'd aged a little by then, though without makeup I still looked unnaturally young, and it served me in good stead. I gained access to places denied to older male journalists; I suppose because I looked so unthreatening, so unsuspicious. Beirut was bleached by the heat, but in the evening the coast became a soft purple, the hills on either side of the bay holding the last of the light. I thought it was beautiful. So did the dead, for different reasons. I gained a reputation for being twice as tough as the men, someone who could walk unflinching through the worst excesses of war. But it wasn't true; my passengers were the ghouls, not I, and what I saw made me weep inside. I never lost the nightmares. And then the dead grew greedier yet.

I was sitting in a bar on El Haifa street, with a group of other journalists when the bomb went off. Most of the terrorist activity had taken place in the banking district, but evidently Al Sabah had decided to enlarge their sphere of activity. I had just got up to go to the bar when there was a sudden blast of light, searing itself onto my retinas. The whispering voices of the dead rose in excitement and fury that they could no longer see what was happening. I staggered back against the table; I could hear the roar of fire. Ears ringing, half blinded, I ran out into the street. The bomb had gone off in the market place. As I watched, a burning awning collapsed in on itself, leaving an iron cage where a stall had been. Somewhere, through the singing in my ears, I could hear screaming.

Closer, closer, whispered the dead, but I was already on my way. At the far end of the market place, a man had been blown against the wall by the blast. I don't know whether he was one of the terrorists, or just a cautious bystander; a gun lay a few feet away. He was covered in blood, one leg shattered below the knee. He had stopped screaming now, and was panting with shock and pain. And the dead murmured

"Not enough. Take the gun and shoot him in the head. It's not enough." They wanted more. I stood entranced, staring at the light of the flames as they reflected from the surface of the gun; sending shadows across the rough plaster of the wall; glistening on spilled blood. "Not enough!" the dead wailed, spoilt children in my head. I found myself bending, reaching for the gun. "Hold it in front of his face, let him be afraid. We want to see!" Moving like an automaton, I picked up the gun. It was hot. It burned my fingers, and I dropped it like a coal. Turning, I ran back through the maze of alleyways to where the emergency services were congregating, and told them that there was a man in the alleyway who needed treatment. Then I walked grimly back to the hotel, disregarding the disappointed chorus in my head.

I sat on the balcony of the hotel until the sun came up, staring out to sea. When the dawn light first appeared over the long line of the mountains, I looked down at my hands. They were small, the fingers locked together like the hands of a frightened child. The dead had given me my life back, and more. Having found a body they could use, they were eking it out, like a precious resource that must be preserved. How long, I wondered in despair, would this go on? I looked up, and the girl was standing at the far end of the balcony. She was not the Celtic shade whom I had seen last time. Dark hair spilled across her face and she wore a long burnous, but the eyes were the same. I wondered whether she created her form out of the land itself, tailoring her appearance to fit local myths. It didn't really matter to me how she chose to present herself.

I said, without preamble, "How long?"

The spirit smiled, not pretending to misunderstand.

Nine years, for every one of your normal span.

Like dog years, I thought, but in reverse. It made sense. I was thirty-one now, but I looked fifteen. A quick mental calculation revealed that at this rate, I might live somewhere beyond the five hundred mark. I stifled a panicky laugh.

The spirit said with remote reproof, *Many would be grateful.*

"I am not." I rose to my feet. "You ask too much, you have become too greedy, insatiable for suffering and pain. I won't pander to you any longer."

And what do you propose to do? the spirit asked, with distant amusement.

"Return me to our original bargain. Let me die."

No. That isn't in my power. You can try, of course. You can throw yourself from this place on which we stand. I can see little enough, but I know that it is high. But we will still let you live, even broken and shattered. Perhaps, the spirit mused, *perhaps it would even be interesting, to experience what you would undergo, in such a form.*

I swallowed a cold lump of fear. I wasn't afraid of death any more, but the scenes to which the dead had led me over the years had fed my imagination until it was bloated with horrors. I could well envisage what it might be like to live on in a ruined shell.

Besides, the spirit continued, *I have told you that we do not possess. You have free will, in the end. All it takes is strength, but perhaps you are not strong enough, to resist the allure of mortal ruin? Maybe you even enjoy it, and we are nothing more than the excuse?*

"That's not true," I whispered, and wondered which one of us was lying. And then the sun touched the edge of the mountains and the spirit was gone. I went back into the hotel room and packed my bag, then booked a flight to London. I faxed the newspaper from the business center at the airport, to inform my editor of my resignation.

Back in Britain, I returned to my sister's house in Scotland. She lived near Lismore, in a small house surrounded by trees. It was a quiet place and in the morning I could walk down to the shore and watch the brown, brackish water lapping over the stones and the herons gliding down the estuary. Everyone accepted my explanation of burnout and post-trau-matic stress. But the dead grew bored. They began to whisper to me again, louder and louder until the world was filled with their voices, like locusts rustling in a field of grain. They spoke of blood and ruin; their voices were seductive and alluring, painting horror in such glowing terms that it was almost impossible to resist. I suppose they were telling me how they saw such things; a different aesthetic from my own. But I remembered the man in the alleyway in Beirut and what they had tried to make me do, and I resisted their call. I already had an idea.

That afternoon, I called the local volunteer bureau and offered my services as a warden on one of the islands off the Scots coast. Setlar was not so remote as to be inaccessible, but it was a quiet place, inhabited mainly by seabirds. The dead, I thought vindictively, could damn well look at something peaceful for a change. Volunteers for such a post are not so easy to come by, and by the end of the following week, I was in residence. I spent long days looking out across the waters of the Firth of Lorn, watching the light as it changed; waiting for storms to roll in. And one by one, the dead fell silent. At first I was thankful, but the quality of that silence gradually made me uneasy, filled as it was with a dreadful, brooding patience. Well, I told myself, if the dead can wait, then so can I.

We saw the year out: June to November, and I elected to stay on the island once the official season was over. As if demonstrating disapproval, an immense storm began on the day that I e-mailed my request to the volunteer section. It hammered down the coast, so that the curve of Mull was lost in rain and the air was full of salt spray. It took its toll on the island, and on other lives, too. On the second night of the storm, I got a distress call.

The call came from the lifeboat service, and it relayed information about a fishing vessel that had overturned on its way back into Oban. The crew were reported as missing; all available personnel were asked to check the shores, in case someone had been washed up. It had hap-pened before; the tides around the Firth are notoriously tricky and often channeled debris through the strait that lay between Setlar and the main-land. I ran down the long path to the shore to search.

I could not see beyond the arch of the rocky headland that sepa-rated Setlar's inner bay from the Firth. It was almost dark, and the rain was driving into my face, blinding me. Behind my eyes, I could sense a sudden, hopeful presence. I played the torch over the shingle, and on the second sweep, I caught a glimpse of something wet and yellow. A life jacket. I scrambled down the shore. The man was lying half in and half out of the water. He was unconscious, but as I began to drag him free of the tide, he came round. He was frozen and bruised by the stones, but he had escaped serious injury. Together, we stumbled up the shingle beach and the winding path of the cliff to the warden's cottage.

As soon as they saw the condition he was in, the dead gave me no peace. They hustled at the back of my eyes, pressure growing moment by moment like a burning in my brain. They whispered, over and over again *Why do you wait, he is helpless, he is half drowned, you are all alone. No one will ever know. Kill him, do it, do it. . . .* —on and on, until with a distant horror I saw that the stranger had put down his cup of whisky-laced coffee and was staring back at me.

"Why are you looking at me like that?" he asked.

"I—I'm sorry, I'm still a bit dazed, I didn't mean—"

"Be quiet," he said, gently enough. He rose from his chair and came to stand in front of me: dark haired, dark eyed, a typical island Scot. He took my chin in his hand and raised my face. I thought of knocking his hand away, but the pity in his face stopped me. He stared for a moment into my eyes with an almost clinical, dispassionate interest.

"Yes," he said. "I thought so. Possessed."

"How do you know?"

"Ah, but I've seen it enough times. My own grandfather, he made a bargain with the dead, long ago. He took them to war and back again; he was one of the ones who liberated Auschwitz." The stranger gave a small, grim smile. "They must have loved that."

In a whisper I said, "What happened to him, in the end?"

"He lived on, ageing one year for every nine. He took to sea, most of the time, but they reached him in the end. They drove him mad."

"Listen to me," I said, "If there is anything I can do—"

"No, there's nothing. You've made your bargain, and you're stuck with it. They'll be with you for the rest of your long years. But they can be—discouraged."

"How?" I said, and I winced at the look in his eyes.

He said, tentatively, "It won't be easy. Or pleasant. But I can help you, if you'll let me."

And once I had heard what he had to say, I agreed, sealing the second bargain of my life.

That was seven years ago. I still look too young to be a mother of two, or so they tell me. I wouldn't know, myself. Sometimes I stand in front of the mirror that hangs in the hallway of our house in Oban, and reach out to touch its smooth, cold surface, and wonder what I would see if I still had my sight. I wonder, too, how long I'll live now that the dead have been deprived of their window on the world; I suspect that it will not be so very long, but as long as I die when my daughters are grown, I do not greatly mind. It seems to me that I have seen enough.

Dancing Day

If I listen carefully, I can hear everything: fires burning, the drift of snow, secrets whispered into walls and voices calling. I have heard many voices across a thousand years, demanding, pleading and finally falling silent, but that day Lilith said that I was still too young to know sense from nonsense.

"You've got a lot of learning to do," she told me, rattling her brassy feathers. She looked at me out of a fierce golden eye. "Not a thought in your head, that's the trouble with you."

But lazy Ishtar from the fire said, "Oh, leave the child alone. Let her make her own mistakes."

It was always the same at home. I did not want to listen and so I went down to the shore to dance. The stars burned molten and far away I could see the other dancer: the one who is always there, spinning at the edge of the world. I felt the sun blaze beneath my feet and the furnace heat of the sky against my skin. In dancing, I forgot who I was, but someone had remembered me.

Her name was Shadineth Massaret. She wanted a wild love, bright as the sun and deep as darkness and so she shut the windows, threw a pinch of incense onto the fire and summoned me. She called me by my own name; raised from the depths of some shadowy Arcanum, written in blood on the day of my making. Much later, Lilith said, "You don't have to answer, you know, just because someone bawls your name in your ear. You're not a dog. I don't know what got into you."

I don't know either. I suppose I was bored, or perhaps I just wanted to see what it was like; that small gray world, filled with dim mayfly souls. Shadineth called my name three times and on the third I answered. Stars rushed by, the air rang like a bell and I fell like a stone into the body of a girl, on a rainy night in Constantinople, in 1923.

I don't think that Shadineth was expecting quite so spectacular a success. She was no professional necromancer: just a bored girl, at a loose end and excited by the thought of the forbidden. We all like to play with fire, sometimes. I was rather surprised at my sudden incursion into the human. Her body was cold; wet as snow and fragile as a shell. Her heart fluttered against her brittle ribs. I tried to tell her that I did not want to hurt her, but my voice sounded thunderous in the vaults of her head. She cried out and clapped her hands to her ears. Somewhere, beyond her, was warmth and I reached out to it, but she screamed again and plucked her hand from the coals in the brazier. Clearly, this matter of possession was something we would both have to work at. I think she fell; the room span up and I found myself looking out of her eyes at the yellow plaster of the ceiling. Her heels drummed the floor. The door burst open and people swarmed in. They picked her up and carried her across to the bed, where they forced something sour and honeyed down her throat. She swallowed convulsively and dropped into dreaming. I had time to think, then, and to consider the consequences of my position.

Possession is such an ambivalent word. The Churches are unanimous in their disapproval, saying that it is common knowledge that people become possessed by demons. Yet we demons know that humans possess us: beguiling us with their desires and capturing us in the webs of their will. We find ourselves imprisoned in cooler flesh than our own, frightened and bewildered. I thought to find a new friend; instead I found myself securely stuck in the chilly veins of an amateur sorceress, now out for the count. I was cold beyond bearing and I wanted to go home. I think I howled.

I was held in her body, afraid and raging, until the morning. The sun came up in a torrent of light above the city and Shadineth flinched as she opened her eyes. I stirred within her, as gently as I could. She rolled over, trying to escape the lodger in her head, and fell off the side of the bed. Servants came running in and helped her back. Then a man came: dressed in a robe the color of dawn. From the sleeve of the robe he drew a small bag and from it he took a pinch of a black powder. An attendant lit the brazier and he cast the powder into the coals. It flared up with a hiss. I watched with interest. He raised his arms to the ceiling and cried out a single phrase. After a moment's reflection, I recognized it. It was an incantation, predictably enough against demons. It was evidently somewhat past its best. I tried to tell him this but my voice roared out from my hostess' stretched throat. A confetti shower of plaster fell from the ceiling and the brazier spat sparks. My voice was too loud; my essence too hot; I was too much altogether for this small, neat world. I gave up, sulking.

The tedious process of exorcism continued throughout the day. Priests and clerics of all descriptions trooped through the House of Lanterns, all bent on becoming the one who liberated its heiress from her besetting succubus. I did my best to cooperate, but nothing seemed to work. Then there was a tapping of heels on the parquet floor and a woman came in. She had dispensed with the customary robes and was wearing a rather modish suit with a rabbit collar. Her title was Luna, and she was a priestess of Cybele: Our Lady of Beasts. She was unwilling to tolerate any nonsense. She threw everyone else out of the room and bolted the door. Then she turned to the poor prone figure on the bed and said, "Right. Enough's enough. I want you out of there on a count of three."

In the smallest voice I could muster I said, "I can't."

My voice was a gale. Words billowed through the room. The windows rattled. The priestess clapped her calfskin gloves to her ears.

"Don't speak. Just nod your head, yes or no."

I managed a little nod.

"That's good. Now, are you trapped?"

I nodded.

"Do you know how we might release you?"

I shook my hostess' head.

"Very well. There's only one thing I can think of, and it's a little risky. Not to you, to Shadineth, so I suggest you listen carefully. If she dies, you will not necessarily be free, and it will take a considerably greater effort to disentangle you: one which is beyond my capabilities."

With care, I nodded. I don't know how she persuaded the family to accept her proposal. I was dimly aware of a disconsolate muttering throughout the hallway as the assembled religious were told that their services would no longer be required. Then an attendant came, with a stronger sedative that sent both my tortured hostess and myself into darkness.

When we awoke, we were no longer in the House of Lanterns but somewhere echoing, filled with a watery light. The first thing that met our gaze was a face: vast, malign and upside down. The carving, which bore an uncanny resemblance to myself, was framed with stone coils of serpentine hair. They had brought us to the cisterns beneath the city; the water reservoirs which served Constantinople even in these modern days. They had brought me to this damp dark place away from the dance of the sun, to keep themselves safe from me. The Luna whispered all this into Shadineth's ear. To my chagrin, I discovered that the Luna was not to be the one to lead the exorcism: this was an honor reserved for the high priestess herself. "But I'll be here," the Luna whispered. "I'll be beside you."

I tried to ask her what was going to happen, for they had not exorcised any of my kind for a very long time. In the old days, more of us had been young and foolish, but now there was only me. Ghosts may possess and be possessed, it's true; but they have no more tenacity than shadows and a breath or a word can send them shrieking into the wind. I was an altogether different proposition.

They had paid for a sacrifice, which surprised me. This was the 1920's, after all. I did not see who it was: perhaps one of the janissaries, whom the alchemists created in their hidden laboratories beneath Pera. Attendants strapped down my hostess' protesting head, so that all we could see was the ceiling.

The Luna whispered in my ear, "Watch the smoke. Watch it drift and die. . . . " over and over until we were both entranced. I began to follow the smoke up into the vault of the cistern and slowly it took me with it, pouring from Shadineth's eyes and mouth. A crimson drop blossomed like an anemone in the water. Someone cried out; a shadow sprang past me into the smoke and I followed, but as my pinions reached free above her head, Shadineth began to fight to keep me in. I wanted only flight and air and sunlight, but she began to reel me down; using the beat of her heart and the pulse of her blood, all the human snares. She was stronger than I; this was not my world. She wanted nothing more, she would have said, than for me to be gone, but the unconscious self is immune to reason. It wants what it wants, and blindly it sucked me back and hooked me in.

The Luna's face was very close; I could smell her narcissus perfume. She was staring into Shadineth's eyes and somewhere she saw mine looking back at her: a spark of gold in an empty head.

"It hasn't worked," she pronounced. The high priestess shoved her aside.

"Of course it's worked. Everyone saw: the demon was cast forth."

"No, it went back in. What did you do that for?" she demanded of me.

I shook the girl's head and, once started, I couldn't stop. It rattled to and fro like a broken puppet.

"Stop that!" She held Shadineth's head still by sheer force. The girl bit her lip and a drop of blood ran down her chin. I chased it with her tongue.

"Oh, I don't know what to do," the Luna said, in despair. "Get them back to the house. We'll try and think of something else."

They took us home to the House of Lanterns and laid Shadineth on the bed. Then they left her, possessed, to wait out another long night. I lay within her, like a seed, waiting. Somewhere in the depths of the night, Lilith came. I dragged the girl's head from her uneasy dreams and opened her eyes. Lilith was leaning against the mantelpiece, examining her taloned nails. Her fiery feathers fluttered in an unknown wind, but in the chamber the candle burned quietly.

I opened Shadineth's mouth and spoke, as though through a ventriloquist's doll.

"Help me," I said.

"Can't, I'm afraid. Not unless you're willing to see her unmade. . . not just dead, child, but unsouled. Do you want that? D'you care?"

They say that we prey on living souls, that we are beyond compassion, but I was young, with a child's fondness. I did not want to see Shadineth hurt. I said so.

"You should have been more careful. If I've told you once, I've told you a thousand times. . . . "

Her bronze skin shivered and ruffled. She blinked golden eyes. I was beginning to feel very sorry for myself.

"Nothing I can do," said heartless Lilith, reaching for the brazier. "I'm sure someone will think of something. Bye."

"Lilith, wait—" I cried, but she was already gone, in a shower of fire.

Life settled down a little after that. Gulan Massaret continued to advertise, covertly, in the esoteric press for the person who might free his daughter. Enough people answered, over the course of the next year:

mathematical mystics from Syria; Gnostic clerics from the Maghreb; the drug makers of Ghent and Antwerp. None of them achieved even partial success. Massaret was reluctant to let his daughter's condition be generally known, for obvious reasons, but it is impossible to keep a secret in Constantinople. The city absorbs lies and confidences and, as befits the cradle of alchemy, changes what it hears. Some said that Shadineth was mad, or ill, or possessed by the spirit of her grandmother, the formidable Alicien.

A surprising number even knew the truth.

The new sciences of the mind began to take a hold in Vienna and Geneva, and Massaret enticed its principal proponents to Constantinople and the House of Lanterns: anything, he reasoned, was worth a try. Shadineth was analyzed for hours. She lay on the couch and stared at the ceiling, and when they asked her to talk about her dreams, she only smiled. At last, despairing, her father had her shut away in the high attics of the House of Lanterns. In the evenings, we would sit behind the filigree bars at the window and watch the lights come on across the city; in all the other gilded cages in which the lost children of Constantinople are kept.

At length, people forgot poor mad Shadineth. Gulan Massaret was given a diplomatic posting to Paris, in an attempt to stop the growing threat of war. He left a handful of retainers to care for his daughter, but it proved to be care in the most minimal sense, for they were afraid. And so, lonely and tormented, Shadineth turned to her constant companion for comfort: to me.

Gradually, over the years, we had achieved a kind of equilibrium. I learned how to be still, and quiet, and gentle. I learned how to speak to her in a small voice, so that she could understand me without pain. Together, we explored the vaults of her mind. She led me through her dreams, and I helped her to understand the mysteries of number and symbol, which together make the rules of the world. I danced for her, and she watched every move and turn I made, spinning down the pathways of her brain. When at last her father came home, years later, we had danced so much that I had almost forgotten who and what I was, and so had she.

Her father was not the same man, either. They had unmade him in the crucible of the internment camps. His mind wandered and soon he took up permanent residence in the rooms below our own. After a few months he died and shortly after that, we discovered that the door to the stairway had been bolted shut. Occasionally, voices floated up through the floorboards; we recognized none of them. No one brought food, but Shadineth did not seem to need it. We kept to the bed after that, becoming absorbed in the play of the sun across the plain of the ceiling. We watched the inconstant light: how it shifted and turned and span away. Darkness and sunlight became the same: only a different day, running round.

Winter came over and again. Frost hid the window and icicles clustered beneath the sill, but Shadineth and I spent all our days in the hollow places of the head and sleep. If we drifted down, we had the thoughts of the city to choose from and other dreams, too, under the snow: the dreams of the lions in the high hills, the multiple mind of the bees in the hive, honey dreaming, slow and other and endless. Sometimes the voices grew louder, closer, but Shadineth and I no longer cared. We were listening to light and the fall of shadows; to warmth and air and winter.

Years ago now, I had told myself that if I trusted Shadineth, she would find her own answer. If they left her alone, she would work out a way. No dramatic exorcisms; no drugs; no long dissection, only

Shadineth herself, taking her own time. And somewhere on the long roads of the mind, we parted company at last: shook hands and said good-bye. I watched Shadineth as she rose from the bed, unlocked the bolts with ease and walked down the stairs. I listened until her footsteps stopped and the voices below, one by one, fell silent. Then I went on my own way, soaring towards the sun and a brighter day.

"What time do you call this?" Lilith asked when she saw me, and I laughed at her and ran through the stars to the shores of the world. Just before I reached it I looked back, once, to where Shadineth was singing, and then I was gone, dancing and away.

The Banquet of the Lords of Night

Severin de Rais hurries through thistledown light, with the dangerous parcel clutched close to his heart, hoping that he won't turn a corner and come face to face with an Unpriest. He's already late, and the Isle de Saint Luce is forbidden territory. Yet even in the midst of his terror, de Rais still thinks it's a pity that he can't pause and marvel, for the Isle is, by old decree of the Lords of Night, the only place in all Paris where light is permitted at this hour. But de Rais cannot stop to admire the lamps; he's running out of time, and if an Unpriest should find what he is carrying. . . de Rais does not even dare think about it. A death sentence, surely. He glances with swift unease up at the shattered stump of Notre Dame, imagining it as it might have looked five hundred years before, filled with candles and prayers and light, before the Lords came and brought the darkness with them, conjuring the great shell which covers the world. The shell lies above the churning storm clouds, too high even to be seen, and de Rais drags his quivering attention back to the present. The metal cover of the precious, precarious parcel is sharp against his chest; the unspells which protect it burn his skin. He wonders in a delirious moment if it will rust if the rain touches it; rust and crumble into nothing more than red ash, like old blood.

The growing rain blurs the lamps of the Isle de Saint Luce so that they look like dandelion clocks, their down blown away on the wind. The light makes de Rais squint and peer, but the parcel warms his breast, in spite of the rain. Heat seeps through him like the taste of honey. The world spins briefly to summer, leaving raindrops scattered in the void. De Rais blinks at this first taste of a season he has never seen, and clasps the parcel even more tightly to his chest. Crossing the bridge which bisects the Seine and leads into the Rue Moins Pitie, de Rais pauses reeling for a moment to catch his unsteady breath. The Seine runs fast with rain swell: a mass of branches tumbles in the current, turning the water to bramble and briar. The risk that he is about to take makes de Rais wonder for a moment if it would be wiser simply to drop the parcel in the river and let the torrent carry it back to the sea, but then he turns away. Above de Rais' head, the curfew bell begins to chime out through the darkness, telling seven o'clock through the gloom. De Rais hurries on towards the Palais.

Behind him, the lights of the Isle are soon lost as he crosses onto the familiar territory of the right bank. De Rais makes his way through dark streets, following his path with meticulously counted steps: along the Quai, down the Tuileries, into the heart of the Lords' Quarter. Should he deviate from that path, he runs the risk of becoming lost in the maze of the city. Occasionally, he detects the faintest gleam of light upon the wet surface of a wall; neon in a blacked-out basement, a candle flickering in a secret room. And then his fears come true. Hastening around the corner into the Rue de Louvre, de Rais runs right into a group of Unpriests. Their long leather coats rustle against the pavement; their heads swivel from side to side. They are clicking like insects in a termite mound, and de Rais shrinks back against the wall, his heart hammering. But their gaze, concealed behind their black lenses, does not turn his way and in a moment they are gone. Why should they challenge him, after all? He's only a lowly pastry chef, and he's not on forbidden ground any more. He's entitled to be in this quarter, the honor signified by the ribbons on his coat. Breathing a long and tremulous sigh, de Rais continues on his way.

He reaches the kitchens of the Palais shortly afterwards, and his lateness is rewarded by a bellow of rage from the head chef. Mumbling insults and excuses beneath his breath, de Rais sidles through the outskirts of the kitchens to collect his work clothes from the store. He fastens the midnight jacket around himself and adjusts the tall smoke-colored hat in the dim reflection of the mirror. His pinched, pale face seems a picture of guilt, but the parcel remains for now in the pocket of his overcoat. De Rais plans to remove it surreptitiously when things quiet down, and hide it at the bottom of the little bread oven in his own small domain. Stepping around the corner of the table, he picks up the chopping board and begins work.

De Rais is a methodical pastry chef, who believes in preparation and planning. The ingredients for today's desserts and pastries have been assembled the night before; the last chores performed by de Rais before he made his weary way homewards. On an ordinary day, tonight and tomorrow would follow the same pattern: home to the attic room in the old Latin Quarter; a few hours' snatched sleep, broken by the sounds from the dingy café downstairs, then back to the Palais early in the morning, with perhaps a stolen hour towards twilight when de Rais can go to the library or snatch a pastis in one of the dreary licensed cafes. But today, things changed. Today, de Rais went to meet the girl: the terrorist, the rebel, the one who gave him the parcel, and perhaps because of that tomorrow will be different too, de Rais thinks with a sudden uplift of his spirits that must surely be noticeable clear across the kitchen. He starts guiltily, and thinks careful, neutral thoughts, but it's not easy to see the expressions on the faces of those who inhabit the kitchens. The head chef jealously guards the ration of candles; everyone else must work in the cold glow of the ovens or simply by touch. It isn't as though they haven't had practice, after all.

Opening the refrigerator, de Rais takes out a container and places it on the table. He opens it carefully, not wanting the essence to escape. The container is full of ice: glassy dark ice from the seas near the southern pole, a place that de Rais knows only from legend. It seems to hold its own glow: it's almost green, like the stories the old folk tell about dawn. With a sharp scalpel, de Rais touches the edge of the sheet of ice, so that it splits and cracks into a nest of slivers. De Rais arranges the shards of ice in the center of each of the twenty-seven sorbet dishes, then reaches back inside the refrigerator for the ingredients of the sauce. He plans a complex, subtle accompaniment to the simple ice: a touch of fragrant Indonesian darkness, gathered close to midnight, redolent of cinnamon and incense and spiced smoke. Placing the darkness in a bowl, he adds a pinch of flavors: twilight from Japan, warm and clouded, with a hint of star anise. Then a touch of evening from the Sinang Delta, water-clear and cool. De Rais stirs all of these elements nine times with an ebony spoon, then pours the swirl of darkness into a silver pan and lights the chilly flame beneath it. He waits, frowning, as a drift of smoke begins to rise from the sauce and then he casts it in a spiral around the little columns of ice and claps his hands imperiously for the serving staff to take it into the dining hall, where the Lords of Night are waiting. The head chef looks up, once, as the procession passes by, and gives a single grudging nod of approval.

Having dispensed with the appetizers, the responsibility for the meal passes on to the head chef for a time, while de Rais busies himself with the desserts. He hopes to get the chance to take the parcel from his overcoat pocket and slip it into the oven, but the head chef has got the apprentices out of his fevered way by sending them over to work in de Rais' corner, a not-uncommon occurrence. Frustrated, de Rais gets on with his own tasks. He prepares fondants of gloom, sorbets of shadows, and sherbets of dusk; each one gathered from the far and unseen corners of the Earth. Then de Rais wipes his weary hands on his apron and steps back to admire his handiwork. Behind him, the booming voice of the head chef says,

"Not bad. Perhaps there's some promise in you after all."

De Rais jumps like a tortured hare. Turning, he snaps, "Don't do that! You startled me."

"Why?" The head chef thrusts his cadaverous face close to that of de Rais. "Nervous? Been doing something you shouldn't? Been gobbing in the fondants again?"

De Rais bridles; he'd never dream of doing such a thing and the head chef knows it.

"Get over there, boy, when you've finished. I want some help to scrub the floors."

The head chef's head jerks in the direction of the apprentices and they scramble after him as he ambles back towards the cold crimson glow of his own territory. Heart pounding, de Rais sidles into the store, retrieves the parcel at last and slides it underneath the iron floor of the little oven. The package is still warm. It seems to radiate its own heat, and de Rais is relieved when at last it's safely out of sight. Then, he goes to where the head chef is waiting and begins to rinse the stone floor clean of blood. He keeps thinking about the package lying in the oven. Once more he rehearses the plan that has been steeping in his mind ever since the girl gave him the parcel.

Once the kitchens are quiet, and everyone has left for the night, de Rais will take the package out of the oven. And then, he will begin to cook. He'll prepare a special dish for the next banquet of the Lords of Night, which will take place tomorrow, on a day that was once called Midsummer. De Rais thinks of the eternal, plunging rain, which he fancies he can hear beating on the pavements above the dungeons of the kitchen, and he shivers as he swabs the bloodstained floor. Mechanically, he goes over the plan once more in his mind, but in the next few minutes, he realizes it might be too late to even think about executing it. The Unpriests have arrived.

They slither down the kitchen stairs, boot-heels clicking on the expensive tiles. De Rais risks a glance, and the nape of his neck grows cold. The people in this group are no ordinary Unpriests. Their long coats bear the Lords' own insignia, and there is a woman with them, dressed in black velvet riding breeches and a leather cuirass. A single dark pearl dangles from one ear, like a bead of jet. Her eyes are hidden behind thick dark lenses. Her head swivels from side to side. This is the closest that de Rais has ever been to one of the creatures of the Lords of Night, and she makes him feel hollow and numb. He stares grimly down at the high, polished heels of her boots. The language that she speaks is archaic, formal, and barely intelligible; she enunciates slowly, evidently for the benefit of the head chef who, as a mere servant, might not be expected to understand her.

"The Unchurch has had word that an attempt is to be made on the lives of the Lords of Night, by non-persons, by dream-sellers, by ghosts. The servants must submit to be searched."

"An attempt on—?" The head chef's thin face quivers in shock. "By whom?"

"I told you. Non-persons. Those who deny darkness, who seek That which is Not."

"By what means?"

"Unknown," the Unpriest says, stiffly, then concedes "By myself, at least. The Lords, of course, know all, but in their black wisdom they have not divulged the answer to one as lowly as myself and were I to know that answer, I would be no more likely to divulge it to you. Now. Prepare to be searched."

From beneath the folds of her coat, she takes a device that de Rais has never seen before. It consists of an extending tube, at the end of which is a round, glistening lens. The woman raises it to the level of the head chef's face, and passes it down his body, from the crown of his head to his toes. Fascinated, de Rais nonetheless stares straight ahead, afraid of attracting undue attention, but he glimpses from the corner of his eye the chef's cadaverous form, surrounded for a moment by black energy; an aura of unlight. One by one, the woman passes the device along the rows of apprentices: darkness crackles and snaps. At last she reaches de Rais. She stares at him for a moment, and, swallowing, he raises his gaze to hers but sees nothing. Her eyes are entirely concealed behind the thick obsidian lenses.

She says, caressingly, "You look alarmed, boy. Are you afraid?"

De Rais says what is no more than the truth. "Yes. I am afraid. I have been afraid ever since I can remember."

A thin charcoal brow arches above the lenses. The woman says, "Indeed? Of what?"

Boldly, de Rais answers, "Of not matching the expectations of the Lords of Night. Of not meeting the standards that I myself set to serve them."

"You talk like an artist," the woman says, brows still raised.

"I am an artist, madam," de Rais says, with the bravery of absolute fear. "I am an artist of culinary color and its absence, a master of texture and shade, of monochrome uniformity. I drain the delicacies that I prepare of the touch of light and fire and brightness that is bestowed upon them by the flames on which they are conjured into being, so that the palates of the Lords of Night may not be seared for one moment by the tiniest spark of light."

To de Rais' infinite surprise, the head chef turns his head and says, "It's true, my lady. The food that this man prepares is a paradigm of unlight. His concoctions are as dark and smooth and rich as the galaxy's core itself." His glance catches that of de Rais: *I don't like you. But you're still one of us.*

The woman bows her head in mocking acknowledgment. "Well, then, I am honored. But you must still be scrutinized."

She raises the device once more and the lens rotates along its appointed track. The woman puts her head on one side, studies him.

"You absorb light, you say? You purify the foods of darkness?"

"I do."

Something long and thin whips from the tube which holds the lens and lashes de Rais across the face. The impact spins him around and he sprawls backwards, stunned. The Unpriest says, "It shows. There are cracks and flickers along the edges of your soul. It is dangerous work that you do, M'sieu—?"

"My name is de Rais," he says, through bleeding teeth.

"M'sieu de Rais. I had not thought that the life of a pastry chef would be so fraught with hazard. Take care that you visit the Unpriests more regularly, to purge your soul of traces of light as effectively as you purify the foods that you prepare." She turns away.

The rest of the kitchen is searched methodically, and de Rais' heart skips and hops as an investigation is made of his work area, including the little stove. The Unpriest lingers as she examines the pastries and sorbets, and de Rais hides a bruised smile as he sees her stealthy fingers creep out and flick a piece of brittle icing to her mouth. But the metal binding of the package remains secure, hidden beneath the iron floor of the little oven and guarded with unspells. The woman heads for the stairs with an angry flounce and de Rais inclines his head until the beetle-click of her boot-heels betrays her absence. No-one says a word after that, except the head chef, who turns to de Rais and says brusquely, "You. Have you finished?"

"The floor is clean. I have my preparations to complete for tomorrow."

"Go and do it, then."

One by one, the apprentices leave the kitchen. De Rais hovers over his tasks, lingering on slicing and molding and freezing, until the head chef snaps a curt good night, along with instructions to lock up. De Rais listens as the chef's heavy footsteps pound up the stairs and the door slams behind him, then he runs to the stove and takes out the package. It's so hot that it burns even de Rais' callused hands. Cursing beneath his breath, he drops the package on the table and flicks open the complex locks until the inside of the package is revealed. He stares for a moment. The girl who gave the package to de Rais has told him: you will see nothing. Do not expect to be witness to miracle. It is latent, nothing more. But you will be able to touch it. Cautiously, de Rais reaches inside the hot metal binding and feels something smooth and soft and warm. He lifts it from the binding, and to his surprise it comes away easily. He feels it glide across the table and has to put out a hand to stop it from falling onto the floor.

Then, working quickly in case it dissipates, de Rais takes his sharp knife and begins to chop, his hand moving faster and faster with a chef's practiced speed until the contents of the package are in tiny pieces. And then de Rais begins his final great work; the last work that, if all goes well, he will ever perform in the palace of the Lords of Night. He begins to sculpt the substance into sugars and candies, into creams and shadows. At last he passes his hand over the surface of the chopping block and finds only a minute sliver, like a splinter of glass. De Rais is sorely tempted to pop it in his mouth, but he resists the temptation and drifts it onto the curling pinnacle of a sugar tower instead. And then he slips everything into the darkest, coldest recesses of the refrigerator, to wait there till morning. As he turns to leave, he fancies that when he next opens the door of the refrigerator, it will have begun to glow.

Early next morning, before the waking bells toll out across the city, de Rais rises from a troubled night, bundles himself into his clothes and hurries back to the Palais. The rain has stopped, but a thin wind rips down the Tuileries, snatching at de Rais' untidy hair. He does not think he slept, and yet his head is filled with dreams that defy the darkening day; dreams of something that flickers golden down the rainy air. When de Rais reaches the Palais, the head chef greets him with a grunt and a tilt of the head; their yesterday truce still fragile as spider silk.

Quietly, unobtrusively, de Rais slides into his chef's jacket. He takes a deep, shaky breath and opens the refrigerator. It is still and dim within, and undisturbed. De Rais relaxes a little, and his breath mists cold metal. He rests his hands on the top of the refrigerator for a moment, to steady them. Then, he goes about the remaining preparations for this evening's banquet; the less critical, less dangerous things, a frenzy of slicing and molding for the hundred guests of the Lords of Night.

When evening comes, everything is ready. De Rais stands back and exchanges triumphant glances with the head chef, whose face is blue with cold. De Rais dispatches perfumed bowls of dusk to the dining hall, and joins the apprentices for a surreptitious glimpse of the guests as they arrive. His hands are trembling again. He watches as something glides through the great double doors at the end of the vast hall. It stands seven feet high and its armored head drifts from side to side. Its mandibles exude a faint and musty fragrance. Huge smooth claws rustle beneath its midnight robes. It moves with ponderous, swinging slowness down the hall, and in its wake the air seems suddenly thin and darker, as though it breathes in health and light, and gives out nothing. Another follows through the double doors: female, this time. De Rais catches sight of the long out-thrust jaw and the slotted vertebrae of her throat beneath her hood. She places a delicately jointed foot on the thick carpet and teeters forward. De Rais melts back into the shadows. Three hours to go, before the clock strikes midnight.

Downstairs again, and silent in his corner of the kitchen, de Rais watches as the dishes of the main course are carried upstairs. The head chef has excelled himself. The foods he has prepared are rarefied to their finest extreme: all blood and essence. De Rais does not like to think where such food has come from, but he doubts that it has been produced by the meat racks at the edges of the city. Wild things, he thinks, reared in the deep growth of the forests which surround Paris, hunted down. The clock ticks on. The seemingly endless parade of dishes is borne from view. At last it is time for dessert.

De Rais hovers anxiously as the sorbets, each one with its cool, deceptive pool of night around the incarnadined ice, are taken upstairs by the serving staff. Then, still in his dark jacket, he waits for a frozen moment until he is certain that the attention of the head chef is elsewhere, and slips after the serving staff. Apart from a pair of servitors at the far end of the hallway, their glacial gaze fixed on the great bronze doors, the hallway is empty. De Rais hastens to the dining hall, his footsteps muffled by the carpet. He puts his eye to the crack of the dining room door. He knows the risk, he thinks, but he still has to see.

Inside, it is almost dark. A faint phosphorescence illuminates the high, echoing vaults of the hall. Beneath, the shadowy presences of the Lords of Night dine on the last of the meat essences. There is a susurrus of anticipation as the desserts are passed around the hall by the silent serving staff, who then troop from the hall. De Rais, his hearing fine-tuned by anticipation, hears the tiny crack as the first silver spoon touches the first sorbet, and the minute crunch of mandibles upon ice. De Rais takes a single breath. Followed by the rest of its companions, the Lord swallows a single spoonful of captured evening. And explodes.

Latent light, ingested by perfect darkness, electrifies every filament of the Lord's body before it flares up into a great column of brilliance. De Rais, thrown back against the wall, can see nothing but the shattered form of the Lord branded upon his retinas, but he can taste the light which streams out from the dining hall: the hard, clear sunlight of mountain peaks; the roseate depths of sundown over ocean; the golden, glittering brightness of the sun at midsummer noon. It has worked. The Lords are gone in a moment of fire, consumed in the forbidden, latent light so carefully concealed in darkness and ice by the skilful hands of Severin de Rais. And in the eye of his mind de Rais sees that light pouring up from the heart of the banqueting hall, gilding every wall in Paris and running liquid into the river, distributing itself in immaculate proportion until the shell of shadow that covers the world is broken and the hidden sun revealed. Darkness and light, night and day, in balance once again, for everyone.

Except de Rais. For he knows, as soon as that first blaze of magnificence has passed, that the light has been too much for his shadow-born eyes. Once the flashing echoes have faded from the ruin of his sight, there is only night once more: familiar, relentless, and cold. But as de Rais turns to grope his way along the hallway, he is smiling, for in his imagination and his heart and his soul there is nothing but the sun.

Loosestrife

She knew that there was something wrong with her baby, because Ellie's eyes did not follow her as she moved about the room and she had once been told that this was important. She crouched over the baby, passing a hand across Ellie's face.

"Ellie? What's wrong?"

This time, the baby's eyes twitched to follow the passage of her hand and Aud breathed a sigh of relief. Nothing wrong, after all, and probably she was just being silly, but she had been told so often that she did not understand things that once she had taken a fact into her head she clung to it. She thought she understood the baby a little better now and as long as it remained just Ellie and herself, no one else, she thought she could cope. Ellie was doing fine, and if she still seemed to eat so little when Aud gave her the bottle, at least she appeared healthy and well. Aud would surely know if a change occurred; she watched Ellie for hours, noticing every movement, every sound.

Picking Ellie up, Aud stepped carefully over the piles of broken plaster and carried her out onto the little concrete balcony.

"Look," she said. "You can see Big Ben from here. See it? See the big clock? And there's the Houses of Parliament, where all the rich people go." She thought that the distant clock face read ten to eight, or perhaps it was twenty to ten. She could never remember which hand meant which, no matter how often she had been told, and it was so easy to lose track of the time. But Ellie, lying quietly in her arms, would never question her; never ask uncomfortable things like 'what time is it?' and 'what does that say?' and 'what is Parliament?' Maybe when Ellie grew up she would be able to answer these things on her own.

"And then you'll be a help to me, won't you?" Aud said. She and

Ellie watched as one of the boats glided down the Thames, just above the water like a big wing, rising as it came to the barrier. Wealthy tourists came on those boats, Aud's mum had told her, to see what was left of London. This puzzled Aud, too: surely you couldn't leave a piece of a city, not like a bit of cabbage that you tried to hide on your plate. When she had asked where the rest of London had gone, her mum said that it was under the water, that it was all to do with the world getting warmer. But to Aud, London always seemed a cold place.

They did not spend a long time looking out of the window, because it was time for Ellie's nap and Aud had to check that the door was locked. She did this many times a day, worrying in case the gangs came. She could hear them at night, running around the bottom of the flats and she was sure that they got into the lift shaft, even though the lift hadn't been working for years. Sometimes, when she went to the food charity or to collect her money, there was a sharp smell in the hallway. It did not smell like anything natural, but as though someone had been burning something. It made Aud nervous and so she did not want to be seen going in and out of the flat. She made sure that the steel door was locked every time. She always tried to take a different way to get her money, too, even though it meant leaving Ellie alone for longer. Sometimes, she got lost, and that was worst of all.

"Where's Highstone Road?" she would ask some passer-by, who always looked as though they had more important places to go. And once someone had snapped, "You're standing in it. Can't you read?"

"No," Aud said, and the man just stared at her before walking away. She felt stupid, then, but it was true. How was she to know how to read, when her mum had never put her in school, keeping her up night after night for company. Later, when she had signed on with the Deserving Poor board, they had tried to teach her, but it was only a short course and the letters just hadn't seemed to stick. She couldn't tell half of them apart, no matter how hard she tried.

"You can't help it," Danny had told her, when she said that she wasn't going back. "You're just a bit thick, that's all. Nothing wrong with that."

"I know," Aud said sadly, but there wasn't anything either of them could do about it. And Danny seemed to know this, too, because he helped her so much: taking the Council seal off the flat and turning the steel slab into a proper door that you could lock, and bringing her veg from the allotments. Sometimes, now that he was back from Ireland, he even offered to look after Ellie, but Aud always said no. She thought it was kind of him, but she didn't feel that it was right. Ellie was her daughter, not his. She did not like anyone even to hold Ellie, and she would not let Danny get too close.

"At least now you've got the baby, you'll get more money," Danny said. "And you're eighteen, aren't you? That should qualify you for extra benefits."

"I suppose so." Aud was doubtful.

"Oh, come on. You're Deserving Poor, they had you checked, didn't they? Not like me," and Danny laughed, sitting in the ragged-sleeved sweater, head shaved and the code clearly visible just above the nape of his heck. "Undeserving, that's what they said I was. Not that I expected anything else, mind. You're lucky you're not too bright, really."

His gaze fell on Ellie and Aud could tell that he was wondering about the baby again. She had not told him anything about Ellie; it had never seemed the right time, somehow.

He said, hesitantly, "Aud—who's her dad? Not that I've any right to ask, mind. Just wondering. I know she's not mine—well, obviously she isn't. But you don't go out much, and if someone's been bothering you—I'd have put off going to Ireland, if I'd known."

"Just someone," Aud had said. "No one you know."

"Come on, Aud. You don't know anyone except me and Gill and the lot down the Social."

"It was someone I met, all right? Just the once." And that was all she was saying, Aud thought. She clammed up and wouldn't look at him, and after a bit more coaxing he gave up and let it rest. But she didn't want to lie to Danny, and she couldn't tell him about Ellie. Not yet.

Now, she hurried down the stairwell, trying not to stumble over the piles of rubbish that had blown in through the open doors. When she reached the bottom of the stairs she paused and looked around her. The courtyard was empty apart from a few boys and a dog. Aud liked dogs, but not kids: sometimes they shouted things and she did not always understand what they said. It was never nice, she could tell that. But the boys ignored her and so she slipped between the blocks of flats and took the path that led down along the run-off canal. There was a lock at the top, Danny had told her, which opened if the river got too full and let the water out. Aud wondered where it went; she pictured it running dark and secret under the streets. It was a comforting thought. She passed the old railway bridge which crossed the run-off: it was pretty in summer, with loosestrife and nettles and long grass. She had come here with Danny, before he went to Ireland, and he'd told her which flower was which. Because it was Danny who told her, she had remembered. Now, the plants had died back and there was only bare earth beneath the bridge, but she still liked it.

She counted the paving stones as she walked, careful not to tread on the cracks. It was only a game, she knew; she had played it as a kid, but somewhere along the line it had turned serious, started to be important. She thought it had been when Ellie had come: the world became a different place, when you had a child. You became larger and smaller at the same time. But she was doing better than her mum, she knew that: letting Ellie sleep at night, not waking her up whenever she felt lonely or bored, not shouting at her. All the time: Tell me you love me; tell me you love me. You shouldn't have to ask that of a child. It should come naturally, but her mum had never been able to let it rest. The Social had been round a few times and Aud had kept quiet. Her mum knew what they wanted to hear, she didn't tell them anything that mattered and so Aud had stayed, the days not-quite-real, the nights sleepless. She did not know why her mother didn't sleep like normal people; she'd always been that way, her mum had said. After the visit by the social, she had overheard her mum talking to Auntie Julie.

"I don't know why you bother," Julie said. "You could have sold her off—there's plenty of them that want one, even if you don't. Even if she's a bit defective. People can't afford to be choosy these days."

"I've been bossed around all my life," her mum had said, hot and angry. "I just want something I can boss around, now."

"You're lucky you could have a kid," Julie said. "Lots of 'em can't. Something in the water, my dad said, or genetic modifications, or mad cows. If you ever want to get rid of Aud, you let me know. I know a bloke down the market."

"I don't like the idea, all the same," Aud's mum had muttered. "What if he sold her to some pervert? Plenty of those around, too. Look at my old man. 'Keep it in the family,' he used to say. I'd only sell her, Jule, if she went to a good home. And even then—I don't know. We're all right as we are."

And now Aud was lucky, too, for she had Ellie and lots of richer people couldn't have babies. She thought of this as she walked along the canal path, and she felt her luck running alongside her, like a dog. She found the DP office without too much trouble, this week.

"Fifty three euros; here you are. Is it all right like that? Want me to put it in the envelope for you?" The woman at the DP was kind, Aud thought. They weren't all like that: the one on the end always looked at her as though she was in the wrong office, as though she ought to be registered at the Undeserving side and have no money at all, just what she could scrounge off the streets on a beggars' license. She plucked up her courage and asked.

"'Scuse me," she said. She'd wanted to know about this ever since Danny had got back from Ireland. "Could you tell me, what's the rate if you've got a baby?"

The woman frowned. "They'd have to be sure it was a genuine claim, love. Otherwise you could lose your registry and go onto the other list— they're trying to discourage girls from getting pregnant to raise their rate. Because so many babies die, you see, or don't come to term, and a lot of girls think they can fake it—get a false certificate. It's not fair, but that's the way things are, these days." She gave Aud a sharp, sudden look. "You're not pregnant, are you?"

"No," Aud said, suddenly afraid. "It's for someone else. A friend asked me."

"Well, if you have a baby, and they let you keep it, you'd get a hundred euros a week, and some of the charities give maternity benefits, but you'd need to go to them for that."

"Thanks," Aud said. She bundled the money into her purse and went out, quickly. She had not told the DP about Ellie. As far as she knew, only Danny knew about the baby and that was the way Aud wanted things to stay.

It was cold out now. Aud's fingers curled inside the thin gloves as she tried to remember what month it was. November, perhaps, but it was hard to tell because they put the Christmas stuff up so early in the shops. It cheered her up, thinking about Ellie and what to get her for Christmas. It would be Ellie's first.

She was walking through the posh bit now, the little knot of streets they called the Village. Aud liked it here, but she felt out of place, as though at any moment someone might come up to her and ask her to leave for making the place look untidy. There was a group of girls clustered on the corner, dressed in coats with big fur collars and cuffs, high heels. Their perfume drifted through the air; they smelled expensive. They were gathered around a pram, cooing into it. Aud could not help looking. The baby looked exactly like Ellie, except its eyes were blue.

"He's so gorgeous," one of the girls was saying. "You're so lucky."

The girl holding the pram gave a small, smug smile. "I wanted a boy, but they're a bit more difficult than girls."

"When did you get him?"

The girl holding the pram turned and caught sight of Aud and her face grew thinner, as if she didn't want a scruffy person near her baby. Aud felt herself grow hot with embarrassment and she hurried away. To cheer herself up, she started thinking about Christmas again and she kept it up all the way back to the flat, but when she got there, she saw that there was a van outside.

It wasn't like the drugs van, which came every week. It was white, with a logo on the side. Aud could not read what it said, but she thought that the letters were a D and a P: perhaps two Ds, or two Ps. The windows were frosted over; she would not, in any case, have tried to look inside. She wasn't that stupid. She skirted the van and made her way up the stairs. There was no sign of anyone in the stairwell. Once the door was shut behind her, she felt safer. Ellie was asleep on the blanket. Aud waited, listening. Someone knocked. Aud froze. Then, with relief, she heard Danny say, "Who are you looking for?"

"Do you live here?" A woman's voice, which Aud did not recognise.

"No."

"Do you know who does?"

"I came up to see one of my mates. It's not his place—he's staying with somebody. I don't know what their name is."

"You do know that this block's been condemned?"

A pause, then Danny said, "Yeah, so what? Where are people supposed to live if they haven't got any money?"

"Does your friend have a girlfriend?"

"Why don't you ask him?"

Aud found herself moving to the bed, stealthily, so that her feet would make no sound on the concrete floor. She picked Ellie up, willing her to be quiet.

"We'd like to have a word, because someone heard a baby crying up here yesterday."

"Someone wasn't minding their own business, then."

"It's no place for a young child. We just want to help." The woman sounded kind, Aud thought, and she was being very patient with Danny. But they always did sound kind. It didn't stop them messing you around.

Ellie was silent, staring up at Aud's face. Aud swallowed hard, then went out to the balcony. Pulling the window shut behind her, she climbed over the partition that divided the balcony from that of the neighbouring flat. She made her way along the row, avoiding the litter and the needles, until she came to the walkway and the stairs that led down. She stopped and looked back. No one was there. She could still see the van parked outside in the courtyard. She hurried down the stairs, clutching Ellie.

"Don't cry, don't cry. . . . " And Ellie did not utter a sound.

The only place she could think of was the railway bridge. She would wait there for a bit, then go back and see if the van had gone. She thought of taking Ellie into the pub, because it would be warmer, but she was afraid of being seen. If she wrapped Ellie up tightly, perhaps it would not be too cold. There was no one about on the canal path and that made her feel safer.

She crouched under the bridge in the damp dimness, watching the boats going back and forth across the narrow glimpse of the Thames. She lost track of the day. It grew cloudy, but did not rain. Ellie slept and Aud grew cold and hungry. She would go back, look for the van—but then a shadow fell across her. Aud looked up and felt filled with relief, because it was Danny.

"They've gone," he said. "You heard them, didn't you?"

"I thought they'd take her away."

"Probably would have done, too." He squatted on his heels, looking down at the baby in her arms. He said, gently, "What do you want to do, Aud?"

"About what?"

"About the baby."

Aud nearly told him, then, but she clamped her lips shut against the words. She did not want to hear herself say: "I stole her, out of someone else's pram." Because then Danny would surely stop being her friend. Instead, she said something else that was the truth.

"I want to take her away. It's not right, bringing her up in London, in that flat. I try to make it as nice as I can, but—"

"—but it's a dump."

"Yeah, and I can't get anywhere else."

"You're not claiming money for her?"

"No. I haven't told them about her."

She waited for him to ask "Why not?" and it occurred to her then that perhaps he knew, or at least suspected, that Ellie was a stolen child. But he only said, "Okay. Listen, Aud. If you're really serious about leaving, then I can help you. Give you some cash and put you on the boat to Ireland. I've got friends there, the ones I told you about."

"The ones in the farmhouse?"

"It might be a squat, Aud, but it's a nice place. A good place for a kid to grow up in. And I think they'd look after you. They don't like the Deserving Poor business—that's why they left England. And things are a bit easier over there. People help each other out."

"Okay," Aud whispered, and her heart beat fast at the thought of the boat, the sea silver in the cold light, a green place at the end of it. She added, "You're really good to me," and embarrassed, he looked away.

The thought of travelling alone scared her, but in the end, she didn't have to. Danny went with her. His dad was sick, he said, and he might as well see the old man before he died.

"But you've only just got back," Aud said.

"It doesn't matter. You know me, back and forth, to and fro. Don't like to stay too long in one place."

But she wondered why she felt guilty, all the same.

They left at the end of the week. Aud tried to give him some money, and at last he took a bit of it for the bus. She sat with her face pressed to the chilly window, looking out at the motorway. They left London behind, and soon there was nothing but flooded fields and the barbed wire enclaves of the shires, where the rich people lived. Once they saw an armoured car, crossing the great bridge into the Republic of Wales. Aud, frozen with nerves, had to show her DP documents, but they let her through without saying anything. Ellie dozed until they got to the ferry and then she woke up, crying a little.

"Does she need feeding?" Danny asked, frowning.

"I don't think so."

"She doesn't seem to want her bottle much, does she? I though babies were all 'in one end, out the other'. Maybe she needs changing."

"I changed her in the service station," Aud lied. "She had her bottle then."

"Oh, right." And to her relief, Danny lost interest. She spent as much time as she could on the deck, watching the gulls and the waves with silent delight. The rocky Welsh coast was soon gone. Aud leaned against the rail, Ellie held tightly in her arms.

"Mind you don't get cold," Danny said. Before she could stop him, he reached out and drew Ellie's blanket aside to tuck it in more securely.

"This trip is the first time I've really seen her in daylight," he said, smiling. Aud closed her eyes, too tightly; she did not want to see his face change. There was a long moment of silence, shattered by a baby's cry. Aud's eyes snapped open, but it was only a gull, wheeling over head.

She felt him take the baby from her and this time, she let him. Ellie made no protest at all.

After a long time, he said, "Jesus, Aud. Where did you get her?"

Aud did not answer, but he did not sound angry, only bewildered and it gave her a little hope.

"Did you nick her out of someone's car, or what?"

"Her name's Ellie," Aud whispered.

Danny handed Ellie back to her, carefully, and stood with his feet braced, staring out to sea.

"Need a cig," he murmured. She watched him roll up in silence, waiting for him to say something. His hands looked cold. He fumbled with the papers, with the tobacco, with the lighter. Then, after a long breath, he said, "Shouldn't be too long, now. Look. That's Wexford, over there."

His friends lived in the countryside near Cork, and when Ellie saw the place she thought it was the most beautiful house she had ever seen, even if half of it was a ruin. A lot of Danny's friends seemed to live in vans, anyway, so the state of the house didn't really matter. A girl called Jade, with a mat of beaded hair and a big smile, took Aud under her wing and showed her to a warm room with a fire.

"You can crash in here. This'll be your space, and the baby's."

She brought Aud a bowl of stew and once Aud had eaten it, the journey seemed to tumble down on her, all at once. She yawned. She thought she would just sit down for a moment, but when she next looked up, it was nearly dark outside. Jade was sitting with Ellie in her arms.

"It's all right, Aud," she said. "Everything's all right." So Aud went back to sleep. She woke later, and there were voices outside the warm room: Danny and Jade.

"Her name's Ellie, right?" Jade was saying.

"Yeah." Danny gave a tight laugh. "Well, that's what it says on the back of her neck."

"She's amazing. I thought she was a real baby."

"So did I, until halfway across the bloody Irish Sea. When the Social came round, I realised Aud'd nicked her, and I knew what would happen. I thought: just get her to Ireland, with the kid, whether it's hers or not."

"You didn't stop to think about her mum?" Jade said, angrily, and Aud cringed.

"Of course I did! I knew it wasn't right, Jade, but Aud's never had a thing of her own and so I thought: just give her a chance. And then, on the boat, I realised. Huge weight off my mind."

"But Ellie's not plastic, is she? She feels real. Like flesh. And she looks at you, and cries—she even seems to pee and eat, but not as much as a real baby."

"She is flesh, Jade. They grow them, in tanks. They're for rich girls who can't have kids—it's some kind of psychological charity initiative. They cost a fortune. But they don't grow up. They're not much more than a toy, really."

I am dreaming, Aud told herself. I don't want to listen any more. She pulled the blanket over her ears, and huddled back against the wall. In the firelight, Ellie watched her with round dark eyes and did not blink even when Jade came back through the door.

"Shhh," she said, when she saw that Aud was awake. She gave Aud a long measuring look, as though she wanted to say something else. But then she added, "I'll be quiet, okay? I don't want to disturb the baby." And reassured, Aud closed her eyes and slept.

Ancestors' Song

One

Rhen Gher Ushuru is singing the Ancestors' Song as the vessel hurtles towards Yhi. He does not know that he is doing so, unless some slight sound filters down through the ocean of his dreams, nor is he aware that the Ancestors' Song has been echoing within the hollows of his head for some thirteen hundred years. The sides of the vessel are encrusted with ice and pitted with meteor strikes, but the vessel is singing, too. Ancient equipment hums slowly like a cold hive, just below the edge of hearing. It broadcasts the Ancestors' Song out into the void, leaving traces to sink into the static of passing solar systems, and causing children of the multitudinous labyrinth of worlds to blink, uneasy, in their sleep. But Rhen Gher Ushuru's song has now gone unheard for over seven hundred years now, as the vessel leaves the galactic core and speeds out into the Reaches.

Gradually, the kabalistic pattern of stars begins first to approximate, and then to fit, the configuration in the vessel's data banks. The vessel veers, spins and shifts, slowing as it nears a particular star system. Five worlds hang in seeming-below; the fourth is as yellow as an eye, mottled with dark uplands. The vessel has reached Yhi.

Two

The artist crouches at the foot of the darkridge, waiting for the huntress. He has been stalking her now for over a week and she has imprinted herself upon him, filling his head with images. Memories uncurl within his mind like blood through water: a footprint in the soft peat of the moor; the gleam of her eyes in the twilight; the scrape of her nails against bone. The artist is too wary of the huntress to allow himself to be seen, and perhaps too proud. He keeps upwind, padding patiently along the narrow streams that cross the moorland, and he sleeps on the resilient black moss which springs back into shape when he rises, betraying nothing. Leaving so little trace upon the face of the world both excites and frustrates him: he is used to delineating territory, making his mark on the Dreamtime. This patient, imperceptible journey is taking its toll on his nerves. The artist consoles himself with an image: the record of his journey that he will create on his return, made from the materials that will be most attractive to the huntress. And when he lures her to the bower, then she will understand. The thought of impressing the huntress in such a way makes the blood pound in the artist's head. But images of the journey alone will not be enough to lure her. He needs a focus for the work: something to catch her eye and draw her in. He needs prey.

Three

/Yhi/destination/termination_of_voyage/

The message sings down Rhen Gher Ushuru's neural pathways, its catalytic cues luring him from his long sleep. Ushuru wakes, to lie motionless. His long outline is dimly reflected in the glossy ceiling above, but it takes him a moment to realize that the reflection is of a human form, still longer to recognize that it is his own. Slowly, as awareness returns to him, the stasis mesh dissolves away until it lies in a glistening film across his skin. Its bubble breaks over his mouth and Ushuru takes a long, rasping first breath. Rising from the stasis couch, he walks unsteadily to the console mesh and activates the imager. Yhi the legendary, world of the lost, fills the screen. He can see its plains, its moors, its two icy moons. As though activated in turn, Rhen Gher Ushuru throws back his head and sings the last verses of the Ancestors' Song, hearing it tremble through the stale air of the cabin. His voice is rough and unfamiliar; he sings words that he has no memory of ever hearing. Crossed over his breast, his fingers begin to trace the spiral filigree of scars that cover every inch of his skin, etched onto his flesh over millennia by the mnemomechanisms of the vessel. Thus he learns of his journey, reminding himself of who he has been and learning what he has become. At last a fingertip reaches the place between his eyes, where a tiny drop of blood seeps out: a representation of the world of Yhi. Setting the navigation system to a landing point, Rhen Gher Ushuru begins to sing the song of his voyage, wondering and tentative at first, but then stronger and more confident as it progresses. The vessel soars down towards atmosphere.

Four

The huntress' movements have become languid now that she has made her kill and fed. She is heading down the long slope of the darkridge to where two more of her kind wait, reclining in the scanty scrub where the moors meet the golden grassland of the plains. The artist's fists clench in impotent frustration. The two who wait for her are males. He is too far away to see the warrior scars on their pale arms and foreheads, but he is close enough to see that they are large, and powerful. It is likely that they are the woman's brothers: the plains predators often travel in small family packs. She has brought them an offering from her hunt; a little limb hangs from the grassmesh across her shoulder, a remnant of the child she caught that morning. The artist shifts uneasily; hunger stirs him. But it is too dangerous to pursue the pack. He waits, watching, until the woman rejoins her siblings, greeting them with cuffs and cries, and then he turns back across the moorland towards his bower. But as he does so, there is a sound like the world ending. Something is coming down from the sky.

The artist has never seen anything like it before, but the sight stirs his soul. He watches, round eyed with wonder, as the glowing object drifts down towards the moor. Its vanes catch the last crimson light of the sun, glowing a deep, gilded red as they turn. Keeping at a safe distance, the artist watches as the thing settles into the moss. He waits for a little while longer, hoping it might do something amusing or strange, but the vanes fold away with complex delicacy and soon the thing becomes no more than a part of the twilight. Losing interest, the artist stands and lopes back towards his home.

Five

When morning comes, Rhen Gher Ushuru steps wonderingly from the vessel and takes a deep breath of the air of Yhi. He looks around him. Moorland stretches as far as the western horizon. The ground is covered with soft black moss; a pool fringed with rushes quivers in the breeze. The air is warm, and smells of rain. To the east, he can see a long line of forest at the foot of a ridge. Cloud hides the high, distant peaks. Rhen Gher Ushuru puts out a trembling hand and touches the earth. He has stepped into Dreamtime: the ancient, eternal now of his ancestors. He is filled with relief, in finding the planet so unchanged from those first, early reports. He does a quick calculation: Yhi has now been colonized for some forty thousand years. More than enough time to ruin a world; cover its fair face with cities, blight the skies. He thinks of his own birthplace: aramite and steel beneath the plastic heavens. New Narrandera no longer seems real; he has stepped out of history, back into the present. If what he sees here is anything to go by, Yhi is still a world within its own morning. It seems his ancestors have kept to their ideals: to find a world still in its Dreamtime, to live their lives at one with Place. Rhen Gher Ushuru makes a swift, spontaneous decision, not wanting to risk the chance that he might change his mind. Stepping back into the vessel, he sets the appropriate mechanism, shoulders his bow and strides back out onto the moor. Then, he watches from a safe distance as the vessel is swallowed in a rosy billow of fire until nothing is left but a scorch mark on the moss. Ushuru takes a deep, ragged breath of mingled regret and relief. What he has just done is a folly of lunatic courage, but he cannot allow himself the luxury of escape. Now, he is committed to Yhi, and to his dream. Turning, he begins to walk towards his future.

Six

At last, the bower is almost complete. The artist sucks a bloody finger and gives a small, approving grunt of satisfaction. He cannot suppress a rush of pride. Since his return from his study of the huntress, he has been working hard to depict the story of his journey. Though he is incapable of expressing it in words, the artist's principal desire is to create something different to the bowers of his kindred. He is impatient with his memories of his past work: bowers filled with delicate choices of veined leaves, the starry dark flowers from the water forest, the artful stains and pigments of russet earth. Juvenile follies, aping the work of his father and brothers to lure the timid girls of the deep forest, all shy eyes and soft hands. He thinks of the nearest bower to his own: the home of a small, pale person, filled with shells and blossoms. The artist spits into the moss. Such vapid beauty will not attract the huntress. Desire hazes him: he remembers her speed, her strength, her bloodstained fingers and mouth. She needs boldness, passion, richness of color and texture. He has worked hard to create an appropriate vision. He steps across the threshold of the bower, pushing aside the ropes of bone-strung sinew, which clatter gently in the evening breeze with an old, dry sound. Redness fills his vision, a powerful contrast with the somberness of the surrounding territory. The bower smells strong, too; invading every sense. At the center, a complex network of woven boughs await an occupant. The artist has very clear ideas as to what he wants for his centerpiece. It should be a male, and a powerful one, to show off his own cunning and strength. It should be someone in their prime: the huntress will not want old meat, and to present her with a weakling child would merely insult her. Offering her a member of her own kindred is probably not a good idea, either, and the artist feels secretly rather alarmed at the prospect of catching and confining one of the plains predators. However, there are certain individuals who live in the deepforest: solitary, wary and dangerous, but also rather decorative. One of those, the artist thinks, would do very well indeed. Armed with a sling shot and a net of sinew, he sets out for the deepforest.

Seven

Rhen Gher Ushuru has discovered a place for a suitable camp: a hollow beneath a low crest of rock, close to a stream. He unloads his rations from the backpack and studies the sky. Yhi's sun is some way past its zenith. Ushuru sits with his back to the sunwarmed rock and muses on his journey so far.

He has seen nothing that gives any hint of civilization, and he marvels at the integrity of his ancestors, to leave their world so unspoiled. At the back of his mind, there is a very faint stirring of unease at the thought that the colony might simply have died out; that he is literally the only person alive on Yhi, but he dismisses this notion as being due to fatigue. He has come too far to entertain such negativity; his life to date has, after all, been spent in search of Yhi. He thinks back, with a faint smile, to his early childhood in New Narrandera; the stories told to him by his grandfather of the Dreamtime of Ancient Earth, and of the

Rainbow Ancestors who set out for a world named Yhi, to make the Dreamtime come again. He thinks of the early reports filtered back across millennia: that Yhi had been successfully colonized, that people were reverting to the harmonious ways of the oldest ancestors. The great beauty of Yhi, so the reports said, was that there was so little competition for life. Yhi possessed no indigenous mammals, nor were there reptiles or birds. But by Rhen Gher Ushuru's day, nothing had been heard of Yhi for over nine thousand years, and thus was the idea of his great quest born, cradled in the artificial heart of New Narrandera. His own world is obsessed with history, with status; what better place to dream of, than a world which lacks either?

Now, that quest has come to fruition. Rhen Gher Ushuru gazes around him in contented contemplation, tempered with thoughts of what may have become of the colonists. Questions as to whether any-one remains on Yhi are soon answered. A scream—of fear, of rage, a human sound—splits the air. Before it has even faded away, Rhen is running up the ridge. A woman is standing with her back to a ridge of rock, her face contorted with fury and fear. She is naked, but her skin is so patterned with whorls of red and black that very little of the pale flesh is visible. Braided red hair falls to her waist; her front teeth are missing. Something is crashing through the scrub. Rhen Gher Ushuru cannot see what it is, but it sounds large. Perhaps things have changed over several thousand years. Thoughts of reconstruction, or imported wildlife, plague his mind. Then the thing in the bushes breaks cover and Rhen Gher Ushuru sees that it is human after all. Nails have become claws; teeth are pointed and sharp. It is male, and at least seven feet in height. It rushes towards the woman. Rhen Gher Ushuru makes his second critical decision of the day. He notches a laminate shaft to the optic sights of the bow, raises it, and fires. The arrow locks on target and the marauder drops, impaled neatly through the throat. Ushuru springs down from the ridge to land beside the woman. She turns, wide-eyed. She stares for a moment at the twitching body of her assailant and then she spins in a swift pirouette and kicks Rhen Gher Ushuru in the stomach. Startled and pained, Ushuru drops to his knees. The iron-hard edge of her foot catches him on the side of the jaw and topples him into the scrub. The world darkens into nightmare.

When Ushuru comes round, the woman is nowhere to be seen. The marauder has been reduced to a bloody tangle of bones, and Ushuru himself has been stuffed securely into a crack in the rocks. He tries to free himself, but is too tightly wedged; a barrier of branches confine his knees and elbows. Despite his discomfort and unease, Rhen Gher Ushuru shakes his head with wonder as he thinks of the woman. Memory of her almost serves to banish fear.

Eight

It is the artist's lucky day, though he himself has no notion of such a concept. The route to the deepforest has taken him along the edge of the scarp, and it is here that he sees the prey. The man has been wedged into a crevice of rock, in the manner of the plains predators. The artist cannot tell whether or not the prey is dead, but thinks it unlikely. The plains people generally treat their prey in such a manner when they have already made a kill, and merely want to establish a larder for some future meal. The artist glances warily about him, but sees no one. Turning his attention to the person below him, he notes that the male is large, with a curious leathery skin covering parts of his body. The flesh of his face and hands are a more normal hue; a broad dark face, reminiscent of the plant-gathering people of the foothills and marked with an intricacy of spiral patterns. Glossy black hair falls in a crest down his back. The artist shuffles forwards, and the prey looks up at him. The artist sees bright eyes, with no trace of fear. The prey's lips draw back, obviously in warning. The artist notes with disappointment that the prey's teeth are the flat molars of a plant-eating person, but there is no doubt that they are in excellent condition. An image floats into the artist's inner eye: of the prey confined in the darkness of the bower. He is the perfect predator, betrayed only by his teeth. The artist decides to take a chance. With the aid of a nearby stone, and keeping his weapon close to hand, he hacks away the wedges and helps the stranger to stand up. The stranger throws back his head and emits a curious sequence of sounds, then he claps the artist on the shoulder and grasps his hand. The artist plucks a handful of fruit from his mesh and waves it in what he hopes is an enticing manner beneath the stranger's nose. Then he leads his new charge back up the slope to the bower.

Nine

Rhen Gher Ushuru is delighted to have located a colonist, though he cannot help feeling that current circumstances could be improved upon. From the corner of his eye, he can see something disconcertingly wet and red. The place has the ripe smell of a meat locker. He does not precisely recall how he came to be in this position, but there is an aching lump on the back of his head, which is tilted backwards. He is unable to move his arms or his legs. Strong capable hands are forcing his jaws apart and something blunt and rough is wedged into his mouth to keep it open. Ushuru swallows, fighting back a fear that exceeds anything he has ever experienced on New Narrandera. The face of his rescuer and captor appears above him: a long, sallow countenance, marked with bars of red earth. The man is silent. He frowns with concentration as he places a hard object against Ushuru's front teeth and begins to file. Ushuru struggles, to no avail. The process takes some considerable time. At intervals, Ushuru's rescuer takes care to drip water and the pulp of a sour fruit down his captive's throat. Whenever Ushuru winces with pain, his captor stops and strokes his head, making soothing noises. At last, the wedge is removed. Gratefully, Ushuru closes his sore mouth and tests his newly sharpened teeth with his tongue. A leaf is dangled above him. Ushuru opens his mouth and lets water drip down his throat. He does not notice the bitter aftertaste until it is already too late.

Ten

Once the laborious process of transforming the plant-eater into something more menacing is over, and the prey is safely confined within the cage, the artist goes outside and sits down on a convenient stone to chew on a mouthful of dreaming root and watch the sun go down. He is extremely satisfied with the situation to date. Now, all that needs to be done is to attract the huntress.

He can see the small pale person approaching from the forest's edge, absorbed in gathering the shells of the snails that collect beneath the outcrops of moss. The artist snorts as he thinks of the pale person's shadowy bower, gleaming faintly against the dark wall of the forest. Images involving weakness and ineffectuality drift through the artist's contemptuous mind. The pale person gives him an anxious glance as he approaches, but the artist ignores him.

Inside his own bower, the prey is making sounds with his mouth again. The artist is aware of a new unease: what if the prey breaks free? What if the huntress has moved on? These thoughts generate so much anxiety that the artist simply rejects them, storing the unsettling images in some latent part of his mind; consigning them to dreaming.

Before him, the twilight moorland seems to ebb and flow like a tide as the dreaming root begins to take hold. The artist's awareness spreads out to encompass the entirety of place: everything transformed into a seamless whole, no separation between himself and the moorland; the songs of dreaming marking each stone, each pool. The world appears to the artist as a multidimensional map, represented in a fluid sequence of images, of which he himself is not the center, but an integral aspect. As he dreams, it seems to him that he can see the huntress, moving swiftly through the dusk, scenting blood, and the artist smiles. He begins to set the lure: imbuing the world with significance, endowing a stone with a sudden, intriguing aspect to catch her eye; causing a leaf to fall enticingly in her path; reeling her in. Slowly, patiently, he watches as she comes, and after a long time, when the world is just at the very edge of darkness, he breaks the dream and looks up, to see her standing on the ridge above him.

Eleven

Rhen Gher Ushuru is dismayed to find himself confined in a narrow cage of what appears to be black bamboo. His wrists and ankles are tightly bound with sinew. What a baffling adventure, Ushuru thinks, yet somehow—satisfying. Imagine how disappointed he would have been had he arrived on Yhi to find a replica of his own hyper-civilized society; filled with gracious, brittle elegance. Yhi is raw, unexpected, sufficiently entrancing to combat the possibility of incipient death. And as Ushuru faces that very real possibility, he finds to his amazement that it no longer matters. His captor has clearly ensnared him for a purpose; the grisly objects around him are arranged in a way that suggests significance. If Ushuru is to die, then it seems that his death will have meaning, and therefore dignity. He is serving a role in Dreamtime; his individuality is becoming translated into archetype. The revelation that his fear of his own death is no longer important to him in no way diminishes Ushuru's determination to survive, however.

He has no idea where his strange captor has vanished to. And then there is a sharp, scuffling sound from the entrance to the bower. Bones rattle and clatter as the captor races in. Someone snarls. Rhen Gher Ushuru's shaved eyebrows elevate to the top of his forehead. The red haired huntress is standing before him, his captor close behind. The woman gives Ushuru a searing glance, and spits. Turning, she gives a slashing, backhand blow to the captor's head. He falls, wailing, onto the soft earth floor. The woman reaches out and overturns the bamboo cage. Bound at wrists and ankles, Ushuru cannot move, but invigorated by her aggression he snaps at her hand with his newly sharp teeth. The woman growls. Razor nails score Ushuru's cheek. In an instant of clarity, Ushuru thinks he understands. The captor has stolen the woman's prey—himself—and she is furious. He shuffles rapidly backwards, trying to get out of reach. Hissing, the woman springs. Ushuru head-butts her, and she sits back, momentarily dazed. Then the captor pushes her to one side. Fumbling with Ushuru's bonds, he hauls Ushuru to his feet. It is clear to Ushuru that things are not going as planned for his captor. The man cowers behind him. The woman scrambles to her feet, spitting. She kicks out at Ushuru, but he grasps her ankle and throws her. Within the instant, she is back on her feet. It rapidly becomes apparent that she outmatches both of them. She is lighter than Ushuru, but much faster. The captor has evidently decided that discretion might be preferable to a messy death. He flees from the bower, and Ushuru, driven by adrenaline, follows. Captor and captive sprint out across the moor, temporarily of one mind. Ushuru can hear the woman close behind, her footsteps drumming on the earth and moss of the moor. His captor is ahead of him now, bolting for a break of fronded trees. Their ferny coils catch the light of Yhi's twin moons, and something large and ghostly gleams ahead. The captor catches his foot on a branch and falls; Ushuru helps him up, turning to face their pursuer, who by now must surely be upon them. But as Ushuru turns, he sees that the woman has stopped dead in her tracks. She is gazing straight ahead, to where something gleams in the moonlight.

Ushuru sees that it is a second bower: shimmering with white flowers, shells catching the light of the moon, an antithesis of the macabre bone-decked place that they have just left. In the dim light, the woman's face has assumed a strangely wistful expression. Ignoring her prey, she strides forwards towards the bower. Someone small and frail comes out, and stares. The woman holds out her hands, and walks inside. She does not come out again.

Twelve

The captor has been busy during the night. When Ushuru wakes, the red sun is coming up over the mountains and there is almost nothing left of the bloody bower. The captor has dismantled it, burying bones and wreckage in the soft earth and muttering bitterly as he does so. At one point, bafflingly, he even jumps up and down. Ushuru watches him for a moment, then stands, stretches, and goes across to speak to the man. He explains his plans, although he knows that the man cannot understand him. The identities that they have created for themselves are over, Ushuru says, and it is time for both of them to learn what new roles they may occupy, within the parameters of Dreamtime. The man does not look up, and so, with a strange pang of regret Rhen Gher Ushuru turns and walks away, across the moors of Yhi. The Ancestor's Song drifts back across the morning air; words from an old and other world.

Orchidae

*"After a long time traveling you will enter a silence, and you will know it is winter
by the way your dreams tremble like stones when the wind blows through."*
—*American Indian saying*

My fellow botanists say that orchids cannot bloom in the snow. They say, too, that each ecosystem has its own complement of orchids, from the delicate Lady's Slipper of the English downlands to the flesh-made-flower blossoms of the rainforests, and that every continent of the world has orchids, except for one. I knew now that I could prove them wrong. I'd finally found the evidence at which my father had hinted in his writings. I'd seen the entry, made on the day he died, in the diary he'd kept on that last Antarctic expedition; that lost diary that had so recently, and by so strange and circuitous a route, fallen into my hands. The diary had confirmed the substance of the dreams that had haunted me for years. Now I knew the orchid was there.

With an effort, I drew myself back from my musings to find that David Boston, director of the London Botanical Institute, was peering at me over the top of his gold-rimmed spectacles. Within the musty confines of the Institute, confronted by Boston in his aged tweeds, I felt that little had changed in the hundred years since the Institute's establishment. Boston said, rather petulantly, "I'm not even sure that I heard that correctly, Jonathan. Did you say you wanted to mount an expedition to Antarctica?"

"Yes."

"Would you care to tell me why?"

Perhaps I should have said: Because I have found that lost diary of my father's, and even though everyone thinks that Andrew Haight died a madman, I still believe in him. And because I have dreamed that the endless glare of the sun coaxes life out of a bulb, buried deep in the glacial snows beyond Prydz Bay, once every hundred years. And from that bulb grows a single orchid that blooms for a day at midwinter's heart.

But science does not like to think that it has anything to do with dreams, even though they are the blood that animates its passions, or madmen, even though they are the fuse by which science is driven. I leaned forward and smiled at David Boston.

"I realize that it must sound a quite outrageous claim," I said, carefully self-deprecating. "But I do actually have some solid evidence for it, and as you know, I'm very familiar with the Polar regions. Let me explain."

He seemed doubtful for a moment, but I held his gaze. At last he nodded.

"All right. Go ahead."

I did not mention my father's research. Instead, I span him some fable about adaptive and parallel evolution, the presence of similar flowers in New Zealand and Tierra del Fuego, greenhouse changes in the biosphere creating a possible climate for dormant seeds. I looked into his pale English eyes and after a while, I saw conviction begin to grow. Scientists are the easiest of people to convince of miracles, if they really want to believe, and they always do. Coming to stand behind David, I put my hands on his shoulders and leaned down to murmur into his ear

"Besides, if we do find anything, it would greatly benefit the Institute...."

I let a whisper of sadness enter my voice: resonant of government cutbacks, a perpetual lack of funding, and I felt him sigh under my hands. He nodded.

"I see your point," he said, glumly.

"It's a gamble, of course," I said, playing devil's advocate. "A risk. If you felt that it wouldn't justify the expenditure—which could be considerable, I'm afraid—then I'd quite understand...."

"But I think it's a risk we must take," David protested. "If your conclusions are correct, then this could be a discovery of immense importance."

"My assumptions are purely theoretical, however, and—"

"But, Jonathan, aren't theory and risk the essence of what we do?"

They weren't, of course, but now he was trying to convince me. I gave a small, reluctant nod. "Well, if you think you might be able to give me some small measure of support...." I said doubtfully. Boston put his arm around my shoulders as he led me to the door.

"I'll talk to various people. Should be able to let you know by Monday." As we reached the door he paused, frowning slightly. "You know Roger Anderson's planning an expedition to Prydz Bay?"

"Oh?" I said blandly. "I wasn't aware of that."

"Yes, for the winter months. . . . I'd suggest you contact him, only—" He gave me an uncertain glance. I laughed.

"If you're thinking of those old rumors of a feud between Anderson's father and my own, I can assure you that there's absolutely no truth in them." I looked him straight in the face. "You know what the scientific scene's like: if there's the chance of an angle, the media will play it up. However," and here I took him gently by the elbow, steering him towards the door, "if we do fund my expedition, it might be as well to keep the details under wraps for a little while. Don't want the Yanks getting a march on us, after all."

"Absolutely not," David said, momentarily alarmed. His secretary was sitting at her desk, inputting something into a laptop; she smiled when she saw me.

"Mary," David said. "Can you make sure that Dr Haight has all the information he needs over the next couple of weeks? He'll need archive access."

"Of course," she said, and then I left the cavernous depths of the Institute for the late golden light of a September afternoon.

I took pains to ensure that things went smoothly after that. Funding was obtained, equipment requested and provided, and the relevant papers organized. A week before I was due to fly out to Antarctica, however, I found myself standing next to Roger Anderson at a post-conference do at Imperial College, in front of a table full of canapés. Anderson looked as startled to see me as I was to see him.

"I thought you'd already left," he said. In that nasal East Coast accent of his, even the most innocuous remark sounded like a sneer.

"Am I going somewhere?" I fenced.

"Sure you are," Anderson said, recovering a measure of calm. He selected a salmon canapé, studied it for a moment between finger and thumb as though considering some particularly unappetizing specimen, then ate it. "You're going to the same place I am." Fastidiously, he brushed crumbs from his waistcoat. "Prydz Bay. In a week's time."

"Good Lord," I murmured. "It's a small world, isn't it? We might even bump into one another. . . enjoy cozy evenings around the camp fire...."

"Jesus, you never give up, do you?" Anderson said. "What did I ever do to you?"

"Not you," I said softly. "As you very well know. This is about your father. And mine."

"Yeah, I know all about that. Listen, Haight. My dad was a ruthless old bastard who had an obsession with the polar regions and wouldn't let anyone get in his way. And from all accounts, your old man was exactly the same. I'm sure they understood each other. But all that's past and done with, now. I'm sorry. I'm just not into the whole Victorian paterfamilias feuding trip. This is the twenty-first century we're in. If we can't be friends, then let's at least call it a truce." He held out his hand. I looked down at it. Part of me wanted to give in, to say, "You're right. What's past is past—" and take his hand. But I remembered my father's diary; that last entry written in a shaky hand, telling of the fight he'd just had with the man who was trying to snatch his triumph away from him and speaking of his determination to find the orchid. That man was Anderson's father, and a few minutes later, my father had gone out onto the ice, leaving the diary hidden in a buried box in what was now a deserted research station. He had died, out there in the icefield. And then I thought of the orchid.

In the dream, its dark stem wound around a pinnacle of ice. The bloom was as fragile as glass, glazed a subtle crimson like blood beneath pale skin. Lacking the perversely ingenious mechanisms of its mainland cousins, it was self-fertilizing: a virginal flower. My father's madness and his dreams had made me what I was: I had inherited his obsessions, his desires, and I had inherited, too, a wish so secret that I could hardly bear to name it to myself. I wanted to be free of the past, and free of my father, and finding the orchid was the key to that dream. I could not let go now. I shook my head.

"Okay." Anderson said, with a sigh. "Have it your way. But remember I tried."

"I'll remember," I said, and turned away.

The following week, I flew out to Antarctica. I watched the world turn to silver and blue, the colors of the cold. Stormy petrels wheeled past the little plane and once I glimpsed an albatross on its long glide across the icy seas. I must confess that it was a relief to step out of the plane and find myself beneath the bitter air and brilliant skies of the far south. I find it easy to deal with people, to manipulate and control, but I always prefer to work alone when I can. Here, with the glaciers above Prydz Bay stretching as far as the horizon, my visions no longer seemed overwhelming; my dreams free to expand across limitless space. I had reached the end of the world, and come home.

There was a survey team already in residence at the base camp: Americans, Norwegians, and a British woman. There had recently been a change of personnel, and everyone was in the process of getting to know everyone else. Pleading fatigue, I kept myself to myself for the first couple of days; occupying myself with my preparations and yearning to get out into the snows. I worked quickly. It would take several days to get up into the glacier, and it was not long to the midwinter solstice. Although it was summer here on the other side of the world, the continent remained dangerous and unpredictable. I had no idea as to precisely where the orchid was to be found; I only knew that I would find it. Casually, I mentioned Anderson's name to a member of the survey team, implying that we were well acquainted and hinting with a smile at a degree of friendly rivalry. They were anxious to help. Anderson's team were scheduled to arrive in a day's time. I set out the next morning.

I took the snowmobile out across the snowfield, and did not look back until I reached the edges of the glacier. The survey station was no more than a tiny black square in the distance; beyond it stretched the pale, glittering expanse of the Amery Ice Shelf and the bay beyond. From this distance, seen through the binoculars, the icebergs looked like sails and for a moment I imagined that I was some mythical original inhabitant of this white waste, that the sails were those of the first European explorers, come to desecrate purity.

I headed up into the Lambert glacier, leaving the vehicle at the base and progressing on foot. I pitched a camp high in a crevice of rock, and sat at the entrance to the tent to watch the sun sink as low as it would in these long southern days. The world was a place of light and ice and fire; I could no longer tell the difference between dream and reality, if indeed a difference existed. The sun shot sparks from the icicles which fringed a nearby overhang, and for a moment I thought of a blade flashing in the light. The dreams were coming with a greater intensity now: the rosy tinge of the light staining the glacier and glancing up, I saw the orchid. I knew that it was not yet real. It danced above me: a black bud, glossy as a beetle's wing, cracking open to shoot out its petals in perfect slow motion. Each translucent petal uncurled, stretching to its furthest extent, displaying itself before me. The sun's light caught the red heart of the flower, touching it with the glow of wine, and slowly the orchid's tongue unfurled, long and delicate and forked like a snake's. It seemed to taste the air. In my waking dream, it seemed that I was standing before the orchid, my mouth open to the blistering cold, and the orchid's tongue penetrated my mouth, probing gently within and sending a flood of sweetness down my throat. Then the sun slipped lower and shadows fell across the glacier. The orchid was gone, but I was dreaming it into being, I told myself, I was making it real. I do not know if I even really slept that night.

I climbed high into the glacier over the course of the following day, and when the sun once more sank down towards the horizon I dreamed again of the orchid. Anderson was not far behind me. I had glimpsed the little moving shape of a snowmobile far out on the icefield that morning, and fancied that I could see Anderson's face through the binoculars. I could feel his presence, contaminating the land with flesh and blood, just as I was. I turned my back on him and headed further into the mountains.

On the next night, it snowed. A wind came up from nowhere, moving with terrifying speed across the mountains and bringing a blizzard with it. I crouched in the tent and listened to the wind lashing the walls of the glacier, thinking of the avalanche in which my father had died. That would be the way to go, I thought. You would not rot, not decay into the heat and dampness of the earth, but simply remain in perfect stasis: purified into ice beneath a grave of snow. I owed it to myself to experience such a death, I thought, and I realized then that I had no intention of bringing any evidence of the orchid back to London: not film, not photograph, and not specimen. It would be a violation even to touch it, and I thought of that long red tongue, flickering out to meet mine.

Next day was midwinter. I could feel it in the coldness of my blood, traveling with oily slowness through my veins, and in the slow beat of my heart. I could feel it in the world around me: poised on a pivot between one season and the next, turning to the dictates of the sun. At midnight, I knew from my dream, the orchid would bloom. I hurried, then, heading for the heights of the glacier and taking risks that I would previously have condemned as foolish. When I reached the summit, the clouds were close enough to touch, so close that the world appeared inverted and if I fell, I thought, I would fall into the well of the sky.

At the summit of the glacier was a small pinnacle of rock. I hastened towards it, for I had caught a glimpse of the wiry stem that coiled around it, and fell to my knees in the snow. Reaching out a gloved hand, I cupped the air around the bud: it was tightly closed, its lips pressed together. I bowed my head. From behind me a voice said

"Haight? What the hell are you doing?"

I turned, shock washing over me. It was Anderson. I did not know how he had managed to catch up with me so quickly, and I did not care. The only thing that mattered was that he was here. He took a wary step forward.

"Get away from it," I hissed. "I found it. It's mine."

"What are you talking about?" Anderson said. He sounded genuinely bewildered.

"The orchid," I whispered.

"There's nothing there."

I looked at the orchid. The black bud shook slowly, as if disagreeing with his words.

"Dr Haight. . . take it easy. You're right on the lip of the glacier. . . ."

"Why did you follow me?" I asked, very quietly.

"Why do you think? The rumor mill's been working overtime; there was talk you were onto something really big. . . with the reputation you've got, I wanted in on it. Seems they were wrong."

"No," I said. "They weren't wrong. The flower's here. But I won't let you touch it."

I stood up.

"Careful! Look, I'm going to come towards you. . . don't do anything sudden."

"All right," I acquiesced. I let him come within a couple of feet. He was holding out his hand and I knew what he was about to do. I could not let him touch the flower. My hand went to the ice axe that hung at my belt. It happened so fast that I was not even sure that I had moved at all.

And I saw the orchid bloom, just as it had in my dream: the white petals uncurling with the red, fracturing like glass across the snow. The tip of its tongue reached out to touch the ice, and then was still. I watched it for a long time, and gradually it sank back down into the snow and was gone. I had seen the flower of my father's long obsession, and my own, bloom at last. I fell to my knees where the orchid had blossomed. I had long since ceased to feel the cold and soon, I thought, I would go to join the orchid in the glacier, and perhaps my blood would warm another seed into life, to bloom if spring should come.

Quantum Anthropology

One: Genreth

I first saw the ghost on the shores of Eil Ei Heirath, at the end of a winter's day before dark. I had been hunting, and the bird's blood was still hot in my mouth, but it was only the fourth kill that day. The bodies of the oroth lay soft and heavy in the bag that hung from my shoulder. Turning for home, I scattered a handful of their pale feathers along the hunting path as a sign of respect. And so I was startled when the ghost rose up before me like a shadow out of the snow; I had not earned a haunting from the spirits of birds.

I soon saw, however, that this ghost had a foolish appearance: half human, as if unfinished. It gaped at me as if it had never seen a girl before, and flapped its hands, making meaningless sounds. It wore a low hat and a thick coat. Its skin was pale, but not like my own: I am a northerner, typically so, with skin as wan as ash. The ghost was pink and unwholesome; the color of meat that has started to rot. Its eyes were black and liquid. I sent out my senses, but as I had expected, I could not feel it. It was not a proper part of the world, and so I ignored it: I had heard that such creatures used to haunt the northern lakeshores. But I had better things to do than be troubled by spirits or folk whom the world had spurned, so I brushed past it on the path and did not look back.

I had forgotten it by the time I reached the tower. My sister Irrys was sitting impatiently by the fire.

"You took your time," she said, sourly. It was only envy, I knew. In these last few days Irrys had come down with the chills and visions that can sometimes mark the start of waterfever, and the satahrach had insisted that she stay inside. She was a dreadful patient. She whined to whoever would listen that she was perfectly well, that it was just the heat and stuffiness of the tower that compounded her sickness. She complained that she kept dreaming of her lover Ettar; that he was lost and alone in the mountains above Derenthsara, where ice lies thinly over the ravines, and people hunt humans for pleasure. The satahrach put a gnarled hand on her brow and told her that it was nothing more than inner heat. Meanwhile, I had gone hunting alone.

"You're well enough to sulk, I see," I said now.

"I'm well enough to be out in the winter." She turned her head so that the long hair fell down her back like snow, shining cold in the light of the fire. "So, did you catch anything?"

"Oroth. Four of them."

"Not too bad, then," Irrys acknowledged, grudgingly.

"Oh, come on, Irrys! If you'd caught them yourself, you'd be boasting for days!"

"Oroth are an easy kill at this time of year," she muttered. "They grow heavy; they can't fly. What did you do, throw your coat over them while they waddled about?"

I did not reply to this insult, but smiled a superior smile to annoy her and left my sister sulking by the fire. And between worry for her, and the task of plucking the birds, I did not think of the ghost again.

Two: Daniel Ottrey

They say that over a hundred years ago, several expeditions set out for this little uncharted world, but no one knows what became of them, or even whether they reached Monde D'Isle at all. That was in the days of the Core expansions, when many small craft were launched onto the galactic tides, seeking legends. Now, such expeditions are less common, and more thorough. We have proper equipment nowadays, and a greater degree of bureaucracy. The task of hunting down lost colonies always has that tang of romance, but the visa sections of government offices are not known for their poetry, or their souls.

We were only permitted to stay on Monde D'Isle for a month; sanctioned to make contact with any descendants of the original colonists and undertake preliminary research, but after that, we were obliged to return to the Demesne worlds and submit proposals for further study and a grant application. The current expedition would be difficult enough. I was the only anthropologist aboard. The rest of the crew were interested mainly in soil samples and geological strata, and were scornful of any life form greater than mould. I considered them typically narrow-minded academics. Moreover, this was my first research assignment after the completion of my anthropological training, and I felt that the crew did not take me seriously. It wasn't only that their discipline differed so greatly from my own, but that there could be little common understanding between us. After all, they were dealing with the dull material, empirical world; I, with the fundamental precepts of social interaction.

"So what exactly are the premises on which your discipline is based?" Val Rettino had asked, skeptically. "That the principles of quantum physics can be applied to sociology? That you change things—social situations—just by looking at them, not even by participating in them? Like—what was that ancient experiment?—peering into a box and seeing whether there's a dead cat there or not? I've heard that your discipline isn't considered mainstream, either—isn't it often described as a kind of faith, based on an inadequate comprehension of old ideas about quantum principles?"

By then I was used to such challenges, and had learned to mask my annoyance behind a semblance of objectivity. Rettino was clearly trying to goad me. "You're correct in your initial description," I told him, loftily." We do indeed hold that the very act of observation alters a social context—certainly in the case of trained observers such as myself. This is why one must be extremely careful in undertaking the sort of research that I do." I did not add that it was why I tended not to socialize overmuch with the crew; I feared that it might offend them.

So when the navigational systems of the ship went down, leaving myself and the little lander temporarily stranded on the planet below, I was inclined to regard my predicament as being in the light of an unexpected gift rather than as a curse.

"Rettino says it'll take a week," Ellen Eng told me apologetically over the array. I could see her long prim face veiled with a haze of static, like an interstellar nun.

"But he can definitely fix it?" I was just checking, not yet worried.

"It isn't difficult, apparently, just time consuming. He says there's no way we won't be able to get you offworld. All you have to do is sit tight."

Now, in one of my brief returns to consciousness and reading these words in my handpad journal, I am aware of their irony. Ellen and Rettino were right. The navigational array was easily fixed, though it took longer than expected. But I do not think that rescue is an option, now.

Three: Genreth

Irrys, irritatingly, saw portents for her lover's return everywhere: in the sparks that spat from the sea-coal blaze, in the trail of a falling star, in the shadows in the snow. At last Mithra, our satahrach, got fed up and told her to stop imagining things.

"If it's a proper portent, you'll know it when you see it."

"But what would a proper portent be?" Irrys cried, gripping the arms of the chair so hard that her nails slit the material. The satahrach clucked with disapproval.

"Proper portent? A sign in the air, or in blood on the lintel. A spirit, or ghosts, which attach themselves to trouble like river-leeches. And will you watch what you're doing with your hands! You don't see Genreth fretting and fidgeting over some worthless young man, do you? Why can't you be more like your sister? I don't understand how two from the same litter can be so different."

"Because Genreth's got a heart like a winter stone, that's why," Irrys snapped, and ran out of the room. She was, we agreed, taking it hard.

A day later, however, a proper portent finally showed up. And to my surprise, it took the form of the ghost I had seen on the hunting path.

Four: Daniel Ottrey

I've found them! my excited journal entry reads. It might be more accurate to say that one of them found me. I had gone out into the snow to break the ice down at the spring and replenish the water supply on the lander. With Ellen and Rettino assuring me on the hour that the repairs were going well, that there was no need for worry, and that they'd have me up and out in the next few days, I was prepared to make the most of my adventure. I wrote up my notes, checked the service mechanism of the lander, and then headed out with the canister.

I met the woman on the path. At first, I thought I was imagining things, as though I had conjured her out of air and shadows: the black coat, her pale face and paler hair, eyes like chips of ice. She was carrying a bag and a single feather clung to her lips. She opened her mouth as if to speak and I saw blood on her teeth like a child's fairy story: black as a raven's wing, and white as snow. Red as blood. She looked at me as though I presented some kind of personal affront, stepped past me with disdain, and was gone down the track.

I began to call after her, but belatedly remembered my training. I needed to set the observational parameters of our meeting more carefully. She did not look back. I wanted to see where she was heading, so I followed her down the path. An hour later, I came to a spine of rock. Below, a dark stone tower stood on the shores of an icy lake. A spiral of smoke curled from its conical roof. I saw the tall figure of the girl trudging across the snow; she reached the tower, and vanished inside. I would have followed her down, but it was twilight now and snowclouds were massing over the peaks. I deemed it best to return to the lander.

The snow lasted for a day, but on the morning after that I woke to find a clear, watery sky and pale sunlight. Today, I decided, I would go in search of the girl, and build on our initial contact. Strapping on the snowshoes, I set out down the barely-discernible track, thanking fortune that Monde D'Isle was a wintry world. I was thankful for any echo of my home.

As I drew closer to the tower I could see that it was built from some kind of glazed black brick: it looked solid, and yet not heavy. The glaze reflected the snowlight, lending a curious insubstantiality to the building. The doors were metal, and carved with all manner of fanciful beasts and birds; higher, I could see windows of what looked like waxed paper. Close to one wall was a saddle of stone, its purpose unclear to me. I perched myself upon it to set the lingua franca running, but I was almost immediately interrupted. The doors swung open smoothly on oiled hinges, and two women stepped forth. One of them was the girl whom I had met in the mountains. It was preferable—according to the principles in which I had been trained—that they note me first, so I did not speak. The girl closed the doors behind her, and stopped to adjust a bootlace. She glanced up at me, and paused. She frowned. She said something in a liquid rush of language to her companion. The lingua franca hummed, starting to analyze the speech, and I stepped forward, smiling. The two women glanced at me again, as if I was of no more consequence than the stone on which I had been sitting. Then they turned, and walked away. I was so startled that I violated my training then and there.

"Wait!" I cried, knowing perfectly well that they would not understand me, but nevertheless hoping to distract them, engage them for long enough that the lingua franca could begin its work on their words. They paid no attention to me. I followed them, and found myself traversing the ridge above the lakeshore. The girls glanced up at the ridge, and they could not have failed to see me, for I stood there in plain view. But then they turned back to the lake. I watched them helplessly as they threw a long net out to catch the graceful white birds that waded in the icy shallows. They killed them by snapping the birds' necks with their teeth; an economically cruel gesture that reminded me of a cat killing mice. When they had snared three of the birds, they made their way back up to the tower, walking straight past me and chattering, like the young girls who frequent the boulevards of La Vard's Demesne.

Once more I followed them, as far as the doors of the tower. Again, the girl paused to attend to her troublesome bootlace, and I took my chance. I slipped through the doors of the tower into a dim, quiet hall. The girls stepped in behind me, but though a perfect stranger was standing before them in their own dwelling place, they moved around me, like water around a stone. So much for my careful theories of identity and observation, participation and interference. Frustrated, I was now determined to be noticed, and to discover why I might be so insignificant a thing.

Five: Genreth

"I told you so," I said, when we found the ghost sitting witlessly on the mounting block. I wouldn't have seen it if it hadn't moved. "And Mithra told you too, that the portent would appear. Clearly, it has taken the form of a ghost. Now will you stop whining on about Ettar?"

"It doesn't mean he's alive," Irrys said, tossing her silvery braid. I could see that she was determined to milk every drop of drama from the situation. The ghost followed us down to the lake. I thought I glimpsed it standing on the ridge.

"Ignore it," I told her.

"So, Genreth," my sister said, as we snared the white serai, "What are ghosts?"

She so rarely conceded that I might know more than she did that I was pleased to display my understanding.

"Well," I told her. "The principal kind of ghost is merely the memory of a life. They have left their bodies behind; they are not part of the world as we are. They do not have the connection to it that they had in life."

Irrys was frowning, so I added, "Stand there, by that rock. Now. What is under the ground?"

Without hesitation she replied, "Iron-stone and paitry, like the bricks of the tower. Deeper, I can feel water, and a seam of coldstone crystal."

"And how do you know that?"

She blinked. "I just do."

"Of course you do. That is what it means to be human, to have these abilities. But a ghost is different. Take the one that we have just seen. I cannot sense it; only see it."

"Aren't you afraid of it?"

I paused. It was true that the ghost scared me, I admitted reluctantly to myself, but I'd rather have died than said so to my sister. I replied, "Why should I be? It is only the remnant of a person, and can do us no physical harm. But it is best to ignore it, all the same. If you acknowledge them, they can steal a piece of your soul."

I glimpsed the ghost again when we came back into the tower, but the last thing I wanted to do was to bind it to me by paying it more attention. In the morning, it was gone.

Six: Daniel Ottrey

I wandered through the chilly tower, unchallenged. I met other people on a landing: a middle aged man and an elderly woman. Their eyes were like lamps in the light cast through the paper windows; despite their ancient origins, they looked barely human. I expected consternation, dismay, or anger, but like the girls at the lake, they paid no attention to me. Such extraordinary behavior both confused and infuriated me. I greeted them in my own language, but the old woman flicked her fingers at me in a gesture of dismissal, and continued with her conversation. Forced to play eavesdropper, I set the lingua franca to record, and waited until I had sufficient data for it to analyze what it had learned. I felt embarrassed to be standing there on the landing, in someone else's house, holding the humming box of the translation device. Why did they not acknowledge me? Much of my training had been based on contact and its problems, but I had not considered that I might be invisible. Uneasily I wondered, too, what effect my observation of these people might have upon them. What social waves might I collapse, by watching them so closely?

But despite my puzzling reception, I was nonetheless excited. Once I had cracked the language, I told myself, then I could start to make the correct approaches. Perhaps there was some ritual greeting without which these people could not acknowledge me. Maybe I had unwittingly offended them in some way—easily done, with less developed cultures—and needed to proffer an explanation.

At last the subjects of my study finished their conversation and moved on. After another twenty minutes or so, the lingua franca sang out, indicating that it had reached the first stage of a breakthrough. It had linked the unfamiliar speech to two ancient languages. I went back down the stairs in search of the girl, and eventually found her in the kitchen, gutting a bird with swift, sharp strokes of a knife.

"Madam, I greet you," I said via the lingua franca, adding sincerely, "and may I give apology, for any offence I may unwittingly have caused."

The girl glanced up, frowning. She stared through me as though I was no more than air, and turned back to her task.

"I realize that I don't understand your society—I am a newcomer here. Forgive me if I don't know the correct way in which to address you. Perhaps you would be kind enough to explain matters to me?"

This time she did not even bother to look up. I confess that this enraged me. I stepped forwards, and put my hand on her arm. I was expecting outrage, perhaps fear, though looking back it was a stupid thing to have done—after all, she was holding a knife. But she shook my hand away like a cat twitching its ear when a fly troubles it, and slit the bird's flesh with a single, decisive gesture.

All the principles in which I had been so diligently trained vanished entirely at that moment. I begged her to talk to me. I made, I see now, a thorough fool of myself. But at last the incongruity of the situation struck me: here was I, a recently graduated anthropologist, standing raving in an alien kitchen, pleading to be noticed by a beautiful young woman who showed none of the usual responses that one would expect in such a situation. When she had finished gutting the birds, she picked up the corpses and carried them over to a wooden box lined with ice. Her mouth was set tight; perhaps with irritation. Turning her back on me, she went out of the room.

Seven: Genreth

It was not until the ghost re-appeared—babbling like a week-old infant—that I finally realized what had happened. The satahrach had said that the ghost was a portent, for Ettar. But for the spirit to be so persistent, Ettar must be in grave danger, or even dead. For all my scornful words, I felt very guilty as I walked from the kitchen and went in search of Irrys. She was a silly girl, but she was still my sister, and I knew that she cared about her young man. If I had misjudged the situation, and he really was in trouble…Well, there was not a lot I could do about it now. I was not trained in these matters, but the satahrach was.

I found Mithra in her herb room, standing over a brazier. I told her about the ghost. She was not happy.

"It may be that you're right. But I want you to stay away from that ghost, Genreth. It seems to be haunting you, and that means that it desires your soul. You must not talk to it, or even look at it."

"But surely we should question it—find out what it knows about Ettar?"

"I will see to that. I will summon it, here and now. Go outside, and wait."

I would have liked to have watched, but it was disrespectful to argue with elders, and anyway, I knew from past experience that she'd only refuse. So, reluctantly, I waited outside the herb room, watching smoke seep through the cracks in the door. After an hour or so, the door opened.

"The ghost will not come," Mithra said. "I've tried everything I know." She did not look pleased.

"Maybe it will come for me."

"You are untrained." She added, more gently, "I do not say, Genreth, that you are not capable of that training—indeed, it may be that this is a sign that you are to be my replacement in this regard, which would please me. But the satahrachin training is long."

"Then what am I to do about the ghost?"

"I told you. Pay no attention to it."

"We can't just let Ettar die."

"We don't know for certain that this is what the portent means. Are you prepared to go after Ettar? Try to lay the ghost to rest?"

She looked at me, and I knew what I had to do. I wasted no time. I ran to my room, and took my sword from its place on the wall. I buckled the sheath onto my back, slipped my black-handled knife into my boot, took my good winter cloak and went downstairs. I met Irrys in the hallway. Her face was pale in the dim light, but determined.

"We'll find him, Irrys," I said. "Don't worry. I won't rest until we do."

No sooner than the vow was out of my mouth when the front door opened. There in the doorway, silhouetted against the light and with a foolish smile on his face, stood Ettar himself.

We both gaped at him like a pair of stunned oroth. He smiled back, confident of his welcome. It was a moment before I could utter a single word.

"Well?" he asked, the smile fading a little. "Aren't you pleased to see me, then?"

Irrys flung herself into his arms. I waited until they had finished hugging and kissing, and then I said, faintly, "Ettar. . . Are you all right?"

He looked surprised. "I'm very well. Why?"

"We thought you might be lost, or in trouble," I told him, through gritted teeth.

"Not in the slightest. I had a fine trip. But I'm touched to see you were so concerned about me," he said over my sister's shoulder. The foolish smile widened. "I didn't think you liked me, Genreth."

"I'm glad you're safe," I said, before I forgot myself and hit him, and then I stumped back upstairs, took off my coat and hung my sword on the wall. I turned back to the door, and saw Mithra standing there.

"Ettar—" I began.

"—is back. Now we know, Genreth. The ghost is a deceiver. And surely after your soul."

Eight: Daniel Ottrey

I tried to talk to others of the household, even tugging at the occasional sleeve, but without result. People brushed me off, stepped past me, murmured things that were incomprehensible to the lingua franca. It was a fascinating situation, but I was dismayed to find that it also distressed me. I felt slighted, as though I was nothing. At least the crew of the ship had noticed me. I began to look back on my arguments with Rettino with a certain nostalgia.

Baffled, I decided to return to the lander. I had my handpad with me in the tower, but at least on the lander I would be able to write up my findings in relative safety. The inhabitants of the tower were beginning to inspire me with an obscure kind of fear. But when I went to the main door and tried to open it, I found that it had been locked, presumably for the night. I wrenched and rattled at it, but the locks were sturdy and did not give. I was trapped. Annoyed and alarmed, I made my way back up to the attics, which seemed deserted, and took out the portable communicator. At least I would be able to speak to the crew. By this time, I was beginning to feel a desperate need to talk to someone—indeed, anyone. But then I found that I could not reach the ship: transmission was blocked.

I demanded an explanation from the communicator, but it replied smoothly "Local conditions are not conducive to transmission. It is suggested that composition of surrounding material is to blame."

There must have been something in the stone of the tower that prevented the signal getting through. I even tried leaning out of the window, but that didn't work either, and it was a long way down. The cold air made my eyes water. I looked down at my hand, holding the communicator, and for a moment it appeared curiously blurred and insubstantial. I blinked to clear my vision, and sat disconsolately down on a nearby couch, to wait for morning.

Nine: Genreth

It would be necessary, so Mithra said, to exorcise the ghost, which had been seen around the house all through the previous afternoon. It had not troubled me again, but Mithra thought that it might simply be biding its time, having failed to lure me out into the world. The thought made me cold, and nervous. I was not familiar with exorcism, so Mithra explained. In order to expel the ghost from the house, we must all gather together in the main hall, and, with the assistance of particular chants and herbs, we must will it out of existence. This task must be started at dawn, when the veils that lie between this world and the next become thin. My family grumbled about having to rise at such an hour, but recognized the need for it.

Irrys was disgustingly superior, and said that no doubt it was some fault in my character that had drawn the ghost to me. I was haughty, she said, and too proud. I did not bother to answer this ridiculous assertion, but it was true that I felt both humiliated and alarmed by the ghost's presence. I slept badly that night, and longed for dawn.

At last I rose and opened the window, to see a faint light over the mountains. At that moment, Mithra knocked on the door to summon me downstairs. We congregated in the main hall, in silence. Mithra lit a brazier, threw acrid herbs upon it, and motioned us to sit around it with our hands joined. This was all we had to do: exorcisms require concentration, so Mithra said, rather than skill. But that concentration must be complete. At all costs, we were not to think about the ghost, for such things thrived on human attention like moths drawn to a lamp. We must render our minds blank, so that it could gain no purchase, and remain like this until Mithra had assured herself that the ghost was gone, willed away. I sat gripping Irrys and Ettar's hands, and tried to think about everything but spirits.

Ten: Daniel Ottrey

I must have fallen asleep on the couch, for when I woke, it was already light. I felt stiff and cold. I raised my hands to my face to blow upon them, and gaped in horror. The worn pattern of the rug showed clearly through my palms. My hands had become translucent. As I stared, the flesh returned; it must, I thought, be the result of fatigue. I had to get out of this unfriendly place, and seek refuge in the lander. I went swiftly to the door, but as I reached for the handle, I saw that my hands were once again transparent. I could see through my sleeve. Somehow, I was becoming invisible in truth. It must be some trick of the light, I thought frantically, some optical illusion. All I had to do was reach the door, and—

Eleven: Genreth

Through the trance-like state into which I had fallen, stunned by the herbs in the coals, I saw that Mithra had come back into the room. She was smiling. I raised my head to ask her about the—but no, I must not think of that. Anything but that. I concentrated on Irrys' warm fingers, clasped in my own, and soon nothing mattered but the drugged silence in my head.

Twelve: Daniel Ottrey

—and I was back in the room. My hands were visible again. The red sunset sent a finger of light across the patterned rug. I took a deep, shaking breath, and then knew nothing more.

I have been in this room for three days now, fading in and out of the world. In the brief periods of my return, I have inscribed as much as I can into the handpad, in the unlikely event that someone will ever find it. Most of my notes are speculations, incoherent and frantic, based on the nature of my discipline. All my training in quantum anthropology concerned the effects of observation on the subjects of study, but what of the watcher himself? What effect does observation, or its lack, have upon him? Sometimes it seems to me that I am merely mad. But sometimes I think that the people of the tower are opening and closing the box of reality, and I am flickering across its borders as their attention waxes and wanes, or that my unswerving belief in the precepts of my discipline is causing me to collapse my own wave function, down to smooth zero.

But what is increasingly certain, now, is that even if the crew come for me, there will no longer be any one here to rescue. A mirror hangs on the wall of the attic, catching the changing light. Each time I return, I rush across, and look. Sometimes there is a face in the mirror: a frightened shadow, a ghost. And soon there will be nothing at all.

The Blood Thieves

I knew what the girl was as soon as I saw her. I'd come across one of her kind a few years ago, you see, when there was all that panic about the volcano. All manner of things had come out of the darkness then, and one of them had turned up in my mum's front garden. But that thing had been small and black, with eyes like dead coals. This girl, sitting on a stone in the derelict lot behind the bus station, was beautiful, forcibly reminding me that I had now been girlfriend-less for some two months. Glimpsing her face in the midst of the furs of her sealskin parka, I could see that she'd been crying: the cold had frozen the tears to frosty snail-tracks down the curve of each cheek. I could hear my heart beating in the silent air. I knew that if I had any sense, I should turn and steal away, pretend I hadn't seen her but, as usual, I was too curious.

"Miss?" I said, tentatively. "Excuse me?"

I saw her catch her lower lip with one pointed tooth.

"I know why you're here," she said. Her voice sounded clear and accusing and remote. I found myself stammering.

"Do you? I mean—there's a possibility that the land's up for sale, and I—"

"What are you called?"

Automatically I reached into my briefcase and handed the girl my business card. She took it in little pale fingers and stared at it as though I'd presented her with a dead rat.

"Olaf Olafsson. Two names. Are they yours?"

"Yes, I—"

"Reykjavik. That is what they call this place now, I believe. And this 'Magnusdottir Real Estate Agency'? What is this?" She smiled, thinly. "You see, I can read your runes, thorn and isa and ehwaz , even though they are dead and entombed on paper."

"It's a—a property company. A company that buys and sells buildings."

The girl gave me a look of utter contempt.

"Only your kind would think stones are things to sell. And will you buy and sell this house, too?"

"Which house?"

She gazed around the derelict lot: at the spidery sea grass and the broken beer bottles.

"This is my house," she said. "You do not see it, but it is here. It has always been here, ever since the breaking of First Winter and the great snows. So many have gone to the rocks and the ice, but we remain, I and my child who is sick. And now you would sell it, and build another?" She blinked, and diamonds formed at the ends of her eyelashes.

I heard myself saying, "Look—nothing's settled yet. The buyer hasn't really decided anything."

"Who would buy this? I know how such a place looks to the eyes of your kind. You can never see what is truly there."

I said weakly, "Apparently there's a plan for redevelopment."

"Redevelopment? By whom?" She turned in a whisper of furs and looked straight into my eyes. It was like looking out onto the ice, and the winter glare. It dazzled me and I stumbled backwards.

"The people who want to buy this land are called Anaheim del Marche," I said. "They're a biotechnology company. I'm not sure exactly why they're interested in it."

"They are nothing but home-breakers to me. I charge you, Olaf the Double Named. Find out why they want to steal my land. And do not let them take my house away."

Her voice faded like the wailing of a kittiwake. And then she was gone, and I was alone in the derelict lot with a cold wind blowing off the sea and the cries of the gulls in the winter air above.

I didn't go straight back to the office. Instead, I left the car where it was and walked down Pjorsa Street to Gunderson's bar. I felt a bit dazed, and in need of a beer. I was also hoping that Gunderson himself would be there: if anyone knew what to do, he would. Once inside, I ordered a beer, enquired after the whereabouts of the proprietor and sat down in the corner. After a few minutes, Gunderson appeared from the back regions, wiping his hands on a towel and bringing with him a faint fragrance of herring. All the same, he had tied his gray hair neatly back in a pony tail and he was wearing clean jeans. His single eye was bright.

"Afternoon, Olaf. Got the day off? I can't stay long, I'm afraid. I've got to pick someone up at the airport in a bit."

"Oh, that's okay," I said. "I just wanted. . . " To my dismay, I heard my voice fading away. The bar seemed suddenly very dark. The next thing I knew, I was lying flat on my back on the bench with Gunderson's concerned face hovering over me. I blinked. He seemed to have two good eyes all of a sudden. Then I realized I was seeing double.

"Olaf, man. Are you all right?"

"Don't know."

Gunderson disappeared and returned a moment later with a bottle of Islay malt. He got the stuff at a cutprice rate from one of the ferry captains. It was like taking a sip out of a peat bog: it could have woken the dead. I spluttered and revived.

"I think I've seen something," I told him. A lot of Icelandic conversations begin like this. Gunderson did not appear remotely surprised.

"All right then, Olaf Olafsson. What do you think you have seen?"

"It was in the lot behind the bus station—one of old Sigurdson's properties. His lawyers are selling off the land. I went to have a look at it for a client; they're thinking of purchasing it for redevelopment. But there was someone sitting in the middle of it. A girl. Not a normal girl. You know."

"You saw one of the huldra?"

"Keep your voice down! You're not supposed to say their name!"

The blue eye winked. "Don't worry. Nothing's going to happen. What did she say?"

As briefly as possible, I told him. Then I sat and sipped my whisky while Gunderson considered the matter. At last he said, "Look, I don't have to tell you that things are getting serious when the huldra start manifesting to perfectly ordinary people like you. They don't like us to see them, because it diminishes them; makes them as queasy as you were a moment ago. If she put a charge on you, then you'll have to fulfill it."

I sighed. Gunderson glanced up at the clock.

"I've got to go and meet this flight, but I'll be back about four. Come and see me then."

I watched his lanky figure vanish in the direction of the doorway. I finished my whisky, and my neglected beer, and then I fished out my mobile and told the office I'd be back in on Monday. In the meantime, I told them, I was going to see a client. Then I sat for a moment, trying to think of what I would say to Mr. Ed McNally of Anaheim del Marche when I next saw him. My boss had been insistent that this was the location the company wanted, and now I'd have to talk their representative out of the purchase. "Sorry," I pictured myself saying breezily. "Can't close the deal on the old Sigurdson land, I'm afraid. You see, it's really a fairy's house, and—" McNally already thought Icelanders were weird as hell. I'd seen it in his face when we'd first met, a kind of unease, masked with joviality. Not for the first time, I wondered why the company had chosen to come to Reykjavik, of all places.

In the back of the bar, someone turned the radio on and the strains of "Human Behavior" drifted out into the chilly afternoon light. Björk's voice reminded me of the huldra's own: thin and eldritch and strange. What about inhuman behavior? I reflected, dismally. Who could say anything at all about that?

I made my way to the Intercontinental hotel and found Ed McNally sitting in the bar, staring out across the bleak expanse of the water. A shaft of late afternoon sun glinted from the distant wall of a passing iceberg. I thought it was a magnificent view, but it seemed to depress McNally. He glanced up at me without enthusiasm.

"Ever been to Texas, Olafsson?"

"I'm afraid not." I tried to infuse my voice with suitable regret. McNally just grunted.

"Look," I said. "About that vacant land behind the station. I'm afraid there's a problem with it."

"Yeah? What kind of problem?"

"Terrible legal complications. I'm sure you can imagine what the land laws are like here—half of them go back to twelfth century claims and to be quite honest, by the time we sort it all out, you'll have spent your money twice over."

"That so?" McNally removed his boots from the coffee table. "Well, shit, that's not a problem."

"It isn't?"

"No. Nothing special about that plot, after all. As long as we can get somewhere fairly central."

"Oh," I said, hope rising. "I thought you were set on that particular property."

"Yeah, your boss seemed to think it would be ideal, but sure, I'm open to suggestions."

"Okay," I said. I tried to stop my face from cracking in a huge, relieved grin. "Great. Then maybe I could fax you some alternatives?"

"Sure, whatever. Doesn't matter where the hell it is, as long as it's central, like I said, and in a location that the company can keep secure."

"Secure?" I asked.

"Sure—the lawyers were pretty insistent about that. Don't want people breaking in and stealing the blood samples. Though it's kinda hard to see why anyone would want to."

"Mr. McNally," I said. "What exactly is your company proposing to do here?"

Ed McNally frowned. "Thought you'd have seen it on TV; we did a big feature on your little news show last month."

"I was on holiday for a couple of weeks; must have missed it."

"Haven't seen the posters in your doctor's office?"

"No, I haven't been to the doctor in years."

"Healthy, eh? Well, that's good. See, my client's involved in the field of genetic research. The project they're going to be running here is to take a sample of everyone's DNA, so that they can track genetic markers, study possible diseases and so on. In return, you guys get free medicine for five years."

"But why Iceland? Surely you could do that in the States?"

"As a matter of fact, they couldn't. Here in Iceland, you've got a very small population, and a limited gene pool: it's much easier to trace the markers than it is in a big, mixed population like the US has got. See, there isn't a whole lot of genetic diversity here." He gave me a uneasy glance; he was a stone's throw away from calling us all inbred. "In the States, for example, you've had a whole lot of immigration. There are literally millions of chemical components strung along the population's chromosomes—what our folks say on the publicity material is that it's kinda like trying to find one flat note, sung by one individual, in a chorus where a whole bunch of other people are singing their favorite tunes. Here, in Iceland, everyone's more or less singing the same song."

"I see," I said. I didn't, really, but I was so relieved I'd saved the huldra's house that I didn't actually care. I should have known that things wouldn't be that easy. I left the hotel and headed home, picking up a takeaway en route. Then I called my cousin Sula, the doctor. She knew about science, and Mr. McNally's gene project sounded more than a bit sinister to me. But Sula was enthusiastic.

"I think it's a great idea," she said. "I know there've been some objections about patient's privacy, but the Althing's agreed to it and I don't blame them. Del Marche are mapping for inherited disease, that's all. I think you've been watching *The X-Files* too much."

I was reassured, at least for a while. That evening, I made my way back to the lot behind the bus station with the good news. I had no idea how to summon the huldra, but in the event, it wasn't necessary. As I stepped into the lot, she curdled out of the air. I felt a breath of frost on my cheek.

"Well?" she said. I told her about the deal. She crept closer, and put her hand on my sleeve. She smelled of snow. "The huldra can be grateful," she murmured.

Embarrassed, I said, "It's enough to know that I've done someone a good turn. Wouldn't want you to lose your house, after all."

"The ones who wanted to buy my house. Are they angry?"

"No," I said. "It doesn't matter where they go; as long as they've got somewhere to build a laboratory."

The huldra frowned. "A laboratory? What is that?"

Her presence was magnetic, as though I was iron tuned into the north. I started babbling on about the gene project; repeating what my cousin had told me. I did not know whether it would make any more sense to her than talk of magical spells would to me, although I somehow got the impression that she was disdainful of human ways rather than ignorant. But the huldra was staring at me in dismay.

"So. They are blood-thieves and body-sackers, these people who would buy my house. And what will they do, once they have sniffed out our ancestors' secrets?"

"Well, if they know which strands have markers, they can isolate particular hereditary diseases. That's a good thing, isn't it?" I added, lamely.

The girl turned and spat a glittering lump of ice into the middle of the sea grass. She said, "We are kin, your kind and mine, however little we like it. We have been kindred for generations, since men loved the maidens of the huldra, and women opened their winter windows to let in unhuman lovers. And if these blood-thieves find that there is strangeness in the blood, that other humans do not have? What then, Olaf the Double Named?" Her smile grew malicious. I thought for a moment. The evening seemed to be growing even colder.

"They'll want to know why."

"Yes, Olaf, they will want to know why. And more blood-thieves and body-sackers will come, from all across the gray seas, and perhaps they will try to seek out the huldra, too, and disturb us further. Perhaps there will be so many of them that they will drive us into the glacier fastnesses where even we cannot walk with ease, or out to sea with the selkies."

And not just the huldra, I reflected. As my cousin had said, I was a big fan of Mulder and Scully. If Anaheim del Marche discovered that there was something very strange indeed embedded in the Icelandic genome, then God knows what might happen. Visions of CIA involvement and sinister conspiracies flitted through my mind like ghosts. But I did not see what we could do to prevent the project from going ahead. Out of the sudden shadows I heard her say, "It rests with you, and I charge you again, Olaf the double-named who has saved my house for me: do not let them have their way. We are all kin. And if the blood thieves come, there will be grieving from Akureyri to Hekla, and not the voices of my kind alone."

And then she was gone again, and I was standing in the derelict lot for the second time that day, with a huldra's charge upon me.

Numbly, I walked back to the car and took the road out past Kopavogur. Once I'd reached the head of the fjord I stopped and got out of the car. In one direction I could see Surtsey's sinister mass rising out of the gray seas and in the other, the heights of Hekla's great bulk in the last of the light. The wind tasted of snow. I stood, shivering, until the light began to fade, but no answers came on the evening wind. So I went back into Rejkavik and did what any sensible Icelander would do under the circumstances: I got drunk. And whenever I get drunk, my mouth behaves like a door flapping in the breeze. By midnight, my problem had become common knowledge. That's the trouble with this town: everyone always ends up knowing everyone else's business.

Towards midnight, Gunderson came to sit beside me. His eye glittered like the light on the sea. He never seemed to regard the loss of the other eye as any great inconvenience, but you know what they say about the Icelander who loses a leg in a car crash and tells people what a relief it is—all it did was get in the way of the other one. Gunderson was a bit like that. It sometimes occurred to me that he saw more with one eye than most people did with two.

"So," he said. "Still got problems?"

"Yes, still got problems." I leaned forwards and put my head in my hands.

"So what are you going to do about it?"

"I've no idea." My voice sounded as though it was coming from the bottom of a well. Suddenly, I felt unnaturally sober. "I can't stop a multinational project, can I? If it was environmental—if they were striking for oil or despoiling the landscape, I might have a chance. . . But the gene project is a good thing, isn't it? Given all the investment and free medicine?" Personally, given a choice between my arthritic granny getting her medicine free of charge and a possibly adverse effect on Iceland's most sinister residents, I was inclined to welcome Anaheim del Marche with open arms. But then there was the charge on me, and given the huldrafolk's public relations record, I didn't take it lightly. Gunderson didn't say anything for a moment. Then he murmured, "I have found that in dealing with the huldra, it is best not to be too clever. It's best to follow your heart, and be as true to it as you possibly can. You know they are supposed to be the children of Loki, the old god of trickery? The best way to fight trickery is not to entertain it oneself. It's difficult to outwit the huldra... And now I think it's time you went home and got some sleep."

I knew he was right. It was the time of evening when they were starting to sing drinking songs—how the hero headed out across the glacier alone after the death of his father and knows he will never see the settlement again. That was one of the cheerful ones. It was definitely time to go home.

I spent the weekend fretting, and on Sunday evening I broke the habit of a lifetime and went to church. Initially, it wasn't a lot of comfort. I was still nursing a hangover, and an arctic chill was creeping beneath the door of the church. In front of me, Kara Gunnardottir's child had developed a runny nose, and when the first hymn finished, its howls went on. Everyone gave Kara sympathetic glances; a lot of the children were coming down with coughs and colds at this time of the year. Then an image of the huldra, and our first meeting, dropped into my mind like a stone down a well. So many have gone to the rocks and the ice, but we remain, I and my child who is sick. … For the first time in three days, I had what might turn out to be a good idea. Follow your heart, Gunderson had said.

And so, for the third time in a week, I went back to the lot behind the bus station and waited for the huldra. Despite the cold, my hands were clammy inside the thick gloves; I didn't feel nervous, so much as apprehensive. It reminded me of teenage dates. Then I turned and she was there.

"Olaf Olafsson?" she whispered. She seemed smaller, somehow, and insubstantial. I could see the wall behind her through her body.

"Are you all right?" I said, in some alarm.

"My child is dying."

"I'm so sorry," I said. "But listen to me. We are kin, you said—your kind and mine."

"What of it?"

"If our peoples are really related, then there might be something we can do to help," I told her. She gave a doubtful frown.

"How could a human help my child?"

"I helped you once before, didn't I?" I said. "I saved your house, remember? My cousin's a doctor, and her clinic's still open for the evening patients. If you could bring your child to her, she might be able to do something for it. I know she'll try."

The huldra seemed to shrink into herself.

"Please," I said. "Trust me."

She wavered for a moment in the dark air and then after a long pause she said, "Very well."

My cousin Sula barely blinked when she opened the door of the clinic to find us standing on the step, even though it was perfectly obvious that the girl with me didn't quite hail from the same species.

"Olaf?"

"Sorry to disturb you," I said, "But this young lady needs your help. It's her baby."

The huldra clasped the small bundle in her arms more tightly to her body, as though we might try to take it away from her.

"All right," Sula said after a pause. "You'd better come inside."

Once within the house, the huldra shed garments at a somewhat alarming rate, until she was sitting in a long pale tunic. Her face, which had been pale as snow, was now blotched with pink.

"It's so hot in here," she whispered.

Briskly, my cousin said, "Well, I'll try and be quick. Let's have a look at the baby."

The huldra peeled back the sealskin wrap to reveal a pinched little face like a prune. It was without question the ugliest child I had ever seen. Sula performed a brief examination, with the huldra watching her like a hawk.

"Tell me," my cousin said. "What's the child's diet?"

"Milk, of course."

"And what about your diet?"

"I eat what my people have always eaten. Eggs and lichen and moss."

"No meat?"

"Of course not! Others of my kind might eat flesh, but I'm not a murderer."

"I think," Sula said, "that it would be a good idea to do a blood test."

It took nearly half an hour to persuade the huldra, who by now was pink and damp, that we were not trying to steal her child's blood for nefarious purposes. At last she agreed, and Sula disappeared into the back regions of the clinic with the sample. The huldra insisted on going with her, hugging the wizened child, and I went too. The child watched me all the time, with an ancient, implacable gaze. It had yellow eyes, like a gull. I smiled weakly at it, and it grinned, displaying small, sharp teeth. After various tests, Sula held up the sample to the light and said

"I thought so. Anemia. I'll give you an iron-fortified formula, and we need to talk about supplements."

"Metal?" the huldra said, doubtfully. "What good will that do?"

Something was nagging at me. I said, "Aren't your kind supposed to be averse to iron?"

"Those are the people of the south," the huldra said. She took the container from my cousin and stared at it.

"Come back in a week," Sula said, adding with a rather frosty glance of her own, "And Olaf—I'd like a word in private about bringing patients to see me. Later."

Outside the clinic, I turned to the huldra, but she was nowhere to be seen. I trudged wearily home through the snow, and though I went back to the derelict lot on the following evening, and then again on the day after that, there was no trace of the huldra or her baby.

I was beginning to wonder if I'd imagined the whole thing when there was a knock on the door. I opened it, to find the huldra, with a bundle in her arms.

"The shaman told me to come back in a week," she said, when I asked her where she had been. Evidently she had interpreted Sula's advice literally.

"How's the baby?" I asked. The huldra gave me the first real smile that I had yet seen on her wintry features.

"Look!"

Proudly, she drew the child's hood aside. It was asleep, but its face was round and rosy and surprisingly human now that its eyes were closed.

"He is healed. And I withdraw my charge from you, Olaf Olafssen. I see that I was too harsh, in my pronouncement upon the thieves of blood." She looked down at the floor, uncertain for the first time. "My kind are old and wary, and it maybe that men have changed since the early days. I have judged wrongly. Perhaps it is best that the bloodthieves do come, after all. . . . Thank you, Olaf Olafssen. And good-bye."

"Wait!" I cried, but she was already fading, like snow in spring, and the child woke at last and gave a thin gull's cry as she disappeared.

I did not lose hope of seeing her again. Gunderson just sighed when I poured out my heart to him over numerous glasses of whisky, and said he supposed I'd have to learn. We sold Anaheim del Marche part of the university campus for their laboratory. The whole population was tested, and I gather that the results have contributed significantly towards our understanding of inherited diseases. The Icelandic population is still entitled to free medicine, and I gather from my cousin Sula that some unusual patients have been in receipt of it.

One day in late summer, I went to the lot behind the station as usual and waited, but no one came, and I think I realized then that she was never coming back. I stood there for a moment, feeling lost and foolish, and then I walked back to the car and drove home. As I passed the terminal where the Bergen car-ferry was disgorging its passengers, I had to brake quite hard as a sleek black car pulled out onto the main road. I made an obscene gesture at the driver, but the windows of the car were tinted black and I couldn't see whether or not he'd responded. I'd have taken his number, but there didn't seem to be any plates, oddly enough. An earlier paranoia flicked through my mind: if Anaheim del March had indeed discovered something curious in the Icelandic genome, and if they had chosen to share their information with certain government agencies. . . . I tried to get a closer look at the car but it sped away, heading north into the long summer evening, and I did not see it again.

The Man from the Ministry

One

The spirit's voice, though still clear, had begun to falter a little as she sang. Uneasily, the demon peered sideways, trying to see, but his view was impeded by a crimson edge of rock. He stamped from one foot to another, trying to concentrate, but the sprit's increasingly weak voice seemed to drown out the world. Hopefully, the demon looked up and to his intense relief saw that the hero's feet were now visible, descending rather jerkily from a cloud. With a single blow of his sword, the hero (mighty Xu Xiao, whose eyes flash pinwheel lightning and whose voice makes a whisper of storms) dispatched the dragon and seized the collapsing heroine in his arms. The audience stood in applause as the opera thundered to a close and the curtain fell; not a moment too soon, the demon thought. He was already halfway across the stage, but the singing spirit was crumpling to the floor. Kneeling by her side, the demon gently detached the simpering mask. Beneath it, her face was the color of rice paper, with a thin thread of blood trailing from the corner of her mouth. The cast clustered around, murmuring in consternation. The demon snatched off his own mask, revealing the incongruous face of a fourteen year old boy above the lurid costume.

"Oh, mother," the ex-demon said, sadly.

Two

They carried her back to the dressing room, while Tang called the remedy man. He returned to find that they had laid her across the couch, nesting her among the frills and ruffles of discarded costumes. Tsu Zu's eyelids fluttered and she murmured something which her son Tang failed to understand.

"Don't try to speak," he told her, sensibly. "Just rest."

One by one, the cast took off their costumes and crept away with backward glances. Everyone loved Tang's gentle mother. Even Maiden Min of Third Chorus, whose venomous tongue had made Tang's life a misery on more than one occasion, patted him awkwardly on the shoulder as she left. Miss Ai, the dresser, pressed a wad of greasy notes into Tang's reluctant palm and told him to use it for the remedy man. Then Tang and Tsu Zu were alone. Tang looked down at his mother. She seemed very small, among the discarded costumes, and very pale.

"Don't worry," he told her inadequately. "The remedy man will be here soon." He tried to sound reassuring, to keep the bitterness from his voice, but it was hard. What Tsu Zu really needed was a hospital bed and a dose of antitubercular drugs, not some quack with his dried snakes and bear's gall bladders, but Tang and his mother were so far down the social hierarchy as to be practically invisible. You needed serious money for serious illness, in this town. Tsu Zu's lips were moving.

"Tang. . . . You have to listen to me. You have to take me to her."

"Who?" Tang asked, but he thought that he already knew the answer.

"To the temple. To Kuan Yin."

"Mother?" Tang asked, increasingly frightened. "You're not going to die."

Tsu Zu smiled.

"It's time, Tang. I can see it, like a gate carved from the clouds." She took a deep, shuddering breath, as though it were the scent of the Celestial Peach Blossom that she inhaled, and not the sweat and powder odor of the dressing room. Then her eyes snapped open and Tang could see another, darker place reflected behind them.

"Tang," Tsu Zu whispered. "You've got to take me to the temple. I can't die here. I made a bargain. . . . "

Her mind's wandering, Tang thought. Where was the remedy man? His phone call had been over half an hour ago, and Huang's shop was only just around the corner from the Pellucid Island Opera House. His mother was murmuring again.

"There's something you must know. When you were very young, you were ill. You nearly died. Your father had been posted to the provinces with the other soldiers, and anyway, I knew he wasn't coming back. He was always ambitious, you see, and he didn't want some little chorus girl and her bastard baby keeping him back. . . but that doesn't matter now. You see, my mother had died the year before, of typhoid, and you were all I had. I took you to the hospital but they turned me away; I didn't have any money, and I couldn't afford the health insurance. I carried you home and sat by the window. It was late afternoon, I remember it so well. . . . The air smelled of cooking and heat, and I could see your spirit begin to coil out of your mouth like the smoke from a spiral of incense. I prayed and prayed, to Kuan Yin, to anyone who would listen. When someone is dying, Tang, everyone around them is very close to the edges of life: close enough to see two worlds at once. I was in the cramped apartment on Wu Lu Road, but I was also in someone's office. It was very strange. There was a big desk, and a man sitting behind it with a lot of parchment documents. And I made a bargain, Tang. . . . "

Her voice faded into a fit of coughing. She put her hand to her mouth and it came away speckled with blood.

"Mother—" Tang said, alarmed, and then someone knocked at the door, very softly.

"About time!" Tang snapped. He wrenched open the door of the dressing room.

"Where have you been?" he demanded, but it was not the remedy man who stood there, with his pouches full of herbs and unpleasantness. Instead, an official stood on the doorstep. Tang knew that he was someone important by the correctness of his suit, which was as black as a storm cloud, his white starched shirt, and his smooth moon face.

"Who are you?" Tang asked, too upset to be polite.

Most courteously, the visitor said

"I am here to speak with citizen Tsu Zu. Is she here?"

Tang, prompted by some inner unease, said, "I won't tell you that until you tell me who you are."

The round lips blossomed into an indulgent smile.

"Why, my name is Citizen Ho Han. I've come from the Ministry, to see your mother."

"Why?"

"It is an official matter," Citizen Ho Han said, still polite.

"Oh."

"Perhaps you can tell me if she's here?"

Throughout his short life, Tang had been sure of one thing: that bureaucrats were either fools or dangerous, and this man, smooth as a buried egg, was one of the latter.

He began to push the door shut, but Citizen Han jammed his foot in the crack. Automatically, Tang looked down. Citizen Han's foot was clad in an immaculate black shoe, as shining and polished as a beetle's wing. An impeccable foot, except that it was on the wrong way round. In horror, Tang gave the door a desperate push and Citizen Han's unnatural heel shot from it like a cork out of a bottle.

"I'll come back later, then," Citizen Han's voice said softly, beyond the door.

Tsu Zu had struggled up to rest on her elbows.

Tang said, appalled, "Who was that?"

"I told you," his mother said weakly. "I made a bargain. With the Ministry."

"Which Ministry?" Tang asked.

His mother paused for a long moment, then whispered, "The Ministry of Epidemics."

Tang had a rather tenuous grasp of local government, but he had never come across this particular bureaucratic agency.

"It's not so very different there," Tsu Zu said. "Hell, I mean. It's organized into departments, just like our government is. Each district has a different remit. There's the Ministry of Storms, and one for earthquakes, and one for Epidemics. There's a sub-department for plague, but you had typhoid, and so they sent someone from Epidemics to see me."

"You made a bargain," Tang whispered. "What was it?"

Tsu Zu hesitated. "Your life, for my soul. You see, I was only fifteen when I had you, and death seemed such a very long way away. . . . I should have known better. But the man from the Ministry seemed so kind, and it all sounded so reasonable. I'm sorry, Tang. But it's too late now."

"No, it's not. There must be something we can do," Tang pleaded. He could hear the shuffle of unnatural feet from beyond the door. His mother nodded.

"When I started to become ill, I went to see someone. An old friend of my grandfather's, from Ju Shang province. He gave me something. A remedy. It's in my jewelery box, on the dressing table. In a little red case."

Tang found the case, hidden beneath a mass of gilt necklaces and cheap lacquer beads. It felt exceptionally heavy, as though it were full of lead, but when his mother opened it he saw that all it contained was a long, twisting strip of paper, inscribed with crimson characters.

"Fetch me the incense burner," Tsu Zu instructed. Tang did so, and watched as she curled the paper inside the burner, then set it alight.

"Now, open the door."

"No way."

"Open it!" Tsu Zu hissed, and Tang was so startled by his demure mother's tone of voice that he was across the room with his hand on the door handle before he knew it. Citizen Han beamed at him.

"Mother has returned, then?"

Hating him, Tang opened the door wide and the man from the ministry stepped through. Tsu Zu, with the last of her strength, took a deep breath and blew the smoke from the incense burner towards him. Citizen Han gasped. His eyes bulged like plums. From the incense burner came a steady, insistent crackling, as though someone was chanting the syllables of a name, louder and louder until the dressing room echoed with the sound. Citizen Han span on his inhumanly jointed ankles and began to dissolve. Tang found himself surrounded by a diffuse, acrid cloud. He choked. Dimly, he was aware that his own body seemed to be becoming lighter. He tried to cry out, but only a whisper emerged. In horror, he looked down at his hand and saw that it was already translucent. Citizen Han's plump mouth was wide open. Tang felt himself being pulled towards it. He tried to draw away, but his body did not seem to be there any more and he had no more resistance than dust before a vacuum cleaner. The yellowing plaster ceiling of the dressing room span up and over him, and he was sucked neatly down Citizen Han's throat. For a moment, there was darkness, an electric pause, and then Han exploded, sending both of them spinning out into the celestial abyss between heaven and hell.

Three

It was unpleasant, being so closely intertwined with Citizen Ho Han. In their mutually incorporeal state, they seemed to have become the same entity; seeing through the same eyes, breathing the same stale air. Ho Han exuded a sense of decay; a musty, oppressive sensation, like that of an old sock left in a cupboard. Tang had stopped panicking by now, and was trying to concentrate on the scenes that passed by. Hell, it seemed, was remarkably similar to his native city; at least in terms of planning if not occupancy. They had gone up Battery Road, and crossed over into Shaopeng, but whereas in Tang's city the central district was full of shops and teahouses and offices, here there was only a suggestion of life. Every building was dark and silent. Shadows watched them from the doorways as they passed and Tang sensed a growing anticipation in the air. They knew what the man from the ministry was carrying: a small, succulent spirit, rent prematurely from the body and still warm. Now, Tang understood why they said that ghosts were hungry.

Tang had never failed to honor the dead. His mother had impressed upon him the importance of compensating the ancestors for their current inconvenienced state. He had delivered food and incense and flowers to the legion of departed relatives, supporting them in the loneliness of the afterlife and ensuring that, on those days when the dead strode the city, they would know that he had honored them and stay away. Yet the city was also home to the limitless dispossessed, and when they died, who had they to comfort them? Many of the dead must be hungry indeed: forgotten by their descendants or simply the last of their lines. They waited now in the empty storefronts, and watched him with their avid gaze.

Ho Han paused at the top of Stair Street and gazed down. The derelict buildings of Shaopeng stretched below. Where the Pellucid Island Opera House stood in the real city, rose an immense pagoda. Its peaked roofs were wreathed in cloud. Balconies and balustrades covered its sides; carved dragons writhed. There was a subtle and indefinable wrongness about it.

"What," Tang said into the stifling air, "is that?"

"That is the Celestial Ministry of Epidemics," Ho Han breathed.

"We're going there?" Tang asked in horror. He felt Ho Han's stuffy spirit coil inwards to look at him.

"The relevant paperwork must be completed," the man from the ministry explained and leaped from the top of the steps.

"Don't drop me!" Tang wailed as they sailed through the stormy air towards the Ministry. Even in his current state, he had no wish to be cast down among the needle teeth and hollow tongues of the hungry ghosts of Shaopeng Street. The city wheeled below; glimpsed through the massing clouds. It was as though someone had made a rough sketch of the landscape. The main roads were still present and Tang could see the dark lines of malign sha energy that ran beneath them. The principal buildings of the city were also mirrored. The pagoda towers of the Ministries of Storms, Water, Epidemics and Fire occupied their place and there were other buildings, too, which Tang did not recognize. Fires burned blue in the spaces between the streets and beyond, where the sea should be, stretched a troubled darkness. The storm streamed by and they plunged down, to come to a graceful landing on the steps of the Celestial Ministry of Epidemics.

"Where now?" Tang quavered. Ho Han did not answer. He drifted through the double iron doors of the Ministry and stopped.

The queue, Tang saw, stretched down a corridor so long that the end of it was invisible. A thousand pairs of eyes turned curiously towards the new arrivals. Everyone smiled, politely, and gave a little bow. Ho Han, with Tang indeterminately in tow, began to pace down the line. Tang looked into each face as they passed. Every manner of illness was represented here. He saw traces of smallpox and leprosy; cancer and Jiangsu fever; and illnesses which he could not even name. The polite, ravaged faces turned away once the demon had passed, to resume their passive stare at the opposite wall. They were preserved in a dreadful patience. It is the manner of your death that marks you, Tang thought, not your life at all. What would anyone remember of his mother, except that she had been the chorus girl who had succumbed to a tubercular hemorrhage? Once they had believed that everything had its cure, just as everything has its price, not understanding that disease outruns the mind of man. Time meant nothing to the demons of the Ministry of Epidemics. They, too, had patience. They would wait for millennia, if necessary; trapped in amber or in the heart of a comet; hiding among the intricate spirals of the genetic code or behind the whiskers of a fly. How long had these spirits been waiting? Tang wondered. To him, the ordered line of the dead seemed sad but proper; a progression from the chaos of their last illness to this quiet hallway. Some of them wore costumes that had gone out of fashion a hundred years before, and their wearers seemed frail and thin as paper, bearing their wounds and tumors with the dignity of the dead. The demon blew lightly upon the doors and they swung open without a sound.

Inside the office, it was quiet. The demon closed the door behind her. Tang gazed around him. The office was a cavernous room, divided by screens and apparently cooled by electric fans set into the ceiling. The desks were hidden beneath mounds of paper; Tang recognized the red seals and ornate parchment coils that were thrown into the graveyard fires to placate the restless dead. Presumably, this was where they ended up.

"I have to speak to Lu Yueh," Ho Han said into the air. From around the corner of a desk stepped a small elderly gentleman.

"Good afternoon," he said.

"Good afternoon. I need to make an appointment with the Third Senior Official."

"I'm afraid that won't be possible. Lord Yueh is out of town at the present moment, and is not due to return until after the festival. Perhaps someone else might be able to assist you?" he asked, helpfully. Tang studied him. The gentleman wore a neat, dark robe. His eyes were entirely covered by cataract, giving his gaze a cloudy, indefinite quality. As he stepped forward, Tang looked down and observed that his feet, too, were back to front. The toes of his elegant black slippers pointed behind him.

"I don't think so, no. I need to speak to Lu. It is he to whom I must report." Ho Han said, agitated. An awful suspicion, which Tang had been entertaining for the last few minutes, was now confirmed. In his terror, he had assumed that his mother had made a bargain with one of the very lords of hell, but he had failed to consider that hell functions in a very similar manner to the real world. He had been sucked from life and brought here not by some celestial demon, but by some minor clerk. This, Tang, felt, exemplified the addition of insult to injury.

"So sorry," the gentleman said, unctuously.

"Very well, then," Ho Han snapped in a fury. Wheeling around, he headed for a door set in the wall.

"Wait!" the elderly gentleman wailed, but they were already beyond his reach. Tang could hear him shuffling forward as the door closed. They were in a lift. Ho Han's suddenly embodied forefinger pressed the topmost button, and then they were sailing upwards, so fast that Tang found himself forced against the wall.

Tang had not expected there to be laboratories, but when they stepped out of the lift and into the upper reaches of the Celestial Ministry of Epidemics, he could see the rows of beds and equipment through every door that they passed. A thought occurred to him. He said to Ho Han

"Those people in the hallway—the ghosts—what are they waiting for? Are they going to come here, to be tested?" He thought of his mother. Was she here, among the ranks of the patient spirits? He had not seen her, and was not even sure that she had died, but perhaps she had changed, worn away by death and time. It was a dreadful notion, that even after the expiration of her body, her suffering might not cease. Ho Han did not reply. He was muttering to himself, a litany of his injuries. He must, Tang thought, have suffered a considerable loss of face. Angrily, Ho Han brushed aside the equipment: the silken nets of the drip feeds, the bronze crucibles and frosted tubes, as though they did not exist. The wards were empty. At last they reached the end of the long line of laboratories. They were in a small room, painted an unpleasing and institutional green. Outside the small window, the storms of the upper air continued to rage. Ho Han took an object from a nearby shelf.

"What's that?" Tang said. The demon raised the hypodermic towards the uncertain light and depressed the plunger with a taloned finger.

"No," Tang said. Abruptly, he understood what he was about to do. "No. . . . " but the needle was already sliding through his smoky being. The contents of the hypodermic fastened onto Tang's disassembled molecules with sharp cog teeth. Tang poured into the syringe, writhing painfully through the congealing air. Then Ho Han gave the hypodermic a painful shake, and injected Tang's essence into a squat, opaque jar.

"You!" a voice cried. "What are you doing? That's government property!" Ho Han turned. "Why, it's Citizen Han," the voice continued, with a greasy note of satisfaction. "What a pleasant surprise. I suppose you're seeking to rehabilitate yourself, regain your old position, with this little gift. What a pity Lord Yueh has chosen to take his holiday now, and not at some more auspicious time. Now, give me the jar."

"No," Ho Han whispered. "No, the soul is mine."

Citizen Han's opponent made a dry, clicking noise, like a beetle.

"You always did have an unhealthy notion of private property. As you know very well, all subsumed entities belong to the Ministry; I'll make a note in your file for you, if you like." Tang felt the jar lurch as it was wrenched from Citizen Han's reluctant grasp. "Now, go and enjoy the festivities. I'll see that all the correct records are made."

Tang watched through the sides of the jar as Citizen Han, his shoulders bowed with defeat, went out of the door. Despite everything that

Han had done, Tang was still sorry to see him leave: after all, better the devil you know, he thought. He tried to turn and look at his new captor, but the jar was swiftly wrapped in a swathe of dark cloth, and Tang could see nothing more.

Four

Tang lost all sense of time but then at last the jar was picked up and the cloth whisked away. Through the jar, Tang saw a very ordinary seeming person in a grubby white coat. From his inconvenienced position, Tang could not see the man's feet, but he was not optimistic.

"Ha!" this person said. He turned to someone behind him. "You see? Homo Sapiens animus, to use the Latin term. A near perfect specimen; only slightly damaged."

Tang seemed to hear a voice, so immense that it remained almost beyond the reach of hearing.

"Ideal," the voice said, admiringly. "When can we begin?"

"As soon as you like," the person holding Tang's jar pronounced.

"Wait," Tang breathed, the loudest sound he could manage. "What are you going to do with me?"

"What's that?" the technician said, quite kindly. "I'm sorry, I didn't quite catch—"

"How long have I been here? What are you going to do with me?"

"Who was responsible for your entry?"

Tang laid all blame firmly at the reversed feet of Citizen Han.

"What a pity. Citizen Han has regrettably been demoted to the Ministry of Vermin, the result of a bureaucratic misdemeanor. Never mind. We'll find a use for you."

Tucking the jar in his pocket, he carried Tang down to a lower level and left him sitting on a workbench whilst various tasks were undertaken around him. Tang gained a reasonable idea of what was going on, because the technician continued to provide a running explanation to his companion who, disconcertingly, Tang was still unable to see.

"The relationships between the two worlds are, as I'm sure someone of your superior education is aware, Minister, highly fluid and tenuous. There are rules, you see, laid down by the Hundred Names of Heaven (on whom may a shower of curses perpetually rain) and we must continue to abide by those. Bureaucracy, I'm afraid, but it's quite vital, otherwise the whole system would fall into chaos and disarray. The provision of intact, living human essences is really quite rare—what's that?"

The enormous voice breathed a question.

"No, no, much less so than one would think, actually. When we are lucky enough to obtain a human spirit, we do our best to ensure that it isn't wasted. Some departments, of course, squander them like confetti—the War Ministry is particularly extravagant in that respect, but here at Epidemics we try to further the advance of science as well as fulfill our remit. We don't have limitless funds, after all. This little one, for example—what's going to happen to him, you might ask? Well, he's going to enjoy lasting fame as an entirely new disease."

"What!" Tang squeaked from the jar, but the great, soundless voice was speaking.

"That's how they all start. You need life, you see, as the seed of death." Tang heard the technician's shoe scuffle modestly along the floor. "I'm sure I'm the first one to be modest, but I've had quite a few pass through my humble laboratories: typhoid, malaria, even the more artistic, specialized ones like river fever. . . . "

The technician undertook a number of tests on the contents of the jar, all of them unpleasant. By the time that he had finished, Tang was no longer sure who, or what, he might be. There seemed to be entirely other dimensions to his nature. Yet the time spent in the jar was not entirely without value; Tang was able to reflect on his position. There was, ostensibly, very little that he could do at present, but it seemed from what the technician had said that he would, at some point, be released into his own world, if not in a particularly enticing form. Tang thought with horror of his new role as a lethal virus. He thought of his mother, ensnared by a literally soulless bureaucrat for eternity, simply for wanting her child to live. He found himself expanding into a cloud of rage.

"Compose yourself," he thought. "Compose yourself, and think."

Deep breathing was out of the question, but he managed to bring about a semblance of calm. He swirled up the sides of the jar, seeking ideas.

Someone was sidling around the edge of the desk. Tang tried in vain to see, but then the cover was thrown back over the jar, and it was picked up.

"Excuse me!" Tang whispered. "Excuse me. . . . " but no one answered as, slowly and stealthily, he was stolen away. He felt a jolt, and a sickening lurch; apparently they were back in the lift. Tang could not tell where they were heading. The virus with which he had been combined was filling his thoughts with an insidious haze, underlain by a ferocious will to survive that frightened what was left of his soul. The jar jolted along: whoever was carrying him had begun to run. His bearer muttered and grumbled to himself, and abruptly Tang realized who it was who had taken the jar. Citizen Ho Han, so shamefully transferred to the Ministry of Vermin, was stealing away the prize that he regarded as his own. As they sped down the hallway, the cloth covering the jar fell off and Tang was able to look back at their pursuers. They had abandoned their human forms; assuming that they had ever possessed them. Their eyes glowed crimson and jade green, and their mouths moved rhythmically, like the mouths of insects. Han and his captive in the jar reached the iron entrance hall of the Ministry. The patient rows of the dead had disappeared. Ho Han was alone with his demonic colleagues, and he was laughing. Before Tang realized what he was about to do, he tossed the jar into the midst of the crowd. The jar shattered, and Tang involuntarily streamed forth to disperse into the air. The leading demon shrieked with rage and leaped at Ho Han, banging his head against the iron wall. Tang tried to hold himself together, but he was being torn in many directions, breathed in by the surrounding demons. Evidently, Tang was aerobically transmitted. He eddied into their lungs, through into their fiery bloodstreams. Dimly, he realized with astonishment what Ho Han had done. He had been altered, to become a demon virus. One by one, the demons faltered and fell. Tang felt their souls depart, shrieking, for some lower level of Hell. His scattered particles remained in their desiccating lungs for a few moments, and then began to coalesce into the air. The iron hall was littered with corpses, withered like the carapaces of insects, but virus Tang felt the fierce pull towards hot blood and breath. The demon who had assaulted Ho Han had succumbed, rustling to the floor with its clawed hands still around the unfortunate thief's throat. Ho Han brushed it indignantly aside, and its hands fell away from its wrists so that he remained wearing the fingers like some macabre necklace. His moon face was contorted with a mixture of triumph and rage. The fragment of consciousness that was Tang wondered why Ho Han had not fallen prey to him. He swarmed down Ho Han's throat, and discovered why. Evidently Han had taken the precautionary measure of an antidote. Virus Tang slid from the cell walls like someone trying to climb a buttered pole. It would be necessary for him to change, if he wanted to gain purchase within the bureaucrat's body, and so he began to experiment, mutating faster and faster until first one, and then another, cell began to split and crack. Ho Han coughed. Corpuscles flooded past the component parts of Tang. The man from the ministry was hemorrhaging. Tang slowed the pace of his assault; a virus does not, after all, want its host to expire before it has found a new one. Wheezing, Ho Han stumbled through the iron doors of the Ministry and out into the night of Hell.

Five

Tang's consciousness seemed lodged in Ho Han's head. He was able to see through the bureaucrat's eyes, and to watch the diffuse, frightened thoughts of Citizen Han flash past. Even from his own disadvantaged position, Tang did not envy Ho Han. Not only was he infected with a sentient, hostile virus, but he had also managed to slay half the staff of a government department.

Han, it appeared, had a family. He lived in a small house in the back streets of Hell, occupied by a sour wizened wife and small, perpetually wailing demon child of indeterminate gender. Tang was forced to listen, too, as Han's wife berated him for his incompetence and selfishness. The bureaucrat sat, sweating and shivering with fever, as she droned on in an insidious monotone. It buzzed through Han's head like a wasp in a bottle.

"They'll come looking for me," Han whined. "They'll know. Oh, why, why, why did I do such a stupid thing?"

Despite an intrinsic lack of sympathy, Tang understood. It was a question of face, of honor through vengeance, but Han was quite right. It had been a stupid thing to do. Tang was sure that if they stayed here, the minions of Hell would find them. If Han could be persuaded to run, they might have a chance. He began whispering into Han's inner ear, counseling flight, and he kept this up until the unlucky bureaucrat could stand neither the nagging of his wife or his illness any longer and stumbled moaning out of the house.

Above, the storm clouds of Hell raced overhead, revealing banners of crimson sky. Han staggered down the street, kicking an assortment of small, squeaking things out of his path as he did so. Through his eyes, Tang could see the red characters of a remedy sign appearing out of the shadows, and there was the remedy shop; parchment walls upon a wooden frame. Han fell through the door. Inside, it was hot and quiet. The remedy man was sitting over a plate of something that Tang could not immediately identify. On Han's sudden entrance, he looked up. He had bright little eyes.

"Ghost," Han quavered. "I need your help."

The remedy man patted his lipless mouth with a napkin and said, "What seems to be the problem?"

"I have a fever," Han gasped, with a glance over his shoulder. "Something new, not seen before." The remedy man gave him a beady look.

"How do you know?"

"I can't tell you that," Han said. "But I can pay. I have money." He fished in his pockets and extracted a handful of notes. The remedy man's little eyes lit up with greed.

"Very well. Let me examine you," the remedy man said. He proceeded to ask Han a great many questions, concerning his diet, his habits, and his health in general. Han's answers were illuminating if unpleasing, particularly over the matter of diet.

"Well," the remedy man said at last. "I'm not sure of the precise nature of your illness, but I can prescribe certain basic treatments which may alleviate the symptoms."

He put the suffering Han through a rapid and diverse range of treatment. Needles were placed beneath Han's eyelids, and herbs beneath his tongue. Small cups of smoldering incense were balanced on the pressure points of Han's wrists. Trapped inside, listening to the supernaturally slow beat of Tang's demonic heart, virus Tang grew uncomfortable but remained intact.

"Let me see your tongue."

Obligingly, Han unscrolled the organ in question, which reached almost to his knees.

"I don't like the look of that much. I don't think there's anything more I can do, Citizen. Sorry."

"No!" Han cried. "You have to help me!" but the remedy man clapped his hands and the walls of the shop began to shred into tatters on the rising wind. Looking through Han's eyes, Tang saw that the walls were not made of parchment after all, but human skin. He wondered queasily what the remedy man had done during his lifetime, to end up here. The books, instruments and furniture were whirled up into the storm, and the remedy man himself transformed into a thing like a boneless bat and soared away. Above, among the storm clouds, was an eye; red as a coal and scanning the city below. Desperately, Han dodged into a nearby alley and began to run, blundering through the city. Tang knew where they were now; in the hellish equivalent of Wuan Chih, and then he realized where Han was heading. He was running in the direction of the place where, in the real city, the temple of Kuan Yin stood. But surely, Tang thought, it wouldn't be the same; surely it would have to be some demonic counterpart of the Lady of Compassion? As they neared the temple, however, Tang could see that it was identical to the temple in his own world, with lacquered steps leading up to a low, pagoda-roofed building. Han bolted up the steps and pounded on the door. After a moment, a small window in the gate opened and a gentle, dark eye peered out.

"Demon?" a calm voice said. "What do you want here?"

"Let me in, let me in. I'll repent. Something terrible has happened!" Citizen Han said in a rush.

"You are aware of the penalty for entrance into the Three Levels?" the voice asked.

"Yes, yes, I know. Just let me in!"

The door swung open. Within, the temple was exactly the same as the one in which Tang's mother had so often prayed. A stout iron brazier, filled with sand and incense rods, stood in the center of the courtyard and the place was filled with drifting smoke. Han coughed and stared with dismay at the black spot of blood on his sleeve. His heart was speeding up, to virus Tang he seemed to have become softer and cooler. He felt, in fact, like a human being.

"You're not well," the voice said with remote concern. Han turned. The woman who stood before them was slight, and dressed in a jade green robe. Tang recognized her immediately: Kuan Yin, the goddess of compassion, she who hears the cries of the world. Ho Han fell at her feet.

"Please help me," he whispered. In a flutter of green robes, the goddess knelt so that she was level with his face. Tang stared through her eyes, and glimpsed a vast sunlit plain, and trees that bore stars in their branches instead of fruit. Kuan Yin gave an empty smile and said

"You, demon?" Why should I help you? I know where you come from. I have the cries of the afflicted ringing in my ears from noon to midnight, and now you have come to beseech me because your creation has turned against you?"

"Lady," Tang tried to say. The goddess' head snapped up.

"What was that?"

"A soul," Han whispered, evidently deciding that honesty was the best policy. "A human soul. The seed of my disease."

The goddess stared at him and Tang felt his host flinch from the sadness in her face. She said, with a sigh

"I am bound by my remit of compassion to assist the suffering, and this I will do. However, universal balance must, by the laws of the Tao, be maintained. What, I wonder, would be a suitable punishment for a being whose entire existence has been to perpetrate pain and suffering?" The dark, limitless eyes widened. "I know. . . ." She raised her hand.

Six

Tang re-entered his own body with a soundless clap of divine thunder. It felt hot and heavy after his weightless existence in Hell. On the dressing room couch, his mother stirred and sighed. The small, rotund man at the side of the bed jerked his hand back from her brow with an exclamation. Tang's mother's face was suffused with a healthy golden glow. Her breast rose and fell peacefully.

"It's you!" Tang said, to Citizen Han. He was surprised to hear his own loud voice. Han's face twisted in helpless fury.

"This is your fault," he hissed.

"Don't blame me," Tang snapped, equally indignant. "You started it." Involuntarily he glanced down at Han's perfectly unexceptional feet.

"Of course. You're human now, aren't you?"

"Not only is that indignity enough," the erstwhile demon snarled. "But that intolerable woman has given me a Gift."

"What sort of gift?"

Before Tang could avoid it, Han reached out and touched him on the shoulder. Tang felt warmth and health steal over him.

"You're a healer," he said, wonderingly.

"From now on, for the rest of my life on this miserable plane, I will heal whoever I touch," Ho Han bemoaned. "Oh, what a dreadful fate!"

and rushing past the astounded Tang, he vanished wailing through the door.

Tang, to his considerable relief, never saw the man from the ministry again, but tales gradually began to filter back from the farthest provinces. People were beginning to speak of Han as an avatar, for he healed with a touch or a word. They called him the Reluctant Buddha, and even though he retreated into the snowbound fastnesses of the mountains, he was still pursued by the sick and the suffering, diligent in their quest, thus demonstrating that, in China, it is not what you know, but who, that matters.